I Should Have Kissed Him

Annie Mick

Contents

Prologue

"I'll trade you mine for yours."

"Eww, we already chewed it." I scrunched my nose so hard, my sunburned skin felt the pain of contortion as I held fast to the wad of gum between my cheek and teeth and spoke around it. "That would be like trading spit."

He grinned impishly around his own gum-filled, puffy cheek. "I know. Kinda like kissing without using our mouths. Besides, I got the pink and you got the blue. Each one has its own flavor. Everybody knows that."

"Then why did you choose the pink one?"

"Because it's the same color as your lips. And if you ain't gonna kiss me, Libby, then at least I should know what you taste like."

"Lucas!" I heaved an exasperated sigh – though the idea wasn't exactly appalling. "We're only twelve. We're not supposed to be kissing."

He furrowed his brow and tilted his head. "How old do we have to be?"

"I don't know." I shrugged, my feet planted firmly on the ground on each side of my bike so it didn't tip over. "Like grownups, I guess. Dad says I can't date until I'm thirty."

"Thirty?!" he exclaimed, shocked and wide-eyed. "We should have kids by the time we're thirty."

"Well, that's what dad said. I gotta be a nurse first anyway."

"Okay." He nodded in reluctant agreement, as my dad was one of his favorite people and he trusted his judgment. "We'll wait 'til we're 32. Why do you want to be a nurse anyway?"

I giggled, teasing him with the memory, "So I can show you how to put the Band-Aids on the right way."

He narrowed his eyes, lifting a single brow. "It wasn't my fault. You were still bleeding and they wouldn't stick!" Something caught his eye as he looked over my shoulder down our narrow street and his entire body stiffened. His knuckles turned white as he gripped the handlebars of his bicycle and yanked hard, pulling the front tire off the ground and letting it fall with a slight bounce. "Dad's home. I guess the bike ride is over. Here goes my night."

Goosebumps ran up and down my arms in the Arizona heat. Lucas' dad scared me, and I wasn't the one who had to live with him. The man was just plain mean. He was always shouting as if you couldn't hear him. He threw things when he got mad. I think he drank beer, too – a lot. The sound of bottles clinking in the trash cans on collection day was a point of chatter amongst some of the ladies in the neighborhood. My mom called it gossip and said meanness came in many forms. She also said the ones that gossiped the most were the ones that kept their own curtains closed the tightest. Something about throwing stones and glass houses.

"Is he going to yell at you again?" I asked worriedly, my concern for my best friend at an ultimate high.

"Lucas!" Mr. Monterrey hollered from the car after he slammed on the brakes, leaving a black skid mark on the street. "Get your ass in the house, now!"

Lucas shot me a wry look – the dimple in his cheek appearing as he did – right before pushing the foot pedal forward and starting toward his destination. "Guess that answers that. See you later, Libby."

"Lucas," I called after him before he could get too far away – the overwhelming need to offer him something to look forward to before he returned to his unhappy home. "I'll give you a taste tomorrow."

He backpedaled so hard his bike slid sideways as he came to a stop, his eyes lit with mischief that matched his trademark grin. "A promise is a promise, Liberty Bell. Can't wait."

The sound of breaking glass and screaming rang through the neighborhood approximately two hours later. Voices I knew well.

I'd been putting my bike away in the garage like always after taking the trash out in the evening. I rushed inside to tell my parents so they could intervene and remove Lucas from the mayhem, as they had done a few times in the past.

"Dad's calling the police, Liberty," mom reassured me. She placed her hands on my shoulders and held me back from following my dad out the front door after the call had been placed.

"Is Lucas' dad gonna hurt him?" I asked, the tears hitting my chin before I could swipe them away. "He sounds really mad this time, mom."

She pulled me into a hug to comfort me, though there was no comfort to give. I needed to know my best friend was okay. "The police are on their way, sweetheart."

Sirens bellowed through the air moments later. Tires screeched to a stop, red and blue lights flashed in the darkening evening of the setting sun, car doors slammed. Soon after came the sound I will never forget: the bone crushing echo of a gunshot and the bloodcurdling scream of my best friend that followed.

"Dad! No!!"

I broke free from my mom's hold and rushed out the door but couldn't get past my dad's stealth and strong arms as I tried to get around him on the front lawn and run in the direction of my best friend's house. "Liberty, honey, we need to stay back."

"Dad, please!" I sobbed. "It's Lucas. I have to help him. He's my best friend."

He picked me up and held me in his arms, letting me sob into his shoulder. "Hey," he whispered as he patted my back. "You did help him, sweetheart. You were the one who came rushing in for us to call. Let the police take it from here. They know what they're doing."

Minutes – maybe hours – later, Mr. Monterrey was escorted by two policemen out the front door in handcuffs as an ambulance pulled up in front of the house and the workers rushed inside with a rolling bed. Lucas was carried out of the house, tucked tightly in a policeman's arms, and placed in the back of a squad car.

"If he were hurt, the policeman wouldn't be taking him," Dad reassured me. "He would be leaving in the ambulance. Liberty, they're just taking him away from whatever is going on inside. You need to let them do their job. Wait here with me."

They wouldn't let me talk to Lucas, wouldn't let me see him or hug him; make sure he was okay. The officer carrying him had whisked him away so fast, I only knew it was Lucas by recognizing his tennis shoes.

I wriggled out of my dad's hold and ran down the street after the police car once I realized they were leaving, desperately trying to check on my best friend. Lucas turned in the backseat to see me running after him – his eyes wide and filled with terror as he cried out. His hand reached out onto the rear dashboard as if he were waiting for me to catch up and grab it. His mouth moved in the shape of my name, *'Liberty'*, though the sound didn't reach my ears.

"Lucas!!" I screamed at the top of my lungs as if it might bring him back to me. "Lucas! Don't go!"

The distance between us continued to grow as the car gained speed and I lost mine. I knew in my heart I would never see him again.

My best friend was gone.

I should have given him my blueberry gum.

I should have taken his tutti-frutti.

I should have kissed him . . . goodbye.

Chapter 1

Liberty

"Liberty," Mom starts cautiously in a tone I've come to know so well over the past three years it makes me shiver. It's compassionate but firm. The tone that starts with, "*I'm sorry, but . . .*" This can't be good. It's bad news. It always is. It was when grandma died, even worse when Dad died. And now, I simply wait to see what the next bomb she's about to drop is going to be. "We have to move, honey."

"What?!" I whirl my head so fast, my braid snags on the clasp of my necklace and I lose a few hairs that get caught. "Why?"

"I've taken a job in North Carolina. It'll be good for us. A nice change of pace. It's close to the ocean and . . ."

"No!" I protest in shock, my greatest fear come to life. "Mom, we can't move. How is Lucas going to find me? He won't know where we went!"

"Liberty." She drops her chin to her chest and blows a deep sigh. "You have got to stop this. It's been three years, honey. You can make new friends."

Bursting into the all too familiar tears that seem to never run dry – my fists clenched in frustration, followed by a fast foot stomp – I present my usual argument. "I don't want new friends, mom. I want Lucas!"

She doesn't understand. I haven't made new friends in all the time he's been gone. I don't have friends, I have *classmates*. The house next door is now inhabited by a young family with little kids. There's no one there to wave goodnight to me through the window that faces mine – not that it would matter. They aren't Lucas. I want my best friend. I want my soulmate.

"Liberty," she says slowly, her voice now stern but pained. "It's not up for debate. The school year starts in six weeks and you need to be ready. The movers will be here in ten days. My job starts at the beginning of the month. This is a new start for us. Your dad would want us to be happy."

"Dad's dead, Mom! Lucas didn't die. He'll come back. I know he will."

She shakes her head slowly and closes her eyes, the tears slipping down her cheeks – much like my own – and guilt consumes me. I shouldn't have snapped like that. My mom is lost without my dad; we both are. His sudden death devastated us. She's trying so hard. I hear her cry at night when she doesn't think I can. I bury my face in my own pillow with the hope that she doesn't hear me either. Her shoulders have borne the weight of my tears more times than I can count.

Pulling her into a hug, I whisper, "I'm sorry. We'll do whatever we have to do to make this work."

I glance at the urn on the mantel that sits next to the picture of Lucas and me by the pool in our backyard. *I won't be happy, Dad, but I will be helpful.*

Three weeks later we are completely unpacked and settled into our new house in North Carolina, approximately two miles from the Atlantic ocean. It's a blue cottage house; two bedrooms, two baths. It has a small backyard with a white picket fence around the front. The neighbors from both sides and one from across the street came over to greet us before we were even out of the car. Two of the houses have small children and their parents offered me babysitting jobs on the weekends, if I was interested. The other has a nice older lady that lives alone and brought us some sweet tea and cookies.

Me? I looked for Lucas. I will always look for Lucas. I'll find him, or he'll find me . . . someday. Best friends always do, don't they?

Mom starts her new job tomorrow as a PA for one of the largest law firms in the state. School starts in three weeks. I'll be a sophomore at the high school this year. I've grown some boobs, started my period, and have a small tendency to be a bit hormonal approximately three days a month.

I don't suffer from social anxiety; I choose social sobriety.

I miss my best friend. I miss our bike rides, our long talks, waving goodnight out our bedroom windows before we went to bed. I miss him choosing his favorite color for the day – because he had two – as he gazed into my eyes and tilted his head. *"I think it'll be green today, Liberty Bell."*

Heterochromia is an interesting condition. Some people pretend they don't notice it, some are puzzled by it, others make fun of it, and some find it fascinating. And now with a whole new group of people to deal with, I'm burdened with the task of deciphering the neutrals from the workers who try to solve a puzzle, the bullies, and the easily entertained. I suppose I could wear colored contacts, but why should I change for the rest of the world? *Lucas' words.*

Having two different colored irises can be fun. People stare at the bridge of your nose or concentrate on one eye until theirs are nearly crossed. It's kind of like a wart on your chin. They will look anywhere other than *at* the anomaly. Little will they know, I don't have fingerprints either. Lucas told me I would be a hard-to-catch criminal. Best keep those lockers sealed up tight. Play nice, people.

The first day of school is literal mayhem. Seems some of these students haven't seen each other all summer. They shout, exchange hugs, high-five each other, but when I walk out of my last class of the day and catch a couple in the hall playing tonsil tag right out in the open as if no one can see them, I'm a bit nonplussed.

"She'll be the one wearing the grad gown two sizes too big and waddling her way up on stage to accept her diploma. Preggers by Christmas, I'll bet on it." The whisper in my ear is followed by a giggle as a gentle hand wraps around my bicep and tugs. "Come on, let's go get burgers and fries by the beach. It's within walking distance."

Turning to see the grinning brunette, I hesitate. She holds out her hand to shake mine as she looks me straight in the eyes – both eyes. "I'm Mallory. I live three houses down from yours. I was visiting my dad when you moved in so I haven't had a chance to come over and introduce myself. Howdy neighbor."

"You live by me?" I inquire, surprised there is someone my age close by.

She tugs harder on my arm, leading me away from the steamy exchange in the hall. "Well, actually you live by me since I was there first. Welcome to the neighborhood. Cool eyes, by the way. I'm hetero too." She turns to look at me, flashing beautiful matching gray irises, bobs her eyebrows, and grins impishly. "Not the eyes, my sexual preference. I'm all about the penis. Let's go get those burgers. Their milkshakes aren't so bad either. Not a fan of vanilla myself – the flavor or the sex – but I won't hold it against you if you are."

And that is how I made my first new friend in North Carolina. Mallory Tompkins. Crazy, outspoken, funny, and a good distraction from the emptiness I would feel until the day I find Lucas. And if I never do, until the day I die.

Chapter 2

Lucas

"Ma'am, we found him," the officer reports into the phone as he shoots me a profound look of disappointment, though it's coated with sympathy. "He's safe."

My aunt's cries can be heard through the receiver of the officer's cell phone that he holds to his ear. "Oh, thank God!" she sobs. "Tanner, what on earth were you thinking? Do you have any idea how far from home you are?"

"Ma'am," the officer calmingly reassures her, "you can talk to him in a while. I'm going to take him down to the station, get some food in him, and try to sort this out. We'll make arrangements once I get him back to the station."

"My husband and I are on our way," she tells him – and me – since I hear every word. I'm sitting in the back of a cop car, on the verge of crying like a damn baby. I hitchhiked all the way here – stupid, I know – over 500 miles to find Liberty, only to find out she doesn't live here anymore and nobody knows where she is.

The house next door – my old house, the one my dad killed my mom in – still looks the same. I didn't want to ring the bell, the memories a nightmare I struggle with a regular basis, but since nobody else in the neighborhood could tell me where she was, I didn't have much choice. I broke down and cried when they answered the door, begged them to tell me where Liberty was. They asked if I wanted to come in and talk. I refused. Just looking over the woman's shoulder into the living room was enough to make my heart nearly pound out of my chest; the flashbacks so clear and overwhelming. The man offered me a soda and came out and sat on the front stoop with me. The woman must have called the police while he kept me distracted.

And here I sit. No Liberty. She's gone. I only wanted to see her, make sure we were still best friends. Feel a hug. Hear her giggle. See my two favorite colors. No one would let me call her back then. I couldn't talk to her, couldn't see her. I wrote her letters but she never answered them.

My aunt and uncle came and got me after I stayed in a house with strangers for two days, and then they took me to live with them in southern California. They're nice people. We get along well. They try. But there's no Liberty there.

"Do you remember me, Lucas?" The officer turns in his seat to look at me as I sit in the caged backseat, head hung low, my hopes and dreams dashed. He's the only officer in the car; the other two that accompanied him occupy the car that sits behind us at the curb.

I raise my eyes slowly to meet his. "You know my real

name?"

He nods. "I'm the one that carried you outta here that night."

"You're the one who wouldn't stop to let me see her!" I pound my fist on the cage dividing the front from the back seat, the picture clear as day in my mind. "She was running after me and you wouldn't stop the car!"

"Lucas," he says softly. "I *couldn't* stop. We couldn't take a chance that you would be seen. Your dad was mixed up with some really bad people. If they had seen you, they would have known what you look like. They would have gone after you and used you as leverage with your dad. We couldn't take that chance. We had to get you out of there as fast as possible."

"What kind of people?" I ask. "Is that why my mom's dead?"

"No." He shakes his head. "Your mom is gone because of your dad's temper. Your dad was dealing drugs and owed some dangerous people a lot of money. We didn't want them coming after you. It was too late for your mom. We did what we had to do for your safety."

"He wouldn't have cared," I snap. "He didn't care about me or my mom."

"We couldn't risk it." He dips his chin. "Your safety came first."

It's all making sense now. The name change, the faraway move. A simple memorial service for my mom – rather her ashes – in California, two weeks later. No returning for my things. I'll bet Liberty never got my letters, either.

I feel my chin start to wobble. "Do you know where Liberty is?"

He shakes his head again. "No, buddy, I don't."

"Can you help me find her?"

He sighs deeply. "Lucas, you're both underage. It's not

something we can . . ."

"Do you know what happened to her?"

"Aw shit." He scrubs his hands over his face. "Look, you're a good kid. Been through a lot. Okay, I think you deserve the truth. Mr. Collins passed away a couple years ago. Liberty and her mom moved away last year. No idea where they went. I think they just needed to leave the past behind."

"Liberty's dad died?"

He grimaces. "Yeah. I was on call that night. He had a heart attack."

My heart feels like it's being shredded. Mr. Collins was always so nice to me. He fixed my bike when my own dad wouldn't. He put an extra hamburger on the grill for me . . . every single time. He's the one who bought us our bubble gum. He pulled my loose tooth for me when it was hurting! And Liberty's mom gave me ice cream after as a reward for being brave.

My body buckles in half as sobs wrack my shoulders. "I should have been here for her. It should have been my dad instead."

"No one's told you about your dad, Lucas?" he asks pointedly.

My head rises, tears dripping off my chin that I swipe with a quick hand. "No," I grunt. "He killed my mom. This is all his fault. He can rot in hell for all I care."

He lets out a slow deep breath and shakes his head as if conflicted.

"What about him?" I cave, curiosity turning to hope that he's serving a life sentence in a prison where he's beaten on the daily.

"You really want to know?" His inquisitive brows rise as he dips his chin. I only nod. "Your dad died in prison before he ever went to trial. Those people he was wrapped up with got to him before he could give testimony against them."

I narrow my eyes, the bitterness I've held for years not tempered in the least with the news. "I hope it was slow and painful."

"Lucas, you don't really mean . . ."

"Don't call me that," I snap harshly. "My name is Tanner Carson. Lucas doesn't exist anymore."

There is only one person entitled to call me Lucas. And apparently I'll never hear from her again. I guess I'll never find out what her pink lips tasted like either.

I hate my dad and I miss my mom. But I miss Liberty more than anyone. The officer said it himself:

"They needed to leave the past behind". I guess that meant me too.

Our English lit teacher was spouting quotes in class one day. She only had half my attention, as usual, until she quoted someone named Wendelin Van Draanen who said, "You never forget your first love". Boy did that hit hard. It's the reason I'm here. But I believe she was trying to cross English lit with sex education because it was the last quote of the day and she finished with a stern warning of, "And first love does not mean sex. Keep that in mind, people."

Ha! I think I fell in love with Liberty Collins the day I met her at the age of five. That Van Draanen woman should have clarified there is no age limit. And while your first love may be unforgettable, it might also be the most painful. If I live to be a hundred, I will never forget her. My blonde, blue and green-eyed wonder. The girl who made everything okay no matter how bad it got. The girl I never got to kiss.

I study the two houses that sit side by side – the second story windows that face one another – and remember how we would wave to each other every night before we went to bed.

There's a sickening pit in my stomach, knowing I'll never see it again. I close my eyes and paint the memory in my mind so as to keep it locked away; the finished canvas that I didn't get to sign because circumstances ruined it.

"*Goodbye, Liberty Bell,*" I whisper softly so no one can hear.

Keeping my eyes closed, the vision of my Liberty in that window the last thing I want to picture, I sigh in resignation. "Can we go now?"

"If you promise not to try and run," the officer proffers, "you can sit up front."

The claustrophobic feeling of being contained in a caged backseat of this car is nothing compared to the solitude I've been locked in for the last four years, but a small sarcastic snort escapes my throat before I can hold it back. "I got nowhere else to go. Could you pull up the street a couple blocks first?"

"Sure." He puts the car in gear and the wheels move under us for approximately twenty seconds. "Good enough?"

"Can you see the houses anymore?"

"Nope."

"Perfect," I tell him, then open my eyes and see the second cop car next to us. "Riding up front would be great. Thanks."

Today is the day I leave my childhood behind. They raided the house afterwards. I didn't even get my clothes back. No toys; not that I had many. No baseball cap, no glove, no signed cast with Liberty's autograph. No bicycle. I don't even have a picture to remember her by; only my memories. And what a memory she was. The girl of my dreams that captured a part of my heart that no one else will ever own. How can such a good memory hurt so much?

Chapter 3

Liberty

"Why Arizona?" mom asks, her face filled with worry lines that travel the span of her forehead; hairline to eyebrows.

"Mom," I drawl. "They have an awesome master's program. They didn't blink twice to take me." *Though right now, I kinda wish she would.*

She squeezes her biceps a little harder with the fingers she has pressed into them by way of her folded arms across her chest, leaving indents that I fear will bruise. "You had two others that didn't blink twice either, Liberty. Why not take one of those?"

My stepdad, Tom Mason, whom I've grown to love over the past four years, steps up behind my mom and drapes his arm over her shoulders. "Sweetheart, she's all grown up. The other two choices wouldn't keep her any closer. In fact, Seattle is even farther away. Trust her judgment. We can go see her anytime you want." He winks at me. "Unless of course she gets too busy with the doctors."

Tom came into my mom's life five years ago by way of a friend at work. He's a widower himself with three grown children and has proven to be excellent husband material. He was patient with her – didn't pursue her relentlessly, but certainly didn't give up after her first refusal of a date, either. Mom was dead set against having a man who wasn't her daughter's father in the house while I was growing up. Overprotective is an understatement. She and dad were truly soulmates, and it took a long time to convince her that loving another didn't mean leaving the other behind. It simply meant stretching your heart enough to make room for a good man – not replacing the original.

I roll my eyes at his teasing. "Getting busy with the doctors is Mallory's job. I'll be concentrating on school."

"That's the other reason I'm questioning your choice," mom grunts. "She's going to the same school . . . again. I love that girl, but . . ."

"Hey, Mr. and Mrs. M!" Mallory's timing is perfect as she enters the house through the back door, sans the knock first, as usual. Over the years she and I have become more like sisters, and boundaries are more like tiny mud puddles that you step over rather than tiptoe around. We've attended the same college; on the dean's list every semester. We shared the same dorm room for two years, moving on to an apartment for three years after that, and are now moving on to our master's programs. We have literally worked our asses off; full class loads during the school year and summer classes on top of that. Transferring AP classes from high school gave us both an ass-kicking head start and we're now headed for those master's programs a year early.

I wouldn't put us at Einstein level, but we're not Darwin award winners either. We're nursing students. We've graduated BSNs, but Mallory wants to be a nurse anesthetist and my goal is to be a nurse practitioner. We've both been accepted into the master's program at UACN in Phoenix.

Our celebration upon receiving our acceptance into the program consisted of a few beers at our local haunt, The *Hollow Leg*, and devising a plan to inform our parents that we would be leaving in a month for the other end of the country. I've yet to hear how Mallory's parents took it, but something tells me since my leaving takes me back to the heart of my childhood, it was probably better than what I'm facing at the present time.

"Hello there, young lady," Tom greets her with a smile.

My mom simply sours her expression and grumbles, "Mallory."

Mallory stretches her arms out and pulls my mom into a hug, forcefully injecting herself into her good graces via non-invitation. "Aw, Mrs. M, it's good to see you too. Thanks for the dinner invite. Did you make me some cookies?"

My mom wriggles out of the hug and stares at her, mouth parted in unamused surprise. She furrows her brow then sighs, well accustomed to Mal's somewhat irritating, yet always lovable way of worming a path into your heart. "I guess that invitation must have slipped my mind. What are you hungry for?"

"How about pot roast?"

"Fine," mom agrees, but shoots her a scowl. "You get no wine tonight though. I still question your influence on my daughter."

Mallory's face lights in delightful amusement as she checks

her fingers off one at a time. "Only a little alcohol, no drugs, and neither one of us is pregnant. I'd say I'm the winningest companionship and influence she could have."

Mom gives her a wry look. "You can't get her pregnant. Not exactly a claim you can accredit to yourself, young lady."

Mallory holds a finger up. "Ah, but I keep the bad dicks away. We're picky about our penises. Give me some credit."

Tom rubs his temples with his fingers and grimaces, then wraps his arm around my mom's shoulders. "Honey, the more you egg her on, the worse it gets."

Mal waves her hand through the air like a flag. "I'm just kidding Mrs. M. I let Liberty choose her own penises."

"Mallory!" I shriek, wishing I had a muzzle to put over her big, fat mouth, or a dictionary to remind her once again the definition of discretion. Not that I'm getting any penis, but nobody needs to know that. The most I've ever done is put a hand on one, and I don't think I was very good at it. That, or I was too good. At least that's what the recipient told me. It was over in ten seconds, maybe twenty. I left in a hurry to the sounds of his groaning apologies and pleas to give him time to recover. I spent five minutes in my car dousing my hand in disinfectant rinse and using half a box of tissues to wipe it off before pulling out of the parking lot of the frat house.

"Scratch the pot roast, Mrs. M," Mal says, as if this is normal conversation in front of parents. She giggles and winks at me, knowing exactly where my thoughts have gone, before asking my mom, "I'm suddenly in the mood for hotdogs. Any chance you could fix me one of your special cappuccinos with the frothy head on it?"

"Don't you have a curfew?" I snarl in warning. It wasn't a question. It was more an order of *zip it shut or I'll punch you.* We're almost 23 years old. Neither of us have had curfews since starting college, outside of being respectful of checking in and being home at a decent hour while we lived at home during the summers.

She grins devilishly. "Never when I'm here. My mom prefers it when I visit you guys."

Tom laughs. "Something tells me she'd let you move in if you asked her."

Mom shoots him a seething glare that makes him wince. "That's not even a little funny."

"Actually," Mallow drawls, "that might not be a bad i . . ."

"No!" we shout in unison, a combination of glares thrown in her direction letting her know it wasn't *even a little funny.* I can handle Mallory in daily doses. My mom has suffered enough.

One month later the U-Haul is loaded; Tom and mom driving my Jeep Cherokee that it's hitched to, and Mallory and I driving her Range Rover to Phoenix. Mom and Tom will be flying back to North Carolina once we get settled in our shared condo.

Two weeks from now, school will start. I think I might swing by the old neighborhood for nostalgia's sake. You know, a trip down memory lane.

Just don't tell mom.

Chapter 4

Lucas

"Is Officer Sullivan in?"

The woman at the front desk of the police station looks up, scrunches her nose as if she's swallowed something sour, and clears her throat.

"*Officer* Sullivan?" she throws my inquiry back at me and tilts her head. "We have a Captain Sullivan. Think he's who you're looking for?"

It's been nearly eight years. He introduced himself as officer when I last saw him, but I suppose it could be him. "Big guy, brown hair?"

She chuckles, amused. "You've just described half the population of the United States, kiddo. Captain Sullivan is a big guy with salt and pepper hair." She grins. "It's a hazard that comes with the job."

My mouth twists to the side. This could have been done without him, but I wanted a bit of insight before I took the final leap. Four years of college with an internship and I want to be a cop. Not just any cop though. I wanted the psychology courses and the criminology training behind me. I want to be able to read people; not just arrest them, and I remember Officer Sullivan helping me when I needed it.

He had brought me back here to the station and fed me, stayed until my aunt and uncle showed up; talked them down, assured they didn't get angry. They didn't. They'd been worried sick. He and I talked about Liberty and her parents, the way their home felt like mine more than my own did. How Liberty had been the best friend I'd ever had. That she was the reason I had come back.

Then he left the room for a minute or two and came back with a small white box and handed it to me. "She came here one day and asked me to give this to you if I ever saw you again. I tried to tell her that I probably wouldn't, but she was pretty insistent. Who woulda thought. Lo and behold, here you are."

I lifted the lid to find a note inside.

Dear Lucas,

I don't know if you'll ever get this, but it's so you won't forget me. The X is for the kiss I didn't give you. You will always be my best friend. I hope I'm yours too. If you ever fall in love, you can throw this away. Your wife probably wouldn't want you to keep it. I would understand. The gum will probably lose its flavor so maybe you can just keep the wrappers? The picture is so you never forget what I look like. I have one just like it, but I would never forget you even if I didn't.

I miss you so much.

I hope you miss me too,

Liberty Bell

Beneath the note was a picture of the two of us that her mother had taken as we stood together by their pool, her monogramed charm bracelet that she always wore with an obviously hand-scratched X in the gold next to the scripted *L*, and two pieces of bubble gum – one blueberry and one tutti-frutti – were under that.

"When did she bring this?" I'd asked him, holding that bracelet in my hand as if it were a lifeline.

"She rode her bike here a few months after her dad passed." He shook his head as if in disbelief as he chuckled, and I swore I saw his eyes mist over. "She was one determined young lady."

I never chewed the gum, though I did very carefully press the hardened pieces flat and laminate them, and they're sealed and preserved – pretty well I might add. Hard as a rock and they sit in my watch box along with the charm bracelet, picture, and the note she wrote. Some things you just never let go of, and the lone surviving physical evidence and memory of Liberty Collins is that for me.

She may have had to leave me behind, but she didn't want to forget any more than I did. And she didn't want me to forget her . . . as if I ever could.

When I left this station that night with my aunt and uncle, I didn't plan on ever coming back, but for some reason here I am. Attending USC and staying close to where I grew up seemed to be the sensible thing to do, and the decision to become a cop was not an easy one to make. But once you make it, you don't want to move around from city to city. Find a home and stay put. My aunt and uncle have two kids of their own – it's not like I left them alone. My memories here are mixed – the most wretched imaginable – but it's the place that holds the best one too.

Hard to believe that this many years later I'm still looking for a place to land. I made friends, dated a few girls even, but nothing stuck. Funny thing, I only dated brown-eyed brunettes and a few redheads. My first kiss was totally forgettable. Didn't taste pink at all. My first round with sex was done with my eyes closed and my imagination wide open. It's amazing what you can put *in* your head once you get *out* of your head. Blonde, blue *and* green eyes, perfect palm-fitting tits, a grabbable ass that would fit so well in my hands. I wonder if her giggle is still the same.

I've considered hypnosis to help me forget – because the pain is overwhelming sometimes – but then I remember the good parts. The way her hair would shine in the sun and fly behind her as we raced our bikes down the street. The fact that she gave me two favorite colors because one eye was just as pretty as the other. The day I got to carry her on my back because she fell and skinned her knees. She probably could have walked, but never had anything felt so good. I sucked at placing the Band-Aids because the blood seeped through and made the adhesive wet and they wouldn't stick. But I got to be her hero that day. I made her laugh even though she was injured because the Band-Aids stuck better to my fingers than they did her knees. The day I realized it broke my heart to see her cry, and I would have exchanged my own tears to take hers away. Yeah, that was the day I knew I was in love with . . .

Lost in my thoughts, I don't hear the man approach.

"Luc . . ." Sullivan clears his throat with his blunder. "Tanner? Is that you?"

Extending my hand to shake his, I grin. "Captain, huh? Yeah, it's me."

He pulls me toward him in a side hug and slaps me on the back. "Wow! Somebody grew up. You look good, young man.

What brings you to the 98th?"

"Wondered if I could speak with you about a few things."

"Absolutely," he says without waver. "Come on back to my office. You want coffee? A water?"

"Water would be great, thanks."

"Sylvie?" He looks to the woman at the front desk who seems to be enjoying our reunion.

"I'm on it," she says. "You gonna recruit that one? You know my daughter is available and she's . . ."

"Thirty two," he chides then shakes his head and rolls his eyes as he leads me down the hall, finishing with a harsh grumble, "and she's probably slept with half my force. Stay away from Sylvie's daughter."

"No problem," I say with a snicker.

"Take a seat." Sullivan pulls his chair out from behind his desk and plops down into it. "What brings you in, son?"

"I'm looking to get on the force."

The silence is deafening, and quite extended actually, before a smile lights his face. "Well, I'll be damned. Let's talk about it."

An hour later, papers in hand, I'm leaving Captain Sullivan's office. He places a snug hand on my shoulder and squeezes. "Damn proud of you, Tanner. You're going to make a good cop. I have no doubt the Academy is going to snatch you up in the first round. Put my name on those papers for a reference. I'll be more than happy to back you up."

"Thank you, sir."

He holds a hand up. "Until you're in my department, it's Dan . . . or Sully. You're welcome to have dinner with the wife and me anytime if you don't have anything better to do." He dips his chin and a compassionate smile matches the look in his eyes. "And Lucas," he says softly, "I'm glad to see you're not letting a shitty history hold you back. You'd be amazed how many people do."

"Not all of it was bad," I tell him as the thought of Liberty crosses my mind. "I have some good memories."

"Hang on to them, kid. Sometimes it's all we got."

I chuckle softly. "As if I could ever forget. Thanks for your help. I'll let you know what they say, Sully."

He laughs and pats my shoulder. "I'll probably know before you do."

Six months later, I'm receiving full accreditation to the police force of Phoenix, Arizona; rank of sergeant due to my previous education as well as extra training. Yet, my comrades still call me rookie. It's okay though. They consider me one of their team and they've been nothing less than welcoming.

Best thing of all? I'm in the 98th district under Captain Sullivan's command. He saved my ass a long time ago and it serves as a reminder to do the same for others. I've never asked his age, but I hope his retirement is a long ways off. I kinda like the guy.

Chapter 5

Liberty

"Have you decided yet?" Mallory licks the salt off the rim of her glass then tips it back for another sip of margarita to wash it down.

"I don't think office work would be very satisfying. I like a fast pace, new faces, you know that. Writing scripts for ear infections and birth control isn't exactly what I had in mind. There's a reason I spent the whole summer last year in intensive training with Maxson." I curl my lip and finish, "She was a hard ass, but she knew what she was doing."

Mal scowls. "Hayes was no picnic either." She holds one fisted hand above the other and jams it downward as she mocks the stern doctor. "'If you can't trach a dummy, you won't be able to trach a human'. I was ready to shove that tube up his dick . . . or his ass." She sneers. "Either way, I would have had him breathing. Hard."

I set down my empty glass and lift my hand for the bartender to indicate I'm ready for a refill. I'm only one drink in and the desire for about four more is pretty strong. Abstinence from alcohol and anything fun has my tolerance level pretty low, but now that school is finished, I'm ready to soak my head in a vat of tequila. I'll go back to the acceptable lady-like glass of wine or two after I tie one on tonight.

Mom and Tom, as well as Mallory's parents, left this morning, having spent a week with us after graduation ceremonies were over. Nothing like parental company to keep you sober.

"Okay." Mallory nods in understanding. "You've got four offers sitting on the table at home. Options up the wazoo, but the choice is a no-brainer. Come work at Banner Medical with me. It's the biggest, best pay, fast paced. What's the problem?"

The bartender sets down two fresh refills in front of us. "Thanks," I tell him.

"These are on the two gentlemen at the end of the bar." He rolls his eyes. "Any others you want are *also* on the two gentlemen at the end of the bar. They're apparently feeling generous . . ." he smirks, ". . . or hoping to get lucky."

Without looking in the direction of those two gentlemen, I pull out a twenty, slap it on the bar, and smile. "Let them know if they get any closer, the drinks will literally be *on* them. We're not looking for company or to get *lucky*."

Mallory leans in and glances down to the end of the bar, then nudges my arm. "We could make it easy and have him tell them we're lesbians."

I crinkle my nose at the thought of horny, old men. "That

29

bad, huh?"

"No, actually they're pretty hot." She takes a sip of her drink and hums pathetically. "But it's a girls' night and I promised my best friend I'd behave myself."

"You did no such thing! Behaving yourself isn't even in your vocabulary."

The bartender chuckles and leans forward, chin on his hand, his low voice loaded with sexual innuendo as he winks at me. "We could let her misbehave and I could take you home with me and show you a good time."

I lean forward, matching his pose with my chin on my hand, my voice full of warning. "Or you could do your job and keep your nut sac intact."

"Damn, you got pretty eyes," he whispers huskily. "A man could get lost in those. I've seen heterochromia in brown and blue but I've never seen green and blue. You'd be like waking up with sapphires and emeralds."

"More like topaz blue balls," I reply cockily then smirk, "because I'm not sleeping with you."

His burst of laughter mixed with Mallory's catches me off guard. "Damn, you're feisty." He reaches his hand out to shake mine. "Dr. Michael Knight. And Banner Medical would be a perfect fit for you. I'm not truly a bartender. I'm here helping out my dad tonight because he had two people call in sick." His thumb lightly brushes back and forth over the top of my hand that he hasn't released yet. His voice feels like velvet over my skin as he promises, "And I would handle your body like the rarest diamond, Liberty Collins."

Oh, this guy is smooth. Wait a minute! I paid cash!

Mallory and I exchange shocked glances before I pierce him with a glare. "How the hell do you know my name?"

"I lectured one of your classes last term." His eyes drop to my mouth then shift back to my eyes. "No man would ever forget you."

Funny, I don't remember him. Not that I should. My head has been buried in the books, writing my thesis, clinicals, studying pharmaceuticals, crafting my skills. At other times trying to rid my dreams of childhood ghosts yet Googling a name on the off chance that somewhere out there exists the boy of those dreams. Have you ever seen a movie you'll never forget? A certain scene that's stuck with you year after year? One you'd give anything to rewrite? A happy ending versus the nightmare that was scripted? Yeah, that.

"You know . . ." Mallory taps her hand on the bar, ". . . I think I'm going to make a trip to the little girls room. Be back in a minute." She stops to whisper in my ear on her way past. "If this is his daddy's place, I bet he has access to the back office with a big desk. Go for it. That facial hair looks like a damn good duster to clean out the cobwebs."

I'm going to murder her. At the very least dip her toothbrush in the toilet. Well, tell her I did anyway so she has to run to the drugstore to buy a new one.

Michael breaks the awkward silence that my *former* friend has left behind. "How about a date instead?"

Oh crap! He heard that.

"I don't know if I'm in the right place to start dating. I've got a lot going on at the present time. I just finished school and I haven't decided on a job and . . ."

"You still eat, don't you?"

"When I remember," I admit with a shrug. Food isn't exactly first on my to-do list.

Damn, he is handsome. Blue eyes that sparkle with a hint of mischief when he smiles. Dark hair cut short on the sides and tousled on top. Finely trimmed facial hair edged to perfection around chiseled features.

He lifts my hand to his mouth and kisses my knuckles. "Let me be your reminder. Next Friday? Pick you up at seven?"

My bottom lip finds its nesting place automatically, tucking itself between my teeth as I study his face.

"Stop that," he teases, reaching out with his thumb and pulling my bottom lip from between my teeth, "or I'll have to kiss it and make it better before next Friday."

"Okay, potty break's over," Mallory announces loudly from halfway across the room, breaking our trance. "What did I miss?"

"Us," one of the guys at the end of the bar tells her enthusiastically.

She stops short and eyes each one of them. "Sorry guys. You're too pretty and I can't choose."

"You could have both of us," one proffers with challenge while the other grins.

She studies each one as if contemplating the idea. "Dumb and Dumber at the same time, huh?" She shakes her head and grimaces. "Even I'm not that charitable. Go home, call your mothers and apologize."

"Apologize for what!?" one asks defensively.

"For not being man enough to get the job done solo."

She struts back to where we sit and plops down on the barstool. She picks up her drink and takes a hefty swallow, setting it back down hard. "That'll teach them."

"Teach them what?" Michael asks, a bit perplexed.

"Emotional impotence for doubles," Mallory says proudly. "Threesomes will forever be accompanied by thoughts of their mother, therefore preventing them from performing. My job here is done." She grins proudly. "Just watch."

Michael's mouth twitches as he glances at the two morons

at the end of the bar, who sit with their heads bent, whispering amongst themselves.

Before long their conversation heats up and we hear, "I made her come harder than you did!"

"Oh please," the other huffs. "She was howling when I was doing her. She only moaned when you were inside her."

One throws back the rest of his beer, slams the mug on the bar, and gets to his feet. "Fuck you, Hanson! Find your own. I'm outta here."

As he saunters toward the door, Mallory hollers after him, "Be sure to tell mommy I said hello!"

The one left behind at the end of the bar glares at her. She eyes him expectantly then tips her head toward the door. "Well, go on. Call your mother. Wouldn't hurt to take her to brunch on Sunday either."

He stands and throws money on the bar before he narrows his eyes. "You did that on purpose, didn't you?"

She matches his glare and in a smooth, even tone asks, "You got a sister?"

His brow furrows and a shadow crosses his eyes. "As a matter of fact, I do."

"Younger?" Mal inquires.

"Yeah," he grunts.

She nods slowly. "And how many would you want doing her at a time?"

He opens his mouth, then closes it, incapable of a retort.

"Thought so," she sings. "Do better. Be an example, not a hypocrite."

Mallory may talk a good game, admire the male species, but she's choosy . . . and careful. She's also seen more than her fair share of damages during clinicals at the hospital in the surgical rooms. It's tamed her, humbled her, and made her extremely compassionate. It's changed her perspective on a lot of things. Her mouth may run like a motor express, but her sex life is the speed of an Amish buggy. In all honesty, her skills are limited to quick wit and book smarts. She reads much more about sex than she participates. I learned that about her in high school. She doesn't feel you need to be well-practiced; simply prepared.

She wants love, marriage, stability, kids someday, and a place to call home. She was forced to split her time between two parents in two different homes from the age of six. Says she's also studied how to plan the perfect murder if the occasion presented itself in the form of a cheating husband, because she would never make her own children go through that. I've never asked if she was serious – I don't want to know – but I wouldn't put it past her. However, I have promised her a partner in crime should she ever need one. No fingerprints, remember?

Before the man makes it to the door, she gets in one last dig. "Little sisters like brunch, too. A new Gucci bag if she's too busy to fit it into her schedule."

The man turns and glares at her for a moment before his features soften. He studies Mallory as if deep in thought, then shakes his head as a chuckle escapes. "Well played." He winks. "I'll remember this."

When Michael returns from serving another customer, he collects our now empty glasses. "Ready for another?"

"Yup," we answer in unison.

"So," he hums lightly as he grins at Mallory. "Did you put Eric in his place?"

"Eric?" she asks cautiously.

"The other guy," he informs her, then lifts his brows slowly. "He's head of radiology at Banner. Sounds like you two haven't seen the last of each other."

Mal stares, slack jawed, before she drops her forehead onto her palm and groans, "Oh, fuck me sideways."

Michael chortles. "Pretty sure he would if you asked him to."

"So are you going to take the position with Banner?" Mallory pulls out the little black dress that every woman owns from my closet and throws it on the bed. It's Friday evening and I have approximately half an hour to be ready to walk out the door with Michael. She has styled my hair and assured my makeup is done to perfection. "This one. Just enough cleavage to make him drool, enough leg to make him go all wobbly in the knees, and it hugs your curves so well he can picture you naked."

"I don't want him to picture me naked!"

"Really?" She grins impishly then laughs and turns back toward the closet. "Hmm...let me see if we still have the nun costumes from last Halloween."

"Ha!" I howl. "You in a nun costume. That's hilarious, Mal. Every convent from here to Georgia would have been slamming the doors shut for fear of you knocking."

Mischief flashes in her eyes. "I never was their favorite, was I?"

"You were on their list," I joke, sort of.

"Shit lists don't count." She giggles and holds up a finger. "But I was always at the top." She glances at the bed. "Now put the dress on. It looks fabulous on you."

She heads for the door but I call after her before she can leave.

"Hey, Mal? I am taking the Banner job. They offered me the ICU post-surgical position. Maxson actually recommended me."

"Yes!" She screeches so loud I do believe the neighbors have heard her as she rushes back and pulls me into a hug. "We'll see each other off and on when I do post-op anesthesia checks."

"Yeah." I smile brightly and hug her back. "Whenever we're on the same shifts."

"What does Michael do?" She narrows her eyes. "Not that he isn't on my shit list. He could have told me who that guy was."

"It was kind of funny." I snicker. "I have no clue what Michael does. I didn't ask." I shrug and pick up the dress. "It doesn't matter, Mal. It's just one date."

"Liberty," she says softly . . . and knowingly. "Give the man a chance. You've continued to search for years. There is no Lucas Monterrey that even comes close to the one you're searching for." She wrinkles her nose. "Unless he aged thirty years in your fifteen or was born ten years after. For all you know, he has a beer belly, seven kids, and keeps a transmission in his bathtub in a trailer somewhere deep in the woods in Kentucky."

My eyes must be bulging because the need to blink is overwhelming.

She shrugs. "What?"

"Seven kids?"

"If he was looking to kiss you at twelve, pretty sure he was looking to get laid by the time he was fifteen." Her mouth twists as she eyes the ceiling and calculates, nodding. "Yeah, it's possible. Especially if they had twins."

"You're nuts, you know that?"

She inclines her chin and narrows her eyes. "I'm not the one searching for a long-lost friend from a decade and a half ago. I know it was devastating, Libs, but you've got to move on. And it's not like he's ever showed up at your door. You were just kids. Your first love can't always be your last."

The one thing I've never admitted to anyone, including

Mallory, is that I haven't searched for Lucas simply to find him. It took me years to admit to myself the need to resolve a conflict. I was desperate to apologize. Had it not been for me telling my parents and the police being called, that night may not have happened the way it did. Lucas wouldn't have been taken away. His mom might not have been murdered. Maybe that's why he's never tried to find me. It's been over fifteen years. I took the note and the picture as well as my bracelet and the gum to Officer Sullivan and asked him to deliver it. I was sure he knew where Lucas went, though he denied it. Maybe Lucas hates me after all. I hate myself too.

I nod slowly. "You're right, but it's not like I have social media. I wouldn't be that easy to find."

Or am I hiding?

She smirks. "Because you consider it *anti*social media. You've always hated it. The closest you've ever come is LinkedIn, and only because you had to for business reasons . . . and you use your stepdad's name and no picture!"

"I had to change it because I wanted *job* proposals, not sex propositions!" I snap harshly. "They were creepy!"

"Liberty." She dips her chin and scolds, "Give Michael a chance. He seems really into you." She winks. "If you're a good girl, he could be soon." She blows a soft whistle. "Damn, that facial hair. Mm...mm...mm."

"Get out of here!" I throw a bed pillow in her general direction then glance at the clock. Twenty minutes to go.

"Cobwebs gotta go!" she calls out as she closes the door. "Good dusters usually have a broomstick close by that . . ."

"Shut up, Mallory!"

See? Sex. But we're back on track, memories be damned, head in the game, the only way to move is forward.

Chapter 6

Lucas

"Hey Tanner!" Jinx calls out from the end of the locker room, a lascivious smirk plastering his face. "We're headed out to The Tempest. Wanna join us?"

"The Tempest?" I put effort into not rolling my eyes but it's a challenge. The Tempest is a strip club on the east side that a few of the guys – some of whom are married – frequent on a regular basis. I've been once; not a fan. I prefer to tuck my thumbs into a thong to remove it in private, versus tucking dollar bills into one to watch an ass wiggle in front of me in public. After the bachelor party I attended there, I made the easy decision that the only thing I ever want to see get hard on my buddies is the glares on their faces as I win the poker game we're playing. Small wonder the divorce rate is what it is.

I don't begrudge the strippers their vocations – there are much less honorable ways to make money – but dealing with the fallout when the customers get too drunk, too aggressive, or a wife has discovered her husband isn't at the game he told her he would be, gets old. Admittedly, handling a drunk customer is preferable to dealing with a woman scorned.

"Already got plans," I tell him as I close my locker door. It's not a lie. It's been a long day. There's dinner waiting and a couple of ice cold beers in my fridge calling my name. There's also a game on tonight and my big screen TV to provide all the entertainment I need. Pretty sure I'll have company by way of a few neighbors who will make their way to my door as well. But they're pretty cool and usually show up with extra beer, chips, dip, pizza, and wings.

They're an eclectic group. Two single firefighters, a real estate agent, a hedge fund manager whose main source of income is divided amongst three ex-wives, a 53 year-old erotica writer and a retired truckdriver who we all know keeps her entertained regularly. At least according to the real estate agent and hedge fund manager who live on either side of her condo. The walls are not soundproof, nor are the writer and truckdriver discreet or quiet. I myself don't have two shits to give as long as they don't live on either side of me.

"Spending the evening with mommy?" Jinx teases with a cocky laugh.

I shoot him a sly grin and bob my eyebrows, knowing he has no clue what my history is and it's the only way to get past him and out of here. "The last thing I think about when I have her ass in my hands and her tits in my mouth is my mommy. Have fun while you look but can't touch tonight, Jinx. See ya later."

"What's her name?" he shouts before I can reach the door.

The pang in my chest hits so hard it nearly takes my breath away. What I wouldn't give to be going home to her. At the very least know where she is, what she's doing, who she's with. I really am pathetic. Social media searches for years have been futile, but I can't seem to help myself. Maybe hypnosis wouldn't be such a bad idea after all.

I turn slowly – feigned composure my best friend at the moment – and offer a puckish grin with a chuckle. "Too sweet for your mouth. Spend your dollars wisely. I'm gonna go get mine for free. G'nite Jinx."

Once home and inside, I head for the shower but stop at my dresser first and open the watch box. Jinx's unintentional cocky remark conjured memories that call for a little self-help. Three years of therapy as a kid couldn't wipe that picture out of my brain; my mom on the floor under me, my dad standing over us with the gun. The nightmares that woke me on a regular basis. I never talked about the even clearer picture of the girl running behind the police car, trying to catch up to me; tears rushing down her cheeks like rain as she screamed my name. No, that memory was mine and mine alone.

I finally had a breakthrough the night Captain Sullivan gave me the little white box from Liberty containing her note and the picture along with her bracelet and two pieces of gum. I pick it up from the watch box and open it, gently removing the contents and unfolding the note to read it once again. *"If you ever fall in love, you can throw this away".* There is not a snowball's chance in hell I would throw this away, because I will never fall in love . . . again. And even if I did, she was my first. There will never be another her. I stare at the picture as I brush my thumb over the scratched X on the plate of the bracelet. This is the only childhood I want to remember. This right here is what stopped those damn nightmares. I had something to hold in my fingers, to look at, to remind me that there is good in the world.

Liberty rescued me when no one else could.

Tracing my finger over the face of the beautiful blonde girl in the picture, I whisper, "Where are you, Liberty Bell? If for no other reason, I need to thank you for being my salvation."

I tuck everything back into the box carefully as if it were the most fragile thing in the world and place it back in the watch box, closing the lid once more. I'll run a social media search tomorrow. Again.

"Yes! Yes! Touchdown!" The sofa cushion next to mine sinks back down as Wiley collapses onto it. He's the hedge fund manager. Apparently sitting on his ass most of the day gives him the energy to make a trampoline out of my furniture when he gets excited. Get him out of his suit and tie and into his jeans and T-shirt and it's like the difference between champagne and cheap beer. I myself prefer the cheap beer guy, but I also prefer my sofa be comfortable; free from shooting springs up my ass, and suitable for naps.

"You realize if you break the springs in my couch you're buying me a new one, don't you?" It's not a question, he knows it.

He laughs heartily. "If the 49ers win, I'll buy you a whole new fucking room of furniture, Tanner."

Did I mention his language shifts from businessman to randy teenager with the change in attire as well? He seems to have forgotten there are women in the room. However, an erotica writer probably pens things that would make us all blush. I haven't read her works; no intention to do so. When I get creative in the bedroom, the last thing I need is *"Descriptions from Ava, chapter 7: paragraph 6"* invading my thoughts. I do just fine on own, thank you very much.

"You bet on the game?" Roger, one of the firemen, asks from the recliner he has laid back to near sleeping position. "How are you gonna pay alimony if you lose your ass on this one?"

"Wifey number one received her last payment this month," Wiley announces with a winning grin. "I am six thousand dollars a month richer as of last week. One down, two to go."

Roger cackles, as do a few others in the room. "And the 49ers are your new retirement plan?"

Wiley tips his beer to his mouth and drains half of it in one long pull, releasing a belch. "I only bet three grand. Four to one odds. I'm good."

Eyeing him skeptically, I ask, "And when you lose?"

He shrugs. "Still three grand ahead."

"Wiley." I shake my head and sigh. "I'm questioning you managing my money, and keep your ass planted on my sofa because you will never be able to afford to replace it."

"Tanner," Shelley, the real estate agent, squeezes in next to me on the sofa. "I've been meaning to talk to you about something. I have a niece who's moving here next week from Wyoming. She's just finished law school and will be starting with the Dennison firm downtown. You two would be perfect for each other. She's smart, polished, great personality . . ."

"Shelley," I interrupt with a warning before she can further her description. "I don't do blind dates and I don't do relatives of friends. It's a disaster in the making."

She nearly growls as she narrows her eyes. "You are so stubborn Tanner Carson. You could at least meet her. I hate to see you so lonely."

"Big difference between being alone and being lonely, Shelley." I aim my bottle back and forth between the two single firefighters in the room. "Pick on them."

She rolls her eyes. "I don't shop at secondhand stores. These guys probably had their first STD in high school. I need your powder room. I had too much wine."

As she makes her way to my bathroom, Reece, the other firefighter, can barely contain his snicker as he shoots me a sly grin. "You do realize 'great personality' is code for *real dog*, don't you?"

Even Ava, the writer, chuckles at his comment before Wiley sneaks in a quiet "Woof."

Roger advises as if he's the head coach, "You could put a jersey over her face and take one for the team."

John the truckdriver shrugs casually and whispers, "If you take her from behind, you'll never know the difference."

Ava throws a sharp blow to his ribs with her elbow and he grunts, then winks at her. "Oh, baby. The reason I take you from behind is so I can admire your ass. I love it and you know it. And," he drawls and bobs his eyebrows, "that way you get my whole hand when I smack it."

I pinch the bridge of my nose and groan. Maybe I should have gone to The Tempest this evening. Conversation is definitely overrated sometimes. This happens to be one of them. Maybe I should throw Roger out of the recliner and take a nap.

A week later, I arrive home at nine o'clock in the evening after a long shift and a day I'd like to forget to find a woman standing outside the entrance door to my building. I see her long before she sees me and in those moments, I'm pretty sure she would just as soon I hadn't.

"Aunt Shelley, I swear to God you're either dyslexic or just plain stupid." She holds a piece of paper in one hand and slowly punches numbers into the code pad, speaking each one out loud as she does. When it doesn't render her the successful click of the lock and entrance to the building, she heaves a throaty growl and kicks the glass door. Due to the fact she's in high heels, I don't imagine it felt very good. That, and the shriek that follows is a pretty good indicator it probably hurt like hell.

"Having a little trouble?" I ask as I step forward. She's a pretty brunette; about five foot-six, give or take without the four-inch heels she wears. Her hair is down, done in loose waves around her shoulders. She wears a red dress, cut above the knees, and the front dips low enough to show the perfect amount of cleavage to prove she has it. Perfectly manicured fingernails to match. Brown eyes. Deep red lipstick. Just my type . . . because she's nothing like her.

She spins at the sound of my voice, startled. "Oh, uh, officer. I – I wasn't trying to break in."

"I didn't say you were." I nod at the door. "I asked if you were having trouble."

She stares at me, jaw agape. Yeah, I'm used to it. If I'm in plainclothes, it's generally a prelude to an offer for a blow job. In uniform, I never know what to expect, unless they're trying to talk their way out of a ticket. She holds out the piece of paper in her shaky hand. "Is this the code to get in?"

I take the piece of paper and glance at the numbers. "This is what you put in?"

"Yes!" she snaps harshly. "I'm not stupid. My aunt sent me a text and I wrote down exactly what she sent. I double checked!"

"May I see the text?"

"What!?"

I hold out my hand, indicating my wish to see the phone itself. She hands it over after pulling it from her purse and opening the screen. I see exactly what I had anticipated and hand it back to her.

"I thought you said you wrote down exactly what she sent."

"I did!" she shrieks indignantly. "It's right there!"

Stepping over to the door, I punch in the proper code and open the door a couple inches after the lock releases.

"You got it!" she congratulates me as if I've won the ring toss at a carnival. "Thank you so much."

I let the door close and grin as the lock clicks.

"Why did you do that? It was unlocked!"

"It was," I quip. "And now it's not. Your aunt sent you exactly what you needed to get in. She's not dyslexic and she's not *just plain stupid*. She's actually quite nice. Open the text and try again. You might want to enter *exactly* what she sent you."

Don't ask me why I'm enjoying this, other than the fact she was a bit snippy, insulted a friend, and watching her cheeks turn crimson is a bit of a turn on. It's been awhile. A long while.

She's Shelley's niece, you idiot! Great personality, hell. That's a great rack, nice ass too. Wouldn't need a jersey over her face and I sure would be willing to take her from behind a time or two as well.

"So, I put in the hashtag symbol and then the numbers and then the star symbol?" she asks sheepishly as enlightenment dawns.

My lips tip in a slight smirk. "Well, some of us still call it a pound symbol but if you want to refer to it as a hashtag, feel free. Yes, that is how it's done."

She scowls as if insulted but then enters the code like a champ – albeit with a stiff middle finger that I'm pretty sure she'd rather be waving at me – the door lock releases and she steps inside. Now, one would think after receiving the help she'd just been gifted, she might say thank you. Not only does she not express gratitude, but she yanks the door that I'm holding for her out of my hand and pulls it shut, smirks, and sticks her tongue out in victory; leaving me standing on the other side.

So much for great personality.

As I watch her ass sway with every step toward the elevator, I mutter to myself, "With an ass like that, you could probably overlook her nasty disposition for a couple hours." I wait a few moments to ensure the elevator has closed before entering the code to make my way in. "A gag might come in handy though."

Early the next morning, coming back from a much needed run, I'm sweaty and ready for a shower after five miles in the Arizona heat. Stripping my T-shirt off before entering the building to use it to swipe my face from the sweat dripping into my eyes, I'm met by little Miss Zero Personality standing at my condo door with a plate in her hands.

She stares as I enter the hall from the elevator, her gaze traveling from my happy trail before fixing it on my chest. She's in a sundress, brunette hair in a high ponytail, makeup done to perfection. Ruby red lips. Once again, just my type – because they're not pink.

"I've been knocking for the last five minutes," she huffs indignantly, as if she's been inconvenienced.

"Five whole minutes? It took you that long to figure out I wasn't home?" I smirk and point to my face. "My eyes are up here, sweetheart."

"Wh-what?" she stammers, embarrassed at having been caught and nearly drops the plate from her hands. "I – I – my aunt told me to bring this to you." She shoves the plate toward me but I don't take it. Not after last night; she locked me out. I'm not about to let her off easy. She gets to work for it.

"Your aunt told you to do it?"

"Yes," she grunts and puckers those ruby reds in a luscious pout. "She said I have to play nice."

"Play nice, huh?" I arch a brow as I let my own gaze travel from her head to her toes and back up again. "What did you bring to play nice with?"

She sighs heavily. "Some baked goods. Would you just take it?"

"From the bakery down the street?"

"No!" she denies adamantly. "They're homemade cannoli. Aunt Shelley wouldn't send you store-bought."

I nearly choke on the laughter I hold back. No, sweet pea, Aunt Shelley would definitely send store-bought, and she certainly didn't bake those. Shelley wouldn't know a hot pad from a dishtowel. She knows her whiskey from her wine, she's a pro with takeout menus, knows the best pizza places in town, but the only apron she'll ever wear is the one she stole from the chef – after lurid sex – in memoriam of the quickie they had in the kitchen of the restaurant. And it sure wouldn't be to cook in. If these cannoli are homemade, the courier made them herself.

"Soooo," I drawl, testing her honesty, "Shelley baked me some treats this morning in order for you to play nice?"

She forces the plate forward into my chest, avoiding eye contact, and taking the opportunity to study my pecs once more. "Could you just take it?"

Avoidance. At least she doesn't lie. Ah, an attorney. And an opportunist.

"You want to come in and have one with me?"

She waves her free hand up and down the length of my body. "You – you're all sweaty."

"You can wait while I shower," I tell her, then wink. "Unless you're afraid the temptation to join me might be too strong, and all that work you put into your makeup this morning would be wasted."

Those brown eyes flash with a hint of mischief and defiance at the same time. No green, no blue. No spark to ignite the cold, dead part of my heart. The only organ of my body that twitches is my dick – just like always.

"I'll join you for a cannoli, but I won't be joining you for a shower, Tanner Carson."

I wink once more. "Maybe next time."

She smirks and tilts her head. "Three dates minimum. I'm Miranda Nelson, by the way."

Miranda Nelson. Nope. Sounds flat. No melody, no music, no song. More than that, no bells. Or is that Bell? As in Liberty Bell.

"I'm well aware," I reply, unlocking my door. "Your aunt already told me."

"What else did she tell you?" she demands.

My mouth twitches as I turn to her before opening my door. "That you have a great personality."

From her gaping jaw and the amount of time she holds her breath, I have a feeling she may have a few hidden talents her aunt doesn't know about. I tip her chin up with two fingers to seal her mouth closed. My voice is low as I tease, "I thought you said three dates minimum, Miranda. We can call this number one. I think I'd like to see how you handle that cannoli first."

Chapter 7

Liberty

"You're just too pretty for words, young lady." Mr. Gustafson's speech is strained due to weakness as well as a sore throat. I readjust his pillows after inserting a new version of distributing his meds and reset the machine to start his fluids once again. Upon transport from recovery to the ICU, one of the IV tubes slipped and got caught in the wheels of the gurney and ripped the IV from his arm. Instead of anymore attempts at simple IVs, it needs replacement, so here I am. Veins in the elderly are not always compliant – they have a strong tendency to roll and/or collapse. Their skin is thin and crepey, and it tears so easily. Blood thinners only add fuel to the fire and it appears the poor man has more bruises than skin at the present time. We've had to run a PICC line because his veins collapse so easily. He's two days post quadruple bypass surgery and six hours post intubation.

"She is, isn't she?" Michael's low timbre is aimed more at me than the patient as he steps up behind me, placing his hand on my lower back, but Mr. Gustafson hears every word. I hadn't even heard him enter the room.

"You best be careful there, doc," Mr. Gustafson warns him with a wheeze. "I can say those things because I'm old. If she has a boyfriend, he may not like you gettin' so close." For being so ill, Mr. G seems pretty sharp. The patient coughs and Michael moves in to place his stethoscope over his chest to listen to his heart and lungs.

He chuckles and whispers in his ear, "I am the boyfriend and I'm perfectly okay with getting close."

"So, *cough,* you're the luc, *cough, cough,* guy," Mr. Gustafson wheezes.

Michael smiles. "The luckiest. Now shush, so I can listen to your heart."

Dr. Michael Knight is a cardiothoracic surgeon at Banner Medical, yet the night we met he was bartending for his father because the help had called in sick. He's six years older than I am, but you can't tell. He's compassionate and kind with his patients. He is loved by the staff and has never had a patient who doesn't rave about him. He is also the fantasy hump of every female nurse and doctor in the hospital. Maybe even some of the males.

When the exam is over and Mr. Gustafson is settled in once more, Michael tips his head toward the door and I follow.

"Dinner tonight at six?" he confirms, then winces. "Provided no emergencies."

"Sounds good." I nod and smile. I know his schedule is hell, and it's not like you can order people to not have heart attacks, blood clots . . . or get shot.

He tips my chin up with two fingers, leaving a soft, more than chaste kiss on my mouth. "I'm off this weekend and so are you. I already checked your schedule. Three glorious days. Let's go somewhere. Get away, just the two of us. I miss you."

We've been dating for nearly a year now. Well, dating is the proper term. In our case, it consists of dinner out which generally lasts a couple hours to include interesting conversation and a few drinks followed by a couple hours of some pretty good sex; always at his place due to my having a roommate, and the typical goodbye when it's over as one of us has to work the next day. By my calculations, I think we've spent a total of ten whole nights together in the last year, though he has voiced his wishes it were different. Our schedules seldom meld, but his job is unyielding and mine keeps me busy as well. Michael also teaches a class at the university once a week so that is another time-suck. When we do have time off, quite often it's not together. The week of vacation I've had over the last year was spent in North Carolina visiting my mom and Tom. Mallory and I went together so she could see her parents as well.

I love my job; the one thing in my life I've never questioned, never second-guessed. Funny thing though; with every Band-Aid I place, I picture clumsy fingers trying so earnestly to make them stick. Lucas insisted on washing his hands before he placed them so he *wouldn't get me infected*. It's a pleasant memory, so I don't try to fight it. Small wonder it makes me smile.

"That sounds like fun." I nod in agreement. "Where would you like to go?"

He kisses my forehead. "Leave it to me. Pack a jacket and a couple sweaters. We'll leave Friday night."

"A jacket and sweaters?" I ask warily. "Are we headed into

the mountains?"

He winks. "Something like that. I have to get back to my rounds. I'll call you later." He leaves one last kiss on my mouth and is out the door before I can inquire further. Generally, PDAs would be unacceptable in the workplace, but Michael is discreet and quite frankly, doesn't seem to care.

"I think he's sweet on you." Mr. Gustafson's weak but humorous comment comes from behind me as I watch the door close.

"I'm kinda sweet on him too," I reply with a smile as I make my way back to his bed.

"Well, if you ever get tired of him," he chuckles, then coughs lightly, "I got a grandson that's free. But I think the doc's a keeper."

"You need some rest, Mr. Gustafson." I fluff his pillows once more and check the vitals readouts on the screen. "It's the best way to heal. We'll probably have you up and walking tomorrow."

"Will you dance with me if I make it to the end of the hall?" He coughs again.

"I'll do a cha-cha with you if you can do it without wheezing," Mallory announces as she walks toward us from the doorway. "How's the pain level, Mr. G?"

"There's my other favorite angel," he says through drawn out, tired breaths then tells her, "Can't complain." Mallory leans over him to let him know he has her full attention. His face lights up with the eye-to-eye contact and his brows lift weakly over half-lidded eyes. "Would you listen if I did?"

Mal chuckles lightly and brushes a finger over his wrinkled, age-spotted forehead. "Of course, I would. I'm the head of the complaint department. Lay it on me."

For a natural born smartass, Mallory is aces at what she

does. Need a laugh? She has you covered. Need pain relief? She's got your shot. Need confidence? She's your whisper in the dark. Need a hug? I swear the woman has eight arms.

"I feel like I got hit by a Mack truck," he tells her. "But you warned me so I was ready for it. I'll be okay. Get ready for that cha-cha, young lady." His eyes roll in my direction. "Did you know my heart doc is sweet on her?"

Mallory giggles. "I did know that. Do you approve?"

"Eh," he says groggily, "she could do worse."

"High praises from a man like you, Mr. G." She pats his arm lovingly, the entire conversation having been spent surreptitiously doing skin temperature check, carotid artery check, mental status check; all for her own peace of mind. Mallory is off the clock, as will I be in another hour. "I want you to get as much rest as you can. Don't be shy about that button to call a nurse. I'm going to go home and brush up on my dancing skills. I'll stop by tomorrow ready to tango."

He lifts a weak hand and points his finger. "A cha-cha."

Her face beams in delight before she winks at him. "Sharp as a tack. See ya tomorrow." She looks to me. "I'll see you at home."

"Absolute, intolerable, class-A jackass," Mallory grumbles to herself as I walk in the door. She tears more pieces from the head of romaine lettuce and throws them in the colander. The way she's attacking it, one might think it's actually insulted her personally. She apparently hasn't heard me come in because she continues her tirade in a low, baritone, mocking voice. "You wouldn't know pleasure if it bit you on the ass, little girl. Give me one night and I'll show you pleasure beyond your wildest dreams."

Good grief, she sounds like an audiobook narrator gone bad. She rips open the bag of carrots, grabs a knife, and starts to whack off the ends of each with enough fervor I fear if she misses, she may lose a finger. "Give me one minute and I'll bite your dick off, you pompous jerk. Better yet, I'll shove it in a mammogram machine, squash it flat, and show you what women go through every year." She giggles to herself. "Give a whole new meaning to the *head* of radiology."

A snort escapes my nose before I can stop it and my presence is no longer hidden. "I take it you and Dr. Eric are going rounds again."

"Oh, we went another round all right." She scowls. "He started with the typical *so we meet again* line. Then he asked if I might want to go out sometime. I told him I don't do doubles and I would rather pleasure myself than waste my time with someone who needs a partner because he has an iffy stiffy."

"You did what!?"

"Oh, ho, ho," she snaps angrily, "that's not all, Liberty. He told me the only *doubles* he's ever done were coming twice before he pulled out and the only *iffy* I needed to worry about would be how much of him I could take and how many orgasms I could tolerate before I begged for mercy." She crosses her arms over her chest, dipping her chin. "Doesn't that sound like sexual harassment to you?"

"Hmm," I hum softly. "Sounds more like a challenge. And admit it, you're loving every interaction with the man. Michael has already explained that whole show at the bar was to get your attention."

She goes back to attacking the carrots. "Yeah, well, a simple 'is this seat taken?' would have been a lot more effective."

"But not very original." I place my purse and keys on the counter and sort through my mail. "Due to the goosebumps on your arms just talking about it, I'd say you're looking forward to begging for mercy."

The scowl she gifts me with is met by my lifted brow. She

releases an exasperated breath and drops the knife. "Why does he have to be so damn cocky?"

"Cocky or confident?" I roll my eyes. "Mallory, if you felt for one moment he was harassing you, you would have reported him ages ago. You antagonized him. Just go out with the man. Your perfect opportunity is this weekend. Michael wants to take me away for three whole days." I smirk. "This way, I wouldn't have to overhear you beg."

"Smartass," she growls. "Wait! Michael's taking you away? You finally found a schedule that fits? Where are you going?"

"Don't know yet. He said to leave it up to him and to pack a jacket and sweaters."

She taps her chin with one finger as she ponders the possibilities. "Jacket and sweaters," she says slowly. "So much for a tropical island. It's not ski season yet. He wouldn't do a dude ranch; too much competition. He wants you riding him, not a cowboy."

"Are you quite done?"

She waves her hand in the air. "You can tell me when you get back. Have fun with uninterrupted sex. It's about time."

I shoot her a wry look before heading to my room to pack. "Let me know if the radiologist's dick glows in the dark."

"I didn't say I was going to sleep with him!" she shrieks.

Smiling smugly, I quip, "I don't think that's what he has planned. How would you beg for mercy in your sleep?"

"Lake Tahoe?" I say too loudly as we stop at Gate 42 and I read the destination sign above us. "That's where we're going?"

"It is." Michael wraps his arm around my shoulder and kisses the top of my head due to his height. "Tonight through Monday afternoon, I have you all to myself."

"Do I have you to myself?" I inquire, knowing he has a

demanding job, and an irritating habit of closing his days with telling the staff if they have any questions to not hesitate to call, regardless of whether or not he's *on* call. I don't know if it's an obligatory issue or a control issue.

The instant his brow furrows I know the answer to my question. At least Mal won't have to worry if the radiologist has one ear open for the phone buzzing at the bedside. Hell, he can leave it sitting on the kitchen counter without a second thought. He can turn it off without a care in the world.

"It's only one patient, Liberty," he explains when he notes my disgruntlement. "I asked Arseen to keep a close eye on her. I did a VSD repair yesterday and want to make sure things remain stable."

"I know you did a VSD repair, Michael," I retort. "In case you forgot, I took care of Ms. Hendryx after the surgery and today. But we both checked out at five o'clock . . . for the weekend." Avoiding the well-known fact that Dr. A would be more than happy to suck him like a Dyson and ride him into the sunset, I add, "Dr. Arseen is a competent doctor too."

"I like to be involved in all aspects of the patient's care, Liberty." He pulls me closer and moves me toward the boarding line. "I won't be leaving you. It would only be a phone call if they need anything."

"You mean *she*," I murmur.

"What?"

"Nothing." I duck down to move out of his hold on my shoulders and step away.

"Hey, hey." He gently grasps my elbow and leads me away from the line of passengers. Taking my cheeks in his palms, he bends at the knees and dips his chin to look me in the eyes – both eyes. "Liberty, it's you and only you. I'm doing my best here. This time with you is like breathing fresh air."

Guilt consumes me. There are days I arrive home weary and

weak from long hours and circumstances. I've seen patients die. I've seen them suffer. But their lives, and their hearts, are literally in Michael's hands. His dedication is in large part what attracted me to him. His good looks, sense of humor, smile, and butt like granite are a pretty damn nice bonus.

"I'm sorry," I whisper as I look up to ease that bent posture. "Let's go have some fun."

"Damn, those eyes," he mutters and smiles. "You could talk me into anything." He takes my mouth in a kiss that makes one forget there's anyone around, until throats start to clear and someone reminds us there's a plane to board.

In the tunnel on the way to the plane I side-eye him. "So, you do know the good doctor flirts with you."

The arm around my shoulder tugs me closer as he chuckles. "Once the medical jargon ends, the only voice I hear is yours. The only body I want is yours. The only mouth I want on mine is yours. Don't ever question it, Liberty."

The flight took less than two hours, dinner is over, and the bottle of wine sits on the edge of the hot tub as we sit with glasses in our hands, soaking in the warm bubbling water . . . naked. It's a cabin, in the mountains. Private, quiet, stars as far as the eye can see. Michael wore a condom for the first round in the hot tub; has two more sitting on the edge at the ready for the next rounds. A bit like a branch of the military, I think. Which one is it that is always prepared?

"Mallory and I can't wait to get into the new condo," I start, my head laid back on the edge of the tub staring up at the stars, sated and relaxed. "One more month and it will be ready. No more traveling to the gym; the building has its own. Two pools; one indoor, one out. It has three bedrooms so we're making the extra an office with a Murphy bed for visitors."

Michael's head whips toward me so fast, I swear I hear his

neck snap. "You and Mallory are moving? Together . . . again?"

I nod enthusiastically. "It's actually closer to the hospital and a whole lot bigger than the condo we have now. Ten floors up and a pretty good view. Concrete between the floors so no more thumping of footsteps above us."

"You already signed a lease? The deal is done?" He furrows his brow as I nod again. "For how long?"

"A year. It's pretty standard."

"How long have you had this planned?" His voice is sharp, the sting of which is making me uncomfortable.

"A couple months," I reply, a tad bit defensive because I feel as if I'm being scolded for not asking permission. "Our lease was nearing the end and we can afford a whole lot more now. Besides, it saves us the time and effort of going to the gym, it's closer to work, and it has a pool." I study his face and watch as his brow furrows deeper. "Why do you seem upset?"

"It's another whole year commitment, Liberty," he grunts. "I wish you'd said something. I was planning on asking you to move in with me."

"Wh-what?" I knew we were getting closer. We have fun, we enjoy each other's company, we're close, comfortable. I don't know how I would feel if I didn't have Michael in my life. I mean, geez, he's met my mom and Tom once when they visited here. Yes, they approved. He is more than charming. But live together? This is out of the blue, and I kinda like my current arrangements.

He slides closer and removes the wine glass from my hand, setting both his and mine on the edge of the hot tub. He moves me to straddle his lap and takes my cheeks in his palms. "Apparently I haven't made myself clear. Maybe I don't do things the way I should or say the things I need to say. It started the day I saw you in your class, but you were a student. Off limits. I stumbled the night I met you, I fell the night we had dinner together, and I plunged down that rabbit hole the first time I made love to you. You suck the air out of my lungs every time you enter a room, but you breathe it back into me with every kiss. I want every waking and sleeping minute I can get with you. I thought by now you'd have figured it out. Liberty Collins, I am head over heels, ass over end in love with you."

Michael has never kissed me like he does at this moment. It's deep, harsh, and claiming. He's in full control as one hand wraps in my hair, his arm around my waist, and he maneuvers me into the perfect position to deliver the physical component to match the poetry he's just recited. What woman wouldn't want to hear those words?

I'd like to reciprocate. I love Michael . . . with most of my heart. But am I in love with him? How do you tell the man you love there's a portion of your heart you gave away years ago, and you knew even then it was deemed nonrefundable?

Chapter 8

Lucas

"Why don't you ever call me baby, or honey, or . . ."

"Because it's not your name," I nearly gag. I've never called any woman by a pet name or nickname; not as an adult anyway. If I can't remember it, a groan and a few chosen swear words while I come have always done me well.

"Don't you think it's time we take this a step further?"

Miranda attempts to trace circles on my chest with her fingertip as she lies in bed next to me – a side of the bed she's deemed hers for the last year a couple times a week on a semi regular basis. A spot I honestly enjoy more when it's cool and empty. I like to stretch out when I sleep. No weighty feel of her legs wrapped with mine. No drool on my chest to wipe off when I wake up. No sweating in the night because she's curled into me like a needy puppy. It's a king size bed . . . for a reason!

When I say *attempts* to trace circles, it's exactly what I mean. She's inquired about the tattoo on my chest directly over my heart; the replica of the cracked monument in Philadelphia. Anytime she gets close to it, I brush her hand away, using the excuse – aka lie – the tattoo artist caused nerve damage, leaving me with the unpleasant side effect of pain with touch. It does cause pain, just not physical, and not due to the artist. It's also the reason I've never showered with her, or any other woman. No one needs to see the tiny seven letters tucked within the crack on the bell. It's symbolic of the permanent crack in my heart.

Miranda's made her own friends since settling in at the law firm; most of whom would only rub elbows with me by way of hearing "license and registration, please." They're the typical pinky-lifted-while-you-drink types. The Jameson and Glenlivet drinkers. God forbid you serve them Johnny Walker. She also refuses to take part in our game nights. *A truckdriver and a porn writer? A three-time divorcee? Oh, the horrors!* She always seems to have previous plans or wants me to change mine. Not happening. I like my friends. They're genuine. They might piss on your toilet rim if their aim is off, but they'd never piss on your dream if they knew you had one.

Miranda isn't totally insufferable when she's out of her own element. She's smart, can be witty, has a body made for bending. She's an overall decent person, but . . . she's not *her*. She warms my blood but doesn't make it hot. We are satiety in sessions, much like friends with benefits. For a while, I thought we were on the same page – a chapter; not the whole book.

Placing my chin on the top of her head so she can't see me

roll my eyes, I tease, "A step further, huh? So you want me to tie you up? Lookin' to get a little kinky?"

She slaps my chest hard enough to leave a bit of a sting, probably a nice red mark too. "Tanner! That's not what I'm talking about and you know it."

I do know it. Believe me, I know it. We traveled down this path two months ago, and why she thinks it's not going to lead to the same dead end it did then is beyond me. She wants marriage, kids, the white picket fence. I made myself clear from day one – and every day since – we were just having a good time. I could do exclusive for the sake of convenience and safety, but the moment one of us wanted to move on, honesty was imperative. No games. And she agreed. She was career oriented and ambitious with no interest in ties. *Her words. Until two months ago.*

And kids? I would never burden this world with my father's bloodline. It ends with me. My greatest fear is being anything like him. My uncle is a good man – he did his best during the time he raised me. But my most impressionable years were spent under the same roof with the senior Monterrey – name changes don't mean shit – and I would never want history to repeat itself by way of me. A risk I'm not willing to take. It's also something Miranda is not aware of. She doesn't need to be, because it's never going to happen. I watch her pill pack probably closer than she does, and sex never happens without a condom.

If I could find a physician willing to perform a vasectomy on a 29 year-old man, I'd be shooting blanks. I don't dislike kids, as long as they're someone else's.

"Miranda," I warn in a drawn out tone she's come to know well, "we're not doing this again. If you're not happy with our arrangement, then we should . . ."

"Don't get so touchy!" she snaps before climbing out of bed, snatching the sheet as she does and wrapping it around her. "I was going to suggest you move into my place for convenience." She waves her hand in the air aimlessly as she looks around the room in disgust and huffs, "Or, God forbid, I suppose I could move in here."

Whoa, whoa, whoa. Not in this lifetime, sweetheart. This is my space, my sanctuary. And you can keep your fancy three bedroom-two bath, posh, full-accommodations-with-a-doorman, uppity-ass apartment.

Narrowing my eyes as I slide out of bed, buck naked and uninhibited, and head for the bathroom, I nearly growl, "Thought you pretty much had. You took over two dresser drawers and half my fucking closet. Feel free to empty them anytime."

"You forgot your watch box," she says snidely. "I made room for mine in there."

I whirl and stomp toward my dresser, opening the lid to the watch box, only to find it gone. My heart hammers in my chest so hard, it feels like it's going to explode. "Where is it?"

"Where's what?" she asks casually.

"What the fuck did you do with it, Miranda?" I glare at her, my breaths increasing as the thought of the only piece of my childhood and my beautiful Liberty no longer visible to me tears at my very soul.

She rolls her eyes and snorts. "Bubble gum and a kid's bracelet? Who are Lucas and Liberty and what are you doing with their things?"

"Where is it?" I storm toward her in a desperate rage I can barely control. "What the fuck did you do with it!?" I scream, grabbing her shoulders but before I shake her senseless – I am not my old man and I would never hit a woman – I release my grip. I take a deep breath and demand once more, "Where is it?"

She tips her chin defiantly. "I threw it away. The trash bag went down the shoot after dinner. Good luck with that."

"I'm done," I utter as I run to grab sweats and a T-shirt and pull them on. "Pack your shit and get the fuck out."

I step into my running shoes at the door and head for the stairwell, taking the stairs three at a time down the necessary four floors to the utility area where the containers that catch the trash bags are located. I panic when I see two guys from building services wheeling out the last one into the alley to unload the bags into the city's dumpsters in the alleyway so the trucks can haul them away.

"Wait!" I shriek at the uniformed men. "Don't dump those yet!"

"Mister," one says as he eyes me warily, "the garbage trucks run on a schedule. If we don't get these out on time, they don't get picked up."

"Please," I beg, my breath heaving after my nice stair workout. "I...I lost something. Do you have any idea which bags would have come from 4C?"

"Aw shit," the other replies as he studies the building from the fourth floor to the basement as if trying to map it out. "That bin's already in the dumpster."

"Which one?"

"Oh hell, I don't know." He winces. "Could be any of these three."

I'll search all fucking night if I have to. "How soon are the trucks due?"

He looks at his watch and shrugs. "Half hour maybe?"

"Tanner!" Roger calls out behind me from the same door I'd just come through and sees me with the trash haulers. "What the hell's going on? Thought I heard something out here."

"I – I gotta, I gotta find her." My breaths are shuddered and my voice is weak as I repeat, "I gotta find her, Roger."

He grasps the back of my neck and mutters in my ear,

"Breathe, buddy. I gotcha. You gotta find who?"

"It's a . . . it's a little white box," I stammer, holding my hands up as I stupidly try to depict a visual as if it will help. "Th-there's a picture, and a note, a bracelet, and – and s-some bubblegum."

He slaps me on the back a few times, grasps my shoulder and squeezes it, heaving a sigh of relief. "Thank God. This'll be a piece o' cake. I thought you meant a body."

He pulls his phone from his pocket and places an order, "Yeah, you, Wiley, and John get your asses down to the alley. Bring some flashlights. Tanner needs help."

A few minutes later, the three others join us in the search and we're all in position: one in each dumpster while Roger and I tear open bags on the ground.

"Wait a minute!" Wiley calls from the dumpster he's standing in. "Don't you buy those trash bags with the green ties?"

I look up from my task at hand. "Not sure. Why?"

"It'd make sorting a whole lot easier if we knew where to start."

"How the hell do you know what color ties are on his bags?" Roger asks him.

"I pay attention. The green ones cost more," Wiley answers. "Always wondered why people pay more for one bag than the other."

"I bet you buy the cheap ones that rip before you get them out of the can," Reece grumbles as he moves another bag out of the dumpster to be inspected.

"Hell no!" Wiley exclaims. "I put my shit in bread sacks and toss it. Why would you pay good money for something just to throw it away?"

John calls out from his position in another dumpster, "Says

the man with three ex-wives."

Wiley chuckles. "I was only rentin' them."

John snorts. "So much for getting your deposit back."

"Tanner." Rogers looks up from the mess he's sorting through. "Think I got something here." He holds up what looks like a lifeline to me, but it's open and the contents are missing. However, the bag is at his feet on the ground and my hope is that the missing components are inside.

I make my way toward him, dropping to the ground on my knees. The others hop out of the dumpsters to join us and stand around me, flashlights in hand, aimed at the trash bag and all that is within while I search the contents. In a matter of minutes – what feels like hours – I eventually find every last piece of what I'm looking for. The picture, the note, the bracelet, and the two pieces of bubblegum sealed in clear laminate; one tutti-frutti and one blueberry.

Carefully placing the contents back into the now slightly stained box, I close the lid and clutch it tight to my chest. It's a good thing I'm not standing; I'm shaking so bad my legs wouldn't hold me up. As it is, I'm folded over my knees on the concrete, sobbing like a baby, holding the one and only memory of true happiness I've ever had: the picture of my Liberty, the words of sentiment I've memorized yet still read over and over, and the kiss she wishes she'd given me. The tomorrow I never got. Moreover, the reminder of why I will never love again: because it hurts like a bitch.

It's not until the sound of the garbage trucks arriving at the end of the alley that Roger helps me to my feet. I note the trash has all been placed back in the dumpsters and the area is clean once more. Feeling embarrassed, I swipe my cheeks on the sleeves of my T-shirt. My hands are filthy from being in the dumpster and, quite frankly, I'm not willing to lose my grip on this little white box.

"Let's head up," Roger says as he sets an arm on my shoulder. "You got a key to get back in to your place?" He has good reason to ask. I'm in sweats with no pockets and I obviously don't have my phone with me to use for the code.

"Shit," I mutter, the circumstances of my exit coiling my insides. "When I found out what she did, my only thought was to find it."

"Whoa, whoa, hang on." The anger in his tone rising as he tugs on my shoulder to halt our footsteps. "You didn't toss that by mistake?"

Pretty sure the look on my face tells the whole story when I only say, "Miranda threw it out."

The shock on his face only lasts a moment before fury takes over. "She still up there?"

"I told her to leave. Not sure if she's out yet."

He turns to Reece. "What color drawstrings you got on your trash bags?"

Reece shrugs. "Who cares? Think I'll toss that bitch's shit out the window anyway. She'll be lucky if I don't toss her out with it. Let's go."

Roger slaps my shoulder as we head for the door. "You can shower at my place. I've got sweats for you. Just search the dresser. PD, FD. Pretty much the same team. Wait there until we get back. We'll pack her shit for her, make sure she's gone and your property remains." He turns to the other three who stand behind us. "Boys, we got some fumigatin' to do. There's a snake in Tanner's apartment. Wiley, you got some lettuce stuck on your ass. Unless you're still hungry, leave it out here for the wildlife."

My shower is long over by the time Roger gets back to his condo with a confidence I envy as he sets my phone on the coffee table. I'd found the sweats and a T-shirt easily. Passed on the jersey briefs; commando is fine. There are limits as to what you loan your friends. My clothes are packed in a trash bag – red drawstrings – and waiting to take home with me to put in the washer.

"She's gone, so are her things. If I were you, I'd block her number and change your locks. Stubborn bitch," he grumbles. "When I couldn't find your phone, I called it to hear the ringtone. Funniest thing, her purse rang when the call went through. Didn't have sense enough to turn it off or silence it. Did give me good reason to dump her purse out on the floor though. She had a key to your condo and a used condom in it." He grimaces and shivers. "Tied off and full."

My face fills with mortification. I think I'm going to puke. What was she planning? To freeze my swimmers? Use a turkey baster?

He lifts a brow in query. "Does she know the code to get in?"

"God no! And my phone uses facial recognition to open it."

He heads for the hallway. "Good. I'm gonna grab a shower. The guys went to their places to get one and will return as soon as they're done. Beer is in the fridge, whiskey is in the cupboard. Help yourself."

"Hey, Roger." He stops before entering the hall but doesn't turn around. "Are you going to ask?"

"Do you want me to ask, Tanner?"

Do I want him to? It's not a short story. Certainly not simple. Definitely not poetry. Undeniably tragic. "Not really."

"Beers and whiskey it is." He spins and grins. "Call Mario's and order a couple of pizzas. Add some hot wings. We can watch a few replays. Tell Wiley if he bounces on my couch, I'm gonna make him sit his ass on the floor."

We spend the next two hours soaking up the beers, chowing down pizza and wings, watching a few replays of football on the tube, and talking about anything other than the events of the evening. This included the hot take on a couple of new female EMTs on the squad that Reece and Roger were biting their fists over, a few stocks that Wiley advised us on, the joys of an erotica writer and the benefits of her research (John), and a new nurse in the ER that Reece and Roger have agreed to share if it came to compromise. All the while, the little white box tucked into the pocket of the sweats I borrowed from Roger, safe and ready to take home with me, back where it belonged.

Not one of them asked about tonight. Didn't ask about the girl in the picture – nor the boy – and didn't ask the significance of the bracelet or the importance of what, to some, would seem a trivial token. No, tonight they saw a friend in need; therefore a friend indeed. And I have never felt so lucky to have four such good friends.

Chapter 9

Liberty

"So, is Michael going to Damon's bachelor party in Vegas next weekend?" Mallory inquires as she tips the glass of salty margarita to her lips.

"Surprisingly, yes." I nod and join her in my own sip as I tip my glass back, savoring a larger amount than I should, but it's been a long week. Dinner out for Mexican food and margaritas to wash it down sounded good. "I'm glad to see him take some time off and get away."

"It's four days!" she exclaims, wide-eyed. "That's more than he took when you agreed to marry him! He should have run you off to Paris, for God's sake. Instead, he took you back to

Tahoe for another three-day weekend." She smirks. "Two and a half to be precise. Interrupted by how many phone calls?"

"We're banking our time for a honeymoon." I sigh in exasperation over her consistent jabs at Michael, then scowl. "He wants to take a month."

She shoots me a wry look. "And yet you haven't chosen a date."

"I'm in no hurry," I state for the hundredth time in the last six months. I swear sometimes she's testing me more than encouraging me.

"What are you waiting for? Mardi Gras? Fishing in Michigan? Heaven forbid you leave the country – his phone might ring." She taps her chin with one finger then holds it in the air. "Ooh, I know. Corn pickin' in Iowa. I think they do it in August. Be sure to buy a tube top and cut off jean shorts. Wear a bandana if you can't find a straw hat."

Make that discouraging me.

"Are you quite finished?"

"Not really," she grumbles. "It's twenty guys going to Vegas, Libs. Five, I could understand. How are they even going to know where the groom is? Do they gamble? Go to strip shows? What are twenty guys going to do for four days in Vegas?"

"Worried about the glowing head of radiology?" I tease.

She scowls and grits through a clenched jaw, "I don't care what he does. He can nuke all the vaginas he wants to. She leans forward over the table and looks out across the bar before whispering, "What would you say to us going down to Vegas just to take a peek into the goings on while they're down there?"

"What?!"

"Ssshhh," she orders harshly as she scouts the room once more. "They'll never know. I rearranged my schedule so we both have a three-off during their time away. We could book a quick flight, two-night stay." She shrugs. "Do a little meandering while we're there."

I roll my eyes and snort. "You mean spying."

"Mmmm," she hums. "If the shoe fits. Wouldn't you rather be positive?"

"Positive of what? Mallory, he's never given me reason to doubt him. Where is this coming from?"

Her cheek sinks inward as she bites it and her brow furrows. "I heard through the grapevine that Arseen has decided to make a surprise appearance. That bitch doesn't have fingernails; she has talons. And we both know who she wants to sink them into."

My face scrunches in disgust. "Arseen is going to show up at a bachelor party?"

Mallory smiles sweetly, then sneers. "Surprise."

I trust Michael, don't I? I mean, the touches, the giggles, the over the top flirting from Arseen is unbearable, but Michael has reassured me over and over he thwarts it at every turn. Her condescending attitude toward me has become extremely irritating as well. The fact she's beautiful is no ego boost either. Pretty sure there's Botox and implants involved, but whatever. No other doctor in the hospital treats me the way she does. My work is exemplary. I've never had a complaint from any of the other physicians, but she picks and criticizes every chance she gets. 'I'm too friendly with the patients. I put more effort into spoiling them than servicing them'. If fresh surgical tape has a crease in it, she complains. I've often wished I could put some over her mouth . . . after I've stitched it shut!

Mallory is also right about not having chosen a date. But that's on me. Michael has told me time and again he would marry me tomorrow. Something about being married before I'm 30 haunts me, though. Michael also wants children right away and I'm simply not ready. That sounds like someone else's dream.

"Book the flight," I tell her.

"Already did," she says, batting her eyelids. "Got a suite, too. Same hotel, different floors."

"You what?!" I stare at her in shock, and maybe a little awe. "How do you know what floors they're on?"

She taps her temple with her index finger. "In case you've forgotten, Libs, I'm as street smart as I am book smart." She slaps the tabletop in victory, then narrows her eyes and smiles slyly. "Get ready, we're goin' to Vegas, baby."

An odd sensation starts in the pit of my stomach, akin to nausea. If he finds out I followed him, is he going to be mad? It's not Michael I mistrust, but Dr. Arseen has been on her knees for him for the last year and a half – even at eye-level – and he doesn't even know it. Or does he?

There's something Mallory is not telling me. It's in her eyes. She is in the OR with them often. Maybe she's heard more than she's telling me and maybe, just maybe, she wants to make sure the gossip is simply gossip. Worse yet, maybe she wants to be sure to have my back if it isn't simply gossip and the truth comes out.

Michael's text comes through as I sit at the airport waiting to board, four hours post the bachelor party's flight leaving.

"Arrived in the city of debauchery, though debauching isn't on my agenda. Can't wait to get home to my beautiful fiancé. Pretty sure I'll be out of touch for a while but will do my best to call at least once a day. These cretins have plans. Love you."

I turn my phone to Mallory, showing her the message. "Do you have any idea how guilty I feel right now?"

She reads the message before uttering, "Best to keep your

friends close and your enemies closer, Liberty."

"Is there something you're not telling me?"

She nods at my phone. "Might want to answer that message now, Libs. Sounds like Michael's going to be *out of touch* for a while." She arches a brow. "Can't say as I remember that ever happening. Can you?" She grabs her carry-on and stands. "Let's go, we're boarding."

I hesitate, my fingers wrapped around the handle of my carry-on. Mallory studies me, tongue in cheek, and tilts her head. "If nothing else, it gives you a reason to set a date. Or, every reason to sign another year's lease with me. Door's always open."

We light up the screens on our phones and show our boarding passes to the attendant. As we begin to enter the tunnel to board the plane, male laughter from passengers exiting the passage behind us from a returning flight rings throughout the terminal before one hollers, "Hey! There's my favorite brunette from the hospital! Ready to breathe hard with me yet, baby?"

"Whoa! Check out the blonde," another calls out, adding a low whistle. "Hot damn! Tanner, she'd be a cure-all for anything that ails you. If you don't grab that, I will. What's your name, sugar?"

I continue my trek – ignoring the virtual pass at my ass as that is their only visual – when a sudden rush of tingles hits so hard it makes me dizzy. I take advantage of the wall to steady myself while Mallory spins back and flips them off. "Her name is roll over and stay dead, Roger. She's off limits and not interested. Don't you have a cat to rescue from a tree?"

"I've been offering to rescue your pussy for months now, Mallory," the first voice retorts. "Say the word, baby. I'm all yours."

"Still not looking to get hosed, moron." She turns back and

gently eases me forward. "Don't even look. They're worse than dogs with a boner. Firemen," she grunts. "Those guys start the fires when they show up in the ER. The nurses' drool alone could douse the flames." She releases her grip halfway down the tunnel. "Must have a newbie on the team, though. Damn, that man looked fine."

"Sounds like you know *Roger*."

"Everybody knows Roger," she says with an eye roll. "It's his buddy, Reece, who offers his resuscitation skills with every unfortunate run-in we've had in passing. I'd rather choke him than stroke him, ya know?"

Chapter 10

Lucas

"Damn, I must have eaten something I shouldn't have." I press a hand to my stomach as we make our way through the airport. The sickly rush hit as Roger was teasing the blonde's backside while Reece propositioned the brunette after we deboarded and entered the terminal. Just like Roger to tease a head of hair and a nice ass – the guy who recommended a jersey over Miranda's face if she turned out to be a *real dog*. Mind you, it was a nice ass, but I don't do blondes. It's not really flu-like symptoms; more like a pit in my stomach accompanied by tingles and goosebumps. The hair on the back of my neck is still on end. It's . . . weird. Probably shouldn't have had the breakfast buffet this morning.

We've just come back from three days in Vegas. The guys insisted we get away in order to toss out the old and ring in the new. Turns out, it was a lot more of toss back a lot and take in the nudes; as in drinking ourselves into a stupor and watch a few strip shows. I indulged them one evening of the strippers. The rest of the time was spent tossing back the drinks and time at the blackjack tables. I won big, they won . . . a little. More than enough to cover the cost of the trip and have a good time.

I did collect on my mom's life insurance. My aunt and uncle invested it for me, and my college was paid for by scholarships. I'm not broke by any means, but my sergeant's rank isn't going to put me in the Fortune 500 magazine either. And yes, Wiley does manage my portfolio. But I wouldn't trust the man to sign a Valentine card for me if my hands were broken. I can see it now: *"I'm horny, be at my place by seven sharp. I'll buy you chocolates and flowers for a blow job"*.

"That damn Mallory won't give me the time of day," Reece grumbles as we saunter through the front doors on our way to the parking lot.

Roger slaps his shoulder. "Maybe if you quit offering to resuscitate her and ask her out, you'd have better luck. A little wine and dine, Reece. A touch of finesse without the offer to undress her first."

"I ain't looking to marry her, you dumbass," he protests with a growl. "But I sure wouldn't mind taking her for a spin or two. She's gorgeous. Damn fine ass, sturdy tits. Sassy as hell. The little shit told me she could *de*suscitate me faster than I could *re*suscitate her."

Roger stops short and squirrels his face. "What the hell was that supposed to mean? Like choking? She into kink?"

Reece shakes his head before his low rumbling laugh starts. "I was kinda hoping she meant sittin' on my face. Had me going for a while. But then I found out by asking around that she's a nurse anesthetist. She was not joking."

"Damn, buddy." Roger chuckles as we start our pace toward the lot again. "Make sure you stay at her place if you ever do get the opportunity. Get in, get up, get the hell out. Otherwise, you're gonna be sleeping with one eye open all night long."

I will admit, these guys can get your mind off whatever it's on when you need it most. They've never asked about that night. Pretty much like it never happened. This trip was in celebration of my being *"unhitched, un-bitched, truly single and ready to mingle again"*. They never did like Miranda.

They stood their ground with Shelley on my behalf when she showed up ready to rip me a new one for breaking her niece's heart. Whatever they did was done in the hallway – quietly – and resulted in Shelley returning the next day when I got home from work; a pizza in one hand, a six-pack in the other, and a half a dozen hugs before she left. Not sure what they told her; don't much care. The main thing is Shelley and I are still friends.

I now keep the little white box in my safe that is bolted to the floor in my closet – same place I keep my gun when I'm not home – locked and secure. If I didn't need to remove it so often for self-appointed therapy, I would keep it in a bank security lockbox. I've changed my locks and the code to my door. If I never see . . . Miranda who?

When I get home, the first order of business is to toss my clothes into the washer and check the mail – after taking a peek in the closet and assuring nothing is out of order.

My aunt has sent her usual 'hope all is well' card that brings a smile to my face every time. We try to talk once a week, hit or miss. My Aunt Ruby. She's a good woman, tried her best with a kid who didn't know up from down for a long time. Gently encouraged me to do my best, but also let me know everyone has a day here and there when mediocre effort is okay. Taking a day for yourself is the best thing you can do for you and everyone around you. She'd wink and say, "Otherwise you get all owly. Just ask your Uncle Didge."

I got along with my two cousins, though it took some time. We never fought; they just weren't Liberty. I joined the football team in high school and played quarterback for three years alongside my cousin, Jake, who played center. That is where we made our connection, and we have remained good friends ever since. He's a coach for UCLA; having gone on to a career that fits him well.

My cousin, Rose, is a fifth-grade school teacher. Married, two kids, and happy as can be in a quiet life with her accountant husband.

Picking up the phone, I press the button to call Ruby.

"Tanner," she answers cheerily. "I'm so happy you called. Didge and I were just talking about you."

Yup, I did the right thing. Today is not a mediocre day.

"Hey, Aunt Ruby. I got your card. How are things in California?"

The conversation lasts for the usual thirty minutes. We cover the basics: health, kids, grandkids, an upcoming vacation, and the closing 'I love yous'.

Time to change out the first load of laundry, toss in the second, and some self-appointed therapy.

Reaching into the safe, I remove the white box and pull out the letter and the picture. The same overwhelming sensation of tingles and goosebumps that washed over me at the airport hits once again and I drop to my ass on the floor. My hands shake as I unfold the note and read the words one by one. I study the picture; the grins on our faces, the twinkle in our eyes, the carefree joy of childhood. What I wouldn't give to feel that one more time. If I'd only known that day it would be one of my last.

"Why can't I let you go?" I whisper to the photo in my hand. "You barely feel real anymore, Liberty. I've been longer without you than I ever was with you."

I carefully fold the letter and place the contents back in the box. Closing the lid on the safe, I lock it and put the key back in the drawer.

Dropping my chin to my chest, I groan, "You are so fucked up, Lucas." Running a fast hand through my hair, reminding myself who I am now and reluctantly say it out loud, "Tanner."

I've been Tanner a whole lot longer than I was Lucas as well. Yet, I miss hearing it so much. Tanner was my mother's maiden name, Carson my aunt and uncle's family name. As they adopted me, they felt a whole new change would help me adapt to a whole new life. You'd think I would have grown accustomed after all these years. Maybe I really am crazy.

Chapter 11

Liberty

Mallory holds out her hand to an unsuspecting and extremely surprised Eric, who stands with a group of the morons as they decide what's next on their agenda. "Give me your cell phone and the room pass to your suite right now before I squeeze your gonads so hard you scream like a girl."

This is our second night here and we've observed from afar. Hidden in dark corners of the bars, we've been watching the drunken antics and activities of these professionals-turned-frat-boys for hours. Our hair is tied up in messy buns, makeup free, while every other woman is dressed to the nines. Not allowed into the strip clubs, our imaginations sufficed as the air was filled with filthy conversations regarding the lap dances they enjoyed. Why Damon's fiancé is going to marry the guy is beyond me.

"Mallory! How, how did you . . ." Eric stammers as he stares at her as if she's a ghost. A very scary ghost. His eyes flit to me and the guilt is unmistakable with the sag of his shoulders and the inability to maintain contact.

We watched Michael and Dr. Arseen leave the bar together approximately fifteen minutes ago; both happily buzzed but walking straight, arm in arm, with smiles on their faces. I'm falling apart on the inside, but the threads of anger seem to be holding me together pretty well right now.

"Liberty . . ." he starts on a soft, remorseful whisper.

"Save it," I hiss. "Give her your room pass, Eric."

Mallory doesn't hesitate before reaching into his pants pocket and yanking his cell phone from it. "Where's your pass, asshole? I know you're sharing a suite with him!" We're starting to gain attention from some of the people around us to include a few from the bachelor party. My cheeks are on fire, a mix of ire and humiliation, but I'm in it this far – may as well go for the gold.

Eric reaches into his shirt pocket and pulls out his pass, handing it to Mallory with one hand while the other pulls at the back of his neck. "Liberty . . ."

"You don't get to talk to her!" Mallory shrieks. "You're as low as he is!" She then turns to the staring faces of the bachelor party and finds Damon, the soon-to-be groom. "If you call up there and warn him, you will have no reason for a honeymoon, because I will remove any and all possibility of relations." Her pointed finger makes the round to the others. "And if any of you try, your family lineage will meet its demise with you, because I will remove your jewels sans the anesthesia. Got it?"

Her threat is met with wide eyes and raised hands; palms

facing her. Had they half a brain, they would be covering their crotches. Under any other circumstances, I would be cheering her on with a raised glass and laughing my ass off, because the woman has more balls than a bouncy house. As God is my witness, I swear every pair of jeans in front of her grows saggy between the pockets as testicles shrink.

All the way to the tenth floor in the elevator, I feel like I'm going to retch as I spin the engagement ring on my finger with my thumb. It suddenly feels foreign to me. I've always felt it was too big, audacious. I can't wear it to work. It's a hazard.

"I can do this for you if you want," Mallory offers softly as she reaches out and takes my hand. "Better you find out now, Libs. I'd rather you hate me as a strong, single, independent woman than a married, devasted mother stuck with children to raise on her own."

Ah, memories of her childhood.

"I don't hate you, Mal," I reassure her through a broken whisper. "You've always had my back."

"As you've had mine," she says.

The doors open and we step off together. Down the hall to room 1024 and she holds the pass up. "Which one of us goes first?"

"I don't know if I can do this," I confess weakly.

"Funny," she says with a scowl as we hear the first howl of "*Michael! Yes, yes!*" coming from somewhere in the room, "seems as though they can."

Snatching the card from her hand, I pass it over the lock and shove the door open. The living room is empty but it doesn't take long to follow the trail of clothing and hear the next howl from the bitch in heat from behind the closed bedroom door. I don't hesitate to push down on the handle and throw open the door to reveal the doggy ride taking place on the bed inside.

Ass in the air, Arseen is moaning loudly while Michael takes her from behind; rather vigorously I might add. So much so, they haven't even heard the door open.

When my inability to speak lasts a little too long, my bestie doesn't falter. "Hope you're wearing a condom, doc. Because she fucks everything that walks."

All action stops as Michael pulls out quickly and rushes to cover himself. His breaths are harder now than they were when he was doing his best work. "Liberty!"

Pulling the ring off my finger, I throw it hard, hitting him on the forehead. Too shaken and shocked to cry, too pissed to be quippy, my voice is flat as I leave with one parting remark, "Give it to her. You suck in bed anyway."

He really doesn't. I've just never seen him so . . . voracious. Michael's always had a tendency to be gentle, tentative, cautious with me – as if I might break. I have to nearly beg for harder or faster. Correction: **Had** *to. We're done.*

Mallory pushes the button for the elevator as Michael rushes out of the room barefoot, shirtless; buttoning his pants on the way to us. "Liberty!"

Mal charges back down the hall to reach him before he can make it to where we were standing and shoves her hands to his chest hard enough to falter his footsteps. "You've done enough damage," she enunciates in a voice so low I don't recognize it. "You made your bed. Go sleep in it, asshole."

"Liberty, please!" he yells around her as if she doesn't exist yet doesn't try to move her.

The elevator doors open and Eric stands inside. Mallory makes her way back to me and gently takes my elbow. "Let's go, Libs." When she sees the radiologist standing in the elevator, holding the door for us, she sneers. "Well, aren't you lucky. If you hurry, maybe he'll do doubles with you."

"Mallory." His voice is but a pleading whisper as he reaches for her.

She pulls his phone from her bra and hands it to him. "Your pass is in the room." She tilts her head in Michael's direction. "Better hope dumbass there has his. Otherwise, you're both screwed. Oh wait!" She chuckles sarcastically. "You've got the whore waiting inside. Now get the hell out of the way."

"Mal . . ." he starts again, but before any of us can shift our positions from inside to out and vice versa, Michael is behind me and grasps my bicep, pulling me back.

"Liberty, let me explain."

"Michael," Eric warns as he leaps forward and separates us, holding Michael back. "Give this time to blow over."

Mallory pulls me onto the elevator and pushes the button for the twelfth floor. Looking to Michael as I turn around, I state my case, "It is over."

"Liberty, please," he begs. "I love you."

Squaring him straight in the eyes, for what I deem to be the very last time, I simply reply, "You don't know what love is."

You don't hurt people when you love them – not intentionally. This isn't the worst pain I've ever felt – I can't even cry. It might sting; more like a bad bug bite. I don't feel like I've lost a part of me. I'm not going to lose myself in a world of hurt for years. I'm not going to lose interest in everything I've come to enjoy. I've been there, I've done that. That part of my heart is gone. That was love. That's a hurt you only feel once in your life.

Before the doors are closed Eric shouts, "What the fuck were you thinking!?"

Taking Mal's hand in mine, I give it a squeeze. "Thank you."

"Another year on the lease?"

The doors open to the twelfth floor. "What about Eric?"

She steps off and I join her as we head for our suite. "Eric who?"

"Mal, you don't mean that."

"We were never a real thing, Liberty," she snaps. "I think he's been through half the female staff at the hospital."

"That's not the impression I got from the way he looked at you."

She stops at the door before passing her card over the lock and turns to me. Her face runs a gamut of nearly a dozen different expressions, i.e. batting eyelashes, a cocky smile, pouty lip, puppy dog eyes, feigned wiping of tears, kissy face, and finally half-lidded eyes with a deep heated glow and groans, "Mallory, baby."

"What the hell are you doing?"

She lifts one shoulder in a shrug. "Mimicking. He is good, isn't he?" She slides her pass over the lock, opens the door, and we step inside. "I would rather have a fun guy who is willing to work for it than one who thinks he's got it in the bag just because he makes a shit ton of money and he's hot." She points to her chest. "I already make a shit ton of money." She sniffs haughtily. "And I'm pretty hot myself."

She renders me speechless, until I break into a fit of giggles. She does make a shit ton of money, and she is hot. And she is funny as hell. This is my bestie. It started the day we met and it hasn't stopped since. I know I'll cry, eventually. Maybe when the shock of it all sinks in. But not tonight. It's not worth my tears tonight. My finger feels a lot lighter; comfortable, free from burden. Man, if that doesn't speak volumes.

"Burgers, fries, and a strawberry shake from room service?" she proffers. "You know I hate vanilla."

Mallory Tompkins: Code for "I've got your back".

"Can we hit this minibar to wash it all down when we're

done?" I ask, nodding at the cabinet against the wall.

"You betcha." She tosses her room pass on the console table, plops down on the sofa, picks up the black leather folder to peruse the hotel's menu, and starts to flip through the pages. "Flight doesn't leave until twelve tomorrow. We can sleep it off in time."

"Hey, Mal," I whisper.

Continuing to flip the pages and avoiding eye contact, she warns, "Liberty, if you thank me one more time, I'm going to start feeling like service personnel. Friends catch you before you fall whenever possible. They bandage the wounds if you fall before they can stop you." She looks up from the menu I don't believe she was actually reading and shrugs. "What can I say? My timing's impeccable."

A soft smile blooms as I nod slowly. "Glad your watch was working."

"What flavor shake do you want?" she asks as she studies the menu once again. "And if you say vanilla, I'm going to make you start watching porn. Live a little."

Mal has never hesitated to say, 'thank you', but I'm not sure I've ever heard her say 'you're welcome'. It's as if it's a foregone conclusion. As though she knows I would do the same for her, which I would, without hesitation. Over fourteen years we've been besties, and honestly, I can't wait to sign that lease.

"You want to what!?" Helena Chalmers stares at me from her supervisor's desk at 6:30 Monday morning. Helena is the head of staffing for all PAs and NPs. She also gives final approval for all hiring of RNs and LPNs, but the grunt work of background checks, interviews, and scoring is on other staff. It's a half hour before my shift starts. I could have waited until lunchtime, could have waited until the end of the day, but the sooner we start the process, the sooner I can get out of the post surg unit. My mind was made up before I left Vegas Sunday morning. Mal and I discussed it over four mini bottles of Glenlivet each and came to the obvious conclusion that it would be best if I left the post surg ICU and found another position in the hospital. I don't develop relationships with the patients – they're short-term stays. One of the reasons I took a hospital job versus working in an office.

Once again, a habit developed during childhood: social sobriety. Don't get close, you won't get hurt. Mallory was my exception. Until Michael. Lesson learned.

"Liberty," she says, calmer now that she's taken a breath. "Take a seat."

"That won't be necessary, Helena. If a transfer to another department isn't possible, I'd like to put in my notice."

"No!" she startles. "Liberty, you're one of the best I have. I'd like to know what's going on." She lifts her brows knowingly. "I get tidbits through the grapevine. Unfortunately, you haven't been very forthcoming about any conflicts. Is this about Dr. Arseen?"

I let out a pitiful huff and shake my head – the sight of Arseen's ass in the air and Michael behind her burning my retinae. "Transfer, Helena. That's all I want. Yes or no. St. Joseph's and Abrazo have openings if you can't accommodate me here."

"Well, they'd be lucky to have you, but I'm not about to let that happen." She starts tapping away at keys on the computer. "Have you and Dr. Knight chosen a date yet?" she asks casually, or is that cautiously? I ignore the inquiry, knowing it's only a matter of time before word gets out. She'll have an answer soon enough – grapevine and all. Being in the ICU, I work with Michael and Arseen on a regular basis with post-op patients. I've had more texts and phone calls from Michael in the last day – all of them ignored and deleted – than I've had in the last month. I'm not about to work alongside either one of them.

She stops tapping the keys and looks up, her mouth twisted. "Liberty?"

"What?"

"I asked if you and Dr. Knight . . ."

"I heard you, Helena," I interrupt, my impatience growing as I put full effort into reminding myself she is not the target of my ire.

The printer begins to drop a few sheets into the tray as she whispers, "Oh."

Pointing to the printer, I ask, "Is that a list of openings?" She only nods. I step to the printer and lift the sheets off the tray; three pages, double spaced. I'll be damned if I go back to emptying bedpans and changing sheets. I did that all through nursing school. I'm not above it, but it's not what I do. I'm a nurse practitioner, for God's sake. I've worked my ass off to get where I am.

The position virtually jumps off the page at me.

"This one," I say, laying the paper on her desk, snatching the highlighter from the penholder and smoothing the tip over the job listing.

She studies the page for a moment then looks to me, brows raised in surprise and jaw agape. "The ER?"

Chapter 12

Lucas

"All units available. Suspected domestic dispute at 6307 Falcon Court." The call comes in over the radio as we climb back into the car after helping at the scene of a six car pile-up on the west side of the city. Roger and Reece worked together using the *Jaws of Life* to extract one victim. Two weren't so lucky as to need it. Eight others in total walked away without a scratch. Some days I swear it's like playing Russian roulette just getting behind the wheel.

I tap the button on my shoulder device. "Unit 57 reporting. Three miles out."

"Shit," Carny groans as I hit the siren and pull out onto the road, heading south toward the address. "I hate these fucking calls. If you can't get along, move out, move on, go blow off some steam at the driving range, take a fucking walk."

If only he knew.

Carny has been my partner for nearly a year. We work well together, have each other's backs, are both single, and have come to be pretty good friends. He's a bit cocky, favors himself a lady's man, but he's a serious cop and sharp. Work first, play later.

Two units are already on the scene when we arrive, vested up, McClaren with megaphone in hand.

"Grab the jackets," I tell Carny as I pop the trunk once parked down the street, then radio ahead to let them know we're ready.

"Neighbor says the guy is a real nut case. A lot of screaming, glass breaking," McClaren radios back. "Neighbor also says there's a kid in there, Tanner." My stomach does a double roll with that info and a flashback runs through my mind, but I shake my head to clear it.

A kid.

Two more cars show up by the time Carny and I have our vests on. "Let's take the back," I tell Carny as I nod toward the neighbor's yard when I see a shortcut through. "Slow and easy. Stay low." I toss him a warning glare. "And remember, there's a kid. They can run out of nowhere."

I inform McClaren of our plan and tell him to put that megaphone to use and distract the homeowner toward the front of the house. If he can keep the owner distracted toward the front, hopefully we can gain access through the back.

A smoke bomb isn't going to kill them; just gain us access and stop this madness.

A woman's sobs can be heard as we near the backdoor to

the house and a sudden heart-wrenching shriek pierces the air prior to the ever familiar sound of a gunshot.

"No, Dad! No!!!"

I'm suddenly back there . . . in my twelve year-old mind, but not my twelve year-old body. And it's the current adult body that pulls my gun from its holster and propels forward through the door via one foot kicking it in and charging through without considering the consequences.

"Drop it!" I yell at the man standing over the body lying on the floor. He stares at her as if in shock, his hand shaking as he lowers the gun to his side but his grip still firm on the firearm.

"Drop the gun!" I warn him once more as I step closer, my finger on the trigger, steady and ready should he move. "Drop the gun," I repeat. "You don't want to do this."

The gun falls to the floor at his feet as he continues to stare at the woman as if in disbelief. Carny rushes in behind me, tackling the man to his knees, then onto his belly before placing cuffs on his wrists behind his back. He eyes me warily, shakes his head, and scoldingly grumbles, "Didn't know suicide was on your bucket list today," then pushes the button on his shoulder unit and calls for backup.

"It wasn't," I reply as calmly as I can, holster my weapon, then squat to check for a pulse I know I won't find on the recipient of the bullet. The bastard was pretty precise. That, and you need the back half of your skull to survive. I nod to the where the whimpers of a young boy sound from our left as he crouches in the corner with one obviously fractured arm with the other holding it while he shields his head. "Saving a kid was."

Carny glances at the boy in the corner before he growls against the ear of the man on the floor, "You sonofabitch," as he grinds his knee into his back, then yanks him to his knees. The front door blows open with half a dozen uniforms charging in.

"Hey, buddy." I drop to my knees in front of the kid on the floor, blocking his view, and speak softly. He's probably eight years old, maybe nine. "Do you hurt anywhere other than your arm?"

His breaths are so stuttered he can barely breathe. "M-m-my m-mom."

"These guys are going to help her while I help you, okay?" I lie, my hopes high I can get him the hell out of here before he sees her. "Can you hold your arm steady while I check you?" The whole time I talk, I'm checking his shoulders, legs, neck. All seems stable. "Are you hurt anywhere else?"

"N-n-no," he stammers.

"Carny," I call behind me. "We got an ambulance on the way?"

"A little late for that, isn't it?" one of the uniforms grumbles.

Maybe the guy can't see what's going on over here in the corner. Maybe he hasn't assessed the entire situation. My main concern is getting the kid out, so I'll save punching him for later. Read the room, asshole.

Another adds quickly, "They're running slow right now, Tanner. A little shorthanded. I-17 had a big pile-up. They're routing them to St. Joseph's and Abrazo, but they needed the extra wheels."

"Carny," I call to my partner. "Need a little help here."

He's by my side in an instant. "What are we doing?"

I look to the little boy. "What's your name, buddy?"

"A-ad-dam." The poor kid's fingers are purple and cold. Pretty evident he has a compound fracture due to the unnatural bend in his forearm, but the skin isn't broken. However, there's no way to tell what it's compressing on.

"Adam, I'm Sergeant Tanner and this is Officer Carny. We're going to take you for a ride in a police car so we can get your arm fixed at the hospital. Carny is gonna hold your arm while I carry you. You ready?"

Carny gasps. "We're taking him in the car?" I simply glower then flit my eyes to the situation on the other side of the room to remind him there are things this kid doesn't need to see. Carny nods once before bending to help out, keeping his voice light. "Car it is," he says, then clumsily adds, "You like sirens, kid?"

"Uh, guys." McClaren approaches as we're getting Adam lifted into our arms. "We're going to need reports."

Shielding the little guy's head against my chest to block his view of the macabre scene behind us as I lift him in my arms and Carny carefully keeps his arm held in place, I tell him, "You can find us at Banner Medical. It's the closest."

McClaren is on our heels and warns us as he follows us out onto the porch, "This ain't exactly protocol."

Carny snorts on our way down the steps. "A rose by any other name, McClaren. Take it up with Sully."

"Real funny, asshole!" he yells after him. "This ain't roses. This is bullshit!"

Carny chuckles. "Yeah, but it'll smell as sweet."

Romeo McClaren: The butt of all things Shakespeare. Guess that's one way to shut him up.

I'm kinda hoping Sully's olfactory sense is better than his memory. I can get past the bullshit and the repercussions for going against "protocol". But having to undergo a psychological evaluation because Sully may see my actions today as a Band-Aid over a personal wound might be a bit much.

"I'll hold him in the back," I instruct Carny as we approach the car. "Call ahead and let them know we're on our way. You drive."

"What about seatbelts?" he asks, incredulous. "We'd be writing tickets for people who don't have their kids in car seats at that age."

"You see any little red wagons handy?" I deadpan.

He heaves a sigh as he opens the back door. "I'll run the siren and be careful."

"Good idea." I ease down into the seat with Adam in my arms while Carny guides us. Adam whimpers slightly with the movements but for all this kid has been through today, he's being a helluva trooper. "You doing okay, buddy?"

"Wh-where's m-my mom?" he sniffles.

It's ripping my heart out to watch him. He is me nearly 18 years ago. He's slight, a bit on the skinny side, younger than I was. I didn't suffer any broken bones. I wasn't found in the corner; I was laying over my mother, trying to protect her from him, thinking I would be next. It's all I remember. He was a mean sonofabitch. To this day I hope he suffered – a slow and painful death to pay for all the suffering he caused us – the effects of which still linger for me.

"Your mom is getting help from the officers back at the house," I lie. We need a social worker to help with this. It's not my job to tell him – he's not ready for the truth, though I'm not sure how much he saw.

He shivers in my arms. "C-can y-you call m-my friend?"

"Who's your friend, Bud?"

"J-jessie," he whispers. "She's my b-best friend. Sh-she'll w-wonder wh-where I am."

And I'm dead. I begged for Liberty all those years ago to no avail. His mom is gone. His dad is going to prison. I hope this kid has family that will take him in. Maybe an aunt and uncle that will give him a home and raise him like their own.

I hold him a little tighter, assuring that his arm is stable as Carny turns into the emergency department drive and attendants rush out to the car, pushing a gurney to collect our charge. "I'll see what I can do, okay?"

The transfer to the gurney isn't hard, but I swear Adam whimpers more than he did when Carny and I moved him from the house to the car. Maybe it was the fact I had to let go of the poor kid – turn him over to the unknown. I suppose one of those whimpers could have been in my head; an echo of my own from years ago.

"You got any info on him?" one of the attendants rush to ask.

"His name is Adam. Otherwise, only address and circumstances," I reply as I follow them in, leaving Carny to park the car, then lower my voice, "none of which we want to discuss in front of him."

He eyes me warily, then tips his chin. "Ah, got it."

Carny and I wait in the hallway while they perform their initial examination. Adam is the key to what happened inside that house before we arrived but getting him treated for his injuries is first on the list of priorities. As we stand and wait, I glance down the hall and see Captain Sullivan watching us. As our eyes meet, his brows rise and he points his finger at me, throws a fast thumb over his shoulder, indicating the exit doors past the waiting room area, and mouths the word, "Now!"

"Oh shit," Carny mutters when he sees him. "What kind of flowers do you want on your grave?"

"Make it a cactus, long needles," I growl, "so I can stab McClaren when he visits."

Chapter 13

Liberty

"Liberty." Michael's irritating plea as he sets his tray on the table next to mine in the hospital cafeteria grates on my nerves. "Can we just talk, please?"

He's in his surgical scrubs, dark circles under his eyes, his beard is scruffy instead of the finely trimmed growth that he normally sports. He must have had an afternoon surgery, or one that ran late. I'd pity him . . . if he were someone else – anyone else. It's been a weeks. Weeks of endless phone calls, voice mails, countless texts, persistent buzzing at the door of our building until Mallory threatened him with harassment. I've blocked three different numbers on my phone. I've received more bouquets of flowers than a damn funeral home hosting a celebrity's wake. Mal and I gathered them up and brought them to the hospital and had the volunteers take them to the patients that didn't have any. Someone should enjoy them.

"Ah, what the hell." I toss the last half of my sandwich back down on the plate and start to rise. "I haven't eaten since breakfast. Guess I can do without my dinner as well. You'd make a great weight loss plan, Michael. Ruining appetites everywhere."

He grasps my wrist. "Liberty, stop! I only want to explain."

"And I only want you to drop dead. There is nothing to explain. Your dick in Arseen was pretty self-explanatory." I narrow my eyes and glance to where he's gripping my wrist. "Let go."

He releases my wrist and rakes his hands through his hair, grinding out slowly, "I'd been drinking. The atmosphere was so different. I took her from behind because I couldn't look at her face. I fucked up, Libs."

"No, you fucked *her*. I hope it was worth it."

He squeezes his eyes closed as if in pain. "Nothing is worth losing you, Liberty. Can you not forgive me?"

"Picture me with another man, Michael." My voice is low and taunting as I paint a graphic scenario for him. "Naked. Doing all the things you used to do to me. Probably doing it better. Whispering in my ear, hearing my moans." His face fills with mortification, a heated glare of anger and jealousy flashes across those eyes I thought were aimed only at me. Leaving my tray behind, I slowly walk backwards away from the table. "It'll happen. Lucky you though, you'll only have to use your imagination."

The sound of silverware and a tray hitting the floor as I leave the cafeteria doesn't render me satisfaction. No, unfortunately, it's serving that vicious little creature we all house inside ourselves; vengefulness.

Something else happens with that sound as well: Realization.

"Can we talk?

I only want to explain.

I'd been drinking.

The atmosphere was so different.

I couldn't look at her face.

I fucked up.

Nothing is worth losing you, Liberty.

Can you not forgive me?"

Not once in the last six weeks has Michael said, *"I'm sorry."* How can you ask for forgiveness if you can't apologize? I don't know if I'm madder at him for his excuses or at myself for not detecting his narcissistic tendencies.

Right now, I'm thinking I should have taken Mallory up on her offer to go axe throwing last weekend; might have let me vent a bit of this frustration. For all I know I'll be 40 before I'm naked with anyone again. But he doesn't need to know that.

My pager sounds as I stand at the vending machine pondering what I might stuff in my mouth in lieu of the dinner that was ruined. Lovely, at least I got half a sandwich down. I had 20 minutes left on my dinner break.

As I approach the ER, Gabby, an RN I work with regularly, grabs my elbow and veers me down the hall. "I need you in Room 7. Got a ten-year-old kid with a compound fracture to the left forearm, but once you get a look at the rest of his body, you ain't gonna be too happy."

"Abuse?" I question as we head for the room.

"Oh honey," she groans. "This poor boy has been up against

Satan himself. His mama was killed by his daddy, his daddy is at the jail, and the police brought the boy in the car 'cause they didn't think the ambulance was gonna be fast enough."

"Wh-what?" My head spins because not only does Gabby talk a mile a minute – not to mention her deep bayou accent that would make gators crawl back into the swamp – but her description is drumming up a few memories from a street scene of old.

Not now, Liberty.

"There was a pile-up on I-17 that drizzled some patients over to us and while he's not the most urgent on the list, he does need some TLC. Doc Zimmerman told me to page you and have you handle the boy. He ordered a drip and some pain meds but the rest is on you."

"Alright." I nod quickly. "I've got it. Let's go."

There's a uniformed officer standing outside the door as we approach. He's young, seemingly nervous and unsure as he paces back and forth. "What's he here for? You said the father is in jail." My question is aimed at Gabby, but the officer speaks first.

"We – we need to question him, ma'am," he offers hesitantly. "He was witness to what happened in the home before we entered."

My nose crinkles as I look to Gabby. "How old did you say he is?"

She scowls at the officer while answering me, "Ten."

Lifting my wrist, I glance at my watch. "Most ten year-olds are in bed by now. I doubt he's going to be much help tonight, officer. My main concern is treating the patient. You might be waiting a long time."

He nods. "I'll wait. My partner isn't back yet anyway."

"Wait down at the nurses' station," I clip. "We'll let you

know if there's any possibility of speaking with him tonight. I wouldn't count on much, officer."

The ER staff have his arm in a padded brace to keep it stable, and he's been changed into a hospital gown by the time I enter the room. The bruises on his calves that peek out from under the gown; ranging anywhere from deep purple and bright pink to the faded stages of light green and yellow, make me want to retch. His feet are dirty, but that could be because he hasn't had his bath yet today. Boys will be boys and all.

The little guy has dark brown hair and the biggest, saddest, blue eyes I think I've ever seen. His cheeks are red and streaked with dried tears. He's like a *take me home* advertisement for a puppy shelter.

"Hey there," I greet him as I approach the bed and extend my hand so he can take it with his good one. "I'm Liberty. Who might you be?"

"A-adam," he stammers. "C-can you find m-my m-mom?"

The ER tech on the other side of his bed glances at me, grimaces and ever so slightly shakes his head.

"Well, Adam," I counter, doing my best to give nothing away, "do you think you could let me check you over first? It looks like your arm might be hurt."

He nods shakily. "Then c-could you call Jessie?"

"Who's Jessie?"

"M-my best friend," he whimpers then sniffles. "Sh-she'll wait for me and miss the bus."

Never have I wanted to cry for a patient more than I do right now, nor have I ever wanted to go outside the parameters of my job like I do. The bus? Does he even know what time of day it is?

"Let's get you fixed up first," I whisper as I lean over him and wink, gently pressing the stethoscope to his chest. "You want to look your best when you see her, don't you?"

"Sh-she won't care," he utters as he attempts to lift a shoulder in a shrug then winces with the pain. "She says hearts matter more than looks."

Out of the mouths of babes.

Chapter 14

Lucas

"What in the hell were you thinking, Tanner?" Captain Sullivan stands in the grassy area off to the side of the ER doors, arms folded across his chest – probably in an effort not to punch me at the current moment. I doubt he's going to bury me, but I'm pretty sure I may be looking at a suspension.

Scrubbing my hands down my face, I sigh heavily. "There was a kid in there, Cap. I was vested up."

He squares me with a knowing look, his bushy eyebrows raised while his chin dips. "Sure you weren't *invested*, to the point you broke all protocol and turned it into a suicide mission?"

I challenge him with a quirk of my brow, a bite to my tone that he doesn't miss. "Like you did for a kid I know?"

He drops his hands to his sides and his shoulders deflate. "Tanner, you know I gotta follow department rules. Suspension until a review. You can't go off half-cocked like that."

I shrug. "I get it. At least the kid is alive. Mind if I go check on him first?"

He slaps my shoulder as we enter the hospital once more. "As of now you're off duty. Report to my office at ten in the morning. Don't get too comfy with your time off, I don't plan on you being gone long."

He sees my partner standing in the waiting area. "Carny," he tosses his thumb toward the exit, "you're next."

"I got your back," I mutter as he passes me. "This one's on me."

He snorts softly. "Don't worry about it. I could use a few extra rounds of golf."

"Hey, handsome," the ER receptionist greets me as I reach the front desk. Liz is middle-aged, married, gray-haired, pleasant, and the only one I can actually tolerate when here. The single ones I've encountered have been with or through half the force and/or firefighters and looking for a husband. Quick pass.

"Hey, Liz. I wanted to check on the boy that was brought in from the DA case a little while ago. Can you tell me where to find him?"

She smiles sweetly. "Ah, the one you brought in personally. I heard about it, Tanner. Nice work."

I roll my eyes and keep my voice low. "Wouldn't want to put in a good word with the Cap for me, would you?"

"You send that old buzzard to me," she scowls teasingly. "I'll set him straight. The boy is in room 7. He's in good hands, Tanner. Liberty's got him."

My heart stops beating as every last breath is sucked from my lungs and I'm taken back to the last conversation we ever had.

"Thirty! We should have kids by the time we're thirty."

"Well, that's what dad said. I gotta be a nurse first anyway."

"Okay, we'll wait 'til we're 32. Why do you want to be a nurse?"

"So I can show you how to do the Band-Aids the right way."

Her giggle echoes in my mind so clearly it's as if it were yesterday. Her scraped knees, the piggyback ride, the day I felt someone else's pain and yearned to take it away and make it my own.

"Tanner?" Liz's voice pulls me out of my thoughts.

"You have a nurse named Liberty?"

"Cute, isn't it?" Her eyes flash with mischief and she winks. "Just wait 'til you see her. And she's single." She points toward the double doors. "Down the hall on the right."

If Liz said anything after, I missed it because my feet are moving faster than my brain can keep up. It's a pipedream; has to be. I'm sure there is more than one female named Liberty in this world, but there is only one Liberty who is my world.

I tap lightly on the slightly ajar door and wait; my heart pounding in my chest. She stands next to the little boy's bed, her back to me, his hand in hers as she speaks softly and comforts him.

"We're ready, come on in." I'd know that melodic sound anywhere that still carries a slight rasp. She brushes her hand through the little guy's hair and says, "X-ray is here. They're ready to take you to get some pictures."

Please turn around, Liberty. I've waited 18 years for this.

"Uh," I stammer, searching for the right thing to say yet desperate to speak her name aloud. "Not x-ray," I say instead. As she turns to see who has entered, my knees nearly buckle and I hold the handle on the door for support. I finally . . . *finally* . . . have a fresh picture from the last I ever saw of her; the terrified blonde girl running after me down the street, screaming my name as I was driven away by strangers. And what a picture it is. Heart-stopping.

My favorite colors of blue and green. I can't choose between the two because both are stunning. Thank God she never surrendered to the world's ignorance and tried to cover them with contacts to achieve consistency. She is still my asymmetrical angel. It's been years, too damn many years. Still the pale blonde hair, now tied up in a messy bun. Soft features, slim nose, and that perfect bow-shaped top lip that I've dreamt of kissing since the day she promised I could. *Pink.* She is so fucking beautiful it hurts.

"*Liberty.*" I swear my lips move but no sound emerges.

She squints and her lips part ever so slightly then looks away suddenly as Adam offers, "That's Sergeant Tanner. He helped me. I rode in the police car with him."

"Tanner," Liberty repeats softly as she nods at Adam and her shoulders notably stiffen, then brusquely asks, "What can we do for you, officer?"

My heart takes a dive for my stomach. She doesn't remember me. Not a damn clue. Yes, I have the advantage of her eyes; the unique blue and green, but I would have known my Liberty anywhere. Is it my facial hair? Shit! *Sergeant Tanner.* Look at me, Liberty. It's me! Lucas! See me! I know I'm not that scrawny kid anymore, but I'm in here. My heart hasn't changed. You still own it.

"I, uh, came to check on Adam." My eyes float back and forth between them, but Liberty's stay fixed on him as I make my way toward his bed on the opposite side. "How are you doing, buddy?"

"They said my arm is broken," he says weakly. "Did you call Jessie?"

"Not yet," I admit. "I don't have her number."

He reels off ten digits effortlessly as if they're implanted in his brain; an emergency contact, a lifeline. I pull a pad and pen from my pocket and jot them down. He also informs me of her address and last name so I can speak to her parents if I need to. He is thorough. As weak and broken as he is, he's determined we contact Jessie: his port in the storm.

"I promise you I'll call her, Adam. Best friends are irreplaceable." My next comment is aimed at Liberty, whether she knows it or not. "Sometimes it takes way too long to find them again."

Liberty's chin whips up as if I've struck a nerve, and I simply stare, soaking in the colors I've missed, the adult face I've only imagined over the years; surpassing anything my fantasies may have gifted me with.

"Where's m-my mom?" Adam's question breaks our gaze, his eyes filled with another round of tears, probably the hundredth of the day.

"I'm not sure, bud." It's not exactly a lie but a whole lot better than telling him *most likely downstairs in the morgue*. Either the initial shock hasn't worn off or he didn't see the final results. Denial is another possibility. Hovering in a corner may have been the best thing he did for himself. Eventually, he'll have to deal with it. Hopefully with a good therapist to help him through. Maybe even a best friend by the name of Jessie.

"I hear we got a young man sporting a broken arm in here waiting for me to take him for some fancy pictures." The large, loud, male x-ray tech enters the room unannounced and laughs boisterously. "I won't even make you smile for the camera, pal. Unless you want to. Can you say cheese?"

A wide-eyed, petrified Adam looks at the tech. "Uh," I utter as I shake my head at Liberty before walking to the tech and muttering, "Can we step out?"

The puzzled tech follows me into the hallway. I close the door behind us before speaking. "The kid's old man just got done blowing half his mother's head off tonight. Nothing personal, but do you guys have a gentile female that could take care of him? In case you didn't notice, he's a little squeamish. Your entry would have been okay had he fallen out of a tree. As it is . . ."

"Aww hell," he mumbles, his face a mix of mortification and pity. "Why don't those dipshits warn us what we're walking in on? I was trying to keep things light. He's just a kid. I'll get Gina to do it." He grabs the radio from his hip and exchanges communication with the x-ray lab, then reassures me, "She's on her way."

"Thanks. Appreciate it."

Ten minutes later, Adam is on his way out of the room for x-rays with a female tech; pleas from him for Liberty to join them. After gently explaining that she can't but promising she will see him again, no matter what, the room is quiet once again.

"Thank you for that," she says as she watches the gurney being wheeled down the hall by the replacement. "I know it was you who asked for a different x-ray tech."

"I figured a gentler approach might be better after what he went through tonight."

Liberty swipes a fresh pair of latex gloves from a box on the wall and as she puts them on I note there is no ring on her left hand. It's possible she doesn't wear one at work, and how the chance she could be married hadn't even occurred to me is dizzying. Maybe I am the only one who remembers. Wait! Liz said she's single. She busies herself with gathering a few things around the room and tossing others in the trash, seemingly frustrated, her back to me the entire time.

"Uh. . ." I fumble as I rake my fingers through my hair – blind, deaf, and lost as to how to start a conversation in this fustercluck situation. "You were really good with . . ."

The door suddenly flies open. "Oh my God, Libs!" the brunette breathes hard as she enters the room. She's in surgical scrubs, a half-tied mask hanging on her neck. "I just heard. Are you okay? This had to be like déjà vu for you."

Déjà vu? What the hell is that supposed to mean?

The newcomer takes note of my presence in the room and stops short. "Wait a minute," she says slowly as she narrows her eyes and scans my uniform-clad body head to toe. "You're not a fireman."

"No, ma'am." My brow scrunches in confusion. "Is there a reason you think I should be?"

"First of all, cut the ma'am crap. I'm not your mother," she scolds, then smirks with another slow assessment from my head to my toes. "Though I could call you daddy."

Liberty heaves a sigh of frustration and groans, "Mallory."

"This is the dude that was with Roger and Reece at the airport," the brunette explains then scowls at me. "After one of those infamous trips to Vegas. Was yours of the mattress monkey variety too?"

I lean against the wall and pinch the bridge of my nose, recalling the tingles, goosebumps, nausea, and the pit in my stomach. Liberty was so close and I didn't even know it. I scrub my hand over my face and mumble, "That explains a lot."

Carny sticks his head in the door, a welcome reprieve from the brunette's sass, but a crushing blow that any chance of conversation with Liberty is over. "Cap says they can interview the kid tomorrow, provided all goes well. You ready to roll,

Tanner?" He winks and grins at the two females in the room. "Evenin' ladies."

As I reluctantly move toward the door – my footsteps slow and leaden as my first opportunity being snatched away feels nearly as painful as my exit eighteen years ago did – the brunette quips, "Tanner. That's different. I like it."

"Funny," I deadpan then look back to Liberty to see her watching me go and whisper, "I hate it." Her brow pinches slightly as my gaze lingers for a few moments, soaking in my two favorite colors, before I take my leave.

I'll be back. I know where to find her now.

"Damn, Tanner," Carny breathes a hearty chuckle on the way out of the hospital. "You about set off the fucking fire alarms in there. Did you see her eyes? Almost enough to make you miss those fabulous tits."

Shoving his shoulder to move him along faster, I scowl. "Shut up, asshole. You're driving. I've been suspended. Move it."

Chapter 15

Liberty

Mallory fans her face as she ducks her head back in the door after gawking at the two uniforms as they walk down the hall away from room 7 where I wait for the return of Adam. "Whew! What the hell was that?"

"Those were the officers who brought the little boy in." I busy myself once again with clearing the room of waste and throwing it in the proper receptacles. Adam should be back soon from x-ray, if the orthopedic surgeon doesn't call for him to be moved into surgery immediately. I've seen these types of breaks before. I'll bet a hundred dollars he'll need pinning, not to mention repair of the obvious growth plate displacement at his wrist. Poor kid. Once the pain medication started working, he calmed somewhat, but the break is going to be the least of his problems. The emotional trauma will be his uphill battle; possibly for years to come.

"Not what I meant." She snort-laughs. "Liberty, I could have stripped naked and danced in front of that man and he wouldn't have known I was in the room. Who is he?"

"Adam said his name is Sergeant Tanner. He rode in the police car with him to get here." I shrug, though impressed with the above board efficiency. "Gabby said the pile-up on I-17 hindered transport so they brought him in themselves."

Her face scrunches. "So, the little boy's dad killed his mom, huh? Seems I've heard a familiar story."

I nod slowly, thoughts of long ago invading rent free space they don't deserve. "Yeah. What a world, huh?"

"You gonna be okay?" she asks, her voice laden with concern. "I know this had to hit you hard." Pretty sure she's counting on me opening my laptop and searching for Lucas Monterrey on a whim. I hadn't done it as often when I was with Michael, but I've started my years-old habit again with the breakup.

"I'm fine, Mal," I tell her with a wave of my hand, though I'm not.

"Well," she chirps. "If you need something to take your mind off of it, Sergeant Tanner would be a damn fine place to start. That man had enough heat in his eyes to keep you warm through cold showers. Damn!" She fans her face then arches a brow. "And in case you didn't notice, those eyes were aimed at you. He may be taking a few of those cold showers himself."

What I don't mention is the haunting familiarity of those eyes. Hazel with green flecks. A warmth that reminded me of long ago. I'm an idiot. It was my imagination in overdrive. *Sergeant Tanner.* The way he came in to check on Adam and took the information, promised to call his best friend for him was touching. The cops that come through the ER are usually in and out; more concerned with collecting information and filing reports. I've yet to see one do what I saw tonight – show that kind of compassion – but then tonight was rather unusual.

I've been in the ER for over a month but still acclimating. I've been proposed to, hit on, flirted with, and actually ass-pinched by a drunken bar brawler. Even a couple emergency workers have hinted at a night out. Should Michael and Arseen ever leave the hospital, I may transfer back to ICU post surg. Patients like Mr. Gustafson were much more pleasant.

"If it's any consolation," Mal offers, "my day sucked too. I had to assist Drs. Knight and Arseen in surgery today."

"That must have been fun." My grumble is loaded with sarcasm, but I feel the need to acknowledge her. She would do the same for me in any situation.

"It was, really," she says with a chuckle. "It's always fun to see Arseen put in her place when the lead doctor tells her to 'shut the fuck up or get out' while his hands are buried inside a patient's chest."

The lid on the haz mat container drops loudly back into place as I let it fall and turn to her, my brows lifted to my hairline. "What?"

"I think her crack about the heart pump reminding her of him is what finally did it." She crinkles her nose in disgust. "The woman really has no shame."

My jaw is agape as I stare at her. I really have no words. Thank God I don't need them as x-ray returns with Adam.

"Dr. Evans is consulting with radiology. Said he'll be down as soon as they're done," Gina says after Adam's bed is set and locked once again. She eyes me, her mouth set in a straight line, and she lifts her brows once before letting them fall. Not a good sign. Dr. Evans is the orthopedic surgeon. Adam should not be returning to the ER. The boy obviously needs surgery. She tilts her head toward the door for me to follow and I look to Mallory in a silent plea to entertain Adam.

"Has Social Services been called yet?" Gina whispers once outside the door.

"I don't know." I shrug. "That's on the advocates. Why?"

"That kid needs surgery." Her mouth twists. "Evans needs parental consent."

"If he had any parents," I sneer, though not at the messenger, "we could get it. His mother died at the hands of his father tonight. You're not going to find any parents to give consent. What's the hold up?"

She glances over both shoulders one at a time before she whispers, "I think it's an insurance thing, really."

Eric and Dr. Evans round the corner, headed toward us, and Gina mutters a hurried "gotta go" and takes her leave. I head back into the room to see Mallory carrying a conversation with Adam that makes me smile. For a woman who will be the first to tell you she's not a people person, her people skills are to be envied.

"I love that movie!" she tells Adam excitedly. "I was going to dye my hair red and wear mermaid clothes after watching Ariel. But then I found out you have to have actual boobies to keep that top up." She tugs at the bosom hiding surgical top she has on and shrugs. "So I was out of luck."

I gasp, but the giggle that leaves Adam's throat is so worth it, I can't even care. Leave it to Mal. No better medicine than laughter, no matter the methods to achieve it. I hadn't noticed the door behind me open and in it stand the stern orthopedic surgeon, Dr. Evans, and a grinning Eric.

"You're still pretty," Adam says. "Jessie has brown hair too."

"Well, that settles it." Mallory tips her chin and tugs at her pony tail. "She must be gorgeous."

"Yeah," a tired Adam agrees with a nod.

"What's the plan?" I aim my quiet question toward the surgeon in the doorway.

He nods at Adam and speaks softly to me. "He needs an OR, I need consent. It's not life and death, but it is urgent. Waiting on Social Services."

"For what?" I snap harshly as I glare at him. "So by next week, you may have permission?" My God, by the time they wait to get him through the red tape, they may as well amputate. I look to Eric. "Call Michael. Get him down here."

"Liberty . . ." he drawls.

Pushing on his chest, I force him out into the hallway. "What's the problem? I know he's here. I saw him in the cafeteria. Is he too busy fucking Arseen?"

"What? No!" he denies, eyes bulging. "He hasn't touched her since . . ." His words trail as he sighs deeply. "He's cardiothoracic, Liberty."

"He's on the board, Eric," I point out through gritted teeth. "We have that boy's medical records. He has no allergies. He needs the surgery. What he doesn't need is us continuing to feed him more drugs while we wait. Michael can cut through the red tape. What is the problem?"

He sighs again and pinches the bridge of his nose. "It's not exactly protocol."

"Neither was fucking his colleague," I whisper angrily, "in Las Vegas, while engaged to me. Make. The. Call."

Half an hour later, Social Services has finally arrived while Michael confers with the surgeon and Eric in the hallway.

After ten minutes of Social Services grilling Adam over the events at the house, that which only upsets him and causes tears that Mallory had turned to laughter, I finally drag the woman out of the room – diplomatically because Adam is watching – and confront her in the hall.

"The last thing that little boy needs is to relive the horror he went through hours ago. What he does need right now is surgical correction of the physical damage that was done. What you need to do is to find out if he has family to help him. Where on earth did you get your degree?"

Her chin tilts upward in haughty indignance, as if her eyes need to cast downward on her subject. Not that it does her any good; she's at least three inches shorter than I am. "I need to know what happened."

"The police need to know what happened," I sneer. "His future therapist needs to know what happened. *You*," I emphasize with a pointed finger, fighting back the urge to punch her, "need to find any remaining family he may have and make arrangements for him. Stop badgering that poor child and find his damn family!"

Michael and his two colleagues stare at me from a few feet away. "Have you come to any decisions?" I bark impatiently.

A look of what I would swear is pride crosses Michael's face as his mouth twitches. "We'll get him taken care of, Liberty. They're setting up an OR now."

"Thank you." I nod once and turn to block the social worker's reentry into the room where Mallory keeps vigil by Adam's bedside, distracting him from the goings on in the hallway. The social worker has his hospital records, has quizzed him about any family members he may know of, has his emergency contacts – outside of his parents. She can contact his school authorities if nothing else. She is done here.

Michael is quick with the few steps it takes to reach me and gently grasps my elbow. "He's lucky to have you," he whispers. "I envy him. If I thought begging would work, I'd be on my knees right now. You deserve so much better than I gave. I'll never stop loving you, Liberty, and I am so damn sorry."

Maybe not a total narcissist.

Could I forgive him? I suppose, someday. Would I ever take him back? Never. Infidelity is not just a matter of placing part A into slot B. It may be a physical act, unemotional, driven by lust or simple temptation. But it is, by all means, destruction of the trust and intimacy two people have promised. There is no coming back from that, at least not for me. Which is why I only blink slowly and turn away.

"Liberty," the smirking Dr. Evans calls from his spot next to Eric. "Tell *Miss No Boobies* to scrub in. She'll be assisting."

Sure thing, doc. No problem. She can't castrate me. Though you can bet your sweet ass my segue is going to be "Don't shoot the messenger".

Chapter 16

Lucas

Two weeks! Two fucking weeks! With pay, thanks to Sully, not that I was worried about it. But two weeks?! No, I don't play golf. Sorry, Carny, you're on your own. Not sure what, if any, punishment he got yet. I explained to Sully he was simply covering my back. If he got no punishment, I'll probably get shit for that too. Nine holes is his favorite Saturday morning pastime, eighteen if he can afford it. Depends on whether or not he joined the guys for a visit to The Tempest. *"Trading nine holes for one"*. Yeah, I didn't find it funny, either.

"Hey, Tanner." Roger's voice rings out as he and Reece arrive in the parking lot the same time I do; half past *five o'clock somewhere.* They run identical shifts at the firehouse – 72 hours each – so often leave and arrive home at the same time. "You off today?"

It's not an unreasonable question. I'm not in uniform. Sully informed me last night suspension was inevitable. Why waste a clean uniform? Now, to lie through the psychological evals and pass the reviews and I'll be good. My extensive chat with Sully this morning consisted of one good ass-chewing, one pass from him revealing my history, and a promise from me that it won't happen again. I omitted finding Liberty last night. Hell, she doesn't know I found her. Maybe I am stuck in a past that she's left behind.

But déjà vu?

"I'm off for a while," I grunt as I grab my gym bag from the back of my Jeep, then lower my voice and mumble, "Not that I asked for it." I managed two hours of sleep last night and it was filled with the new, very real, face of Liberty Collins. All grown up, more beautiful than I remembered. A perfect work of art, replacing that picture of the little girl running after me with tears in her eyes. The flawless, porcelain skinned, blue and green-eyed beauty, so close I could have touched her.

Roger's brow furrows. "You didn't get shit-canned, did ya?"

"No, dumbass." I hitch the strap of my bag over my shoulder and roll my eyes. "I didn't get shit-canned."

I did, however, spend a couple hours at the gym beating the piss out of a punching bag. A hundred punches thrown at my old man's face, fifty for the asshole who killed Adam's mom, another fifty for McClaren and his big mouth, a hundred and one for the frustration I'm feeling, and another twenty for the hell of it.

"You look like you need a beer," Reece comments then tilts his head and lifts a brow, "or ten."

"I'm good," I mutter. "Beer ain't gonna solve anything."

"Beer solves everything!" Roger exclaims as he punches in the code to enter the building and pulls open the door.

"Gettin' laid never hurt either," Reece adds with a slap on my back as he follows us in. "Usually works for me."

Roger rolls his eyes and shakes his head. "Which is never gonna happen if you don't stop pissin' a circle around her and just ask her out instead of promising her the ride of her life on your fireman's pole."

Reece grins. "I kinda like playing with her. Mallory's feisty as hell. Makes the game that much more fun." He blows a low whistle. "Can't help but wonder what's under that hospital garb."

The combination of the name *Mallory* and hospital garb captures my attention. "Who are you talking about?"

"The same woman from the airport," Roger reminds me. "He got a fresh dose of her sass last night. We were at the hospital helping with transport after the disaster on the interstate when he ran into her. Probably been rockin' a hard-on ever since." He warns Reece with a pointed finger, "I got dibs on the blonde though. Between those eyes and that ass," he groans as if in pain. "Hard choice between being on top or taking her from behind."

"Stay the hell away from Liberty!" The threatening growl leaves my mouth as if on autopilot. Blonde, eyes, ass. Who else could he be talking about?

Two sets of shocked and wide eyes turn my way. "Whoa," Roger hums, holding a hand up. "Didn't know you'd laid claim, Tanner."

"25 years ago," I grumble, stabbing the elevator button. Good God, it was that long ago. When we were five. A lifetime. The doors open and we step on together.

"Kindergarten crush?" Reece taunts.

Don't ask me why, but I glance at Roger, knowing he's the only one who clearly saw what I put back in the little white box that night. "Bubblegum buddy."

One brow lifts while the other furrows in contemplation; he's a multitasker. "Go get your shower, you smell like shit," he orders quietly as he and Reece exchange a look. "You got half an hour. We'll be back with the beer. I could use a good bedtime story tonight."

"Your old man killed your mom?" Reece looks horror stricken. "In front of you?" I continue to slowly peel more of the label off the bottle in my hands and nod slowly. "And your name isn't really Tanner Carson?"

"Legally it is. I haven't been Lucas Monterrey since I was twelve years old."

"Damn," he breathes on a whisper. "And Captain Sullivan is the guy who . . ."

"I think we've been over that already, dipshit," Roger growls and points to the last bottle in the six-pack on the coffee table. "Hand me another beer."

I've spilled my story as they listened patiently, awestruck and a bit mortified. Liberty's and my history, the night of the murder, our separation, my life leading up to last night to include how I ended up with the little white box, and finally, the fact she had no idea who I was.

"That picture you have," Roger looks thoughtful as he asks, "it was taken close to the last time you were together?"

"About two weeks before, I think."

"Go get it."

The two of them examine it together, shoulder-to-shoulder, brows scrunched, before Reece looks up and snickers. "Nice chicken legs."

"Fuck you," I mutter. "I was just a kid."

Roger elbows him, scowls, and grunts in my defense, "Knock it off," before he bursts into laughter. "Sorry, buddy, but he is right." He points to the scrawny, wet, happy kid in the picture. "If this is what you're going by, it's no wonder she didn't recognize you. That's like comparing Moby Dick to a guppy. Jesus, Tanner, she was taller than you in this. You've got facial hair. You're six foot-two, and weigh, what, 200 pounds?"

"195 and it's solid muscle," I challenge.

Reece sweeps a rather effeminate hand gesture through the air and performs a perfect impression and haughty voice of someone we'd all like to forget, "And ten of it is his dick alone." He rolls his eyes and smirks. "At least according to Miranda."

Squeezing my eyes closed, I shiver. "Don't ever do that again."

I open them to see Roger staring at his friend in disbelief . . . and abhorrence. "That was downright spooky. You just made my asshole pucker."

"It worked pretty well when I called Boonie, pretending to be his mistress," he says of their coworker at the firehouse with a casual shrug. "Scared the livin' shit out of him when he thought she was pregnant. He hasn't cheated on his wife since."

Roger continues to stare, his jaw agape. "That was you?!"

"When you say, 'I do'. . ." Reece simpers, ". . .it should also mean I won't. You put a ring on your finger, it should also metaphorically be on your dick."

"The guy was ready to piss his pants!" Roger howls.

Reece winks and grins. "Bet his balls tightened up a bit, too."

"They shriveled up inside his taint, Reece!"

Reece tips his beer in a cheers and smiles cockily. "Gives a whole new meaning to no place like home."

As miserable as I am, these assholes still make me laugh. Not sure if that was their goal, but they do achieve it.

"Okay." Roger polishes off the last of his beer, sets the bottle down hard, and releases a loud, obnoxious belch. "Operation Lucas is about to get under way. Reece, order some Chinese with extra fortune cookies. Tanner, grab a pen and paper." He holds up a hand then points toward the kitchen. "Oh, as long as you're headed that way, grab another six-pack out of the fridge."

Reece is already on his feet, sorting through the menus on my kitchen counter, but hesitates and looks to Roger who's pulled out his phone and studying the screen. "What are you going to do?"

Roger studies the screen, squinting as he enters info, and speaks slowly. "Doing a little Amazon shopping. Gotta find a Liberty Bell replica and . . . some . . . tutti-frutti and blueberry bubblegum."

Reece looks impressed as he nods at me. "That's rather ingenious. I didn't think he had a romantic bone in him."

"I have one, Reece," Roger says firmly as he continues to tap on the screen. "I prefer to call it a bone-er. And the ladies love it."

I roll my eyes. "Sounds about right. What are we doing with that stuff?"

"*We're* not doing anything with it." He lifts his chin and grins, then sets his phone down. "You're going to have them delivered, piece by piece, a few days apart, anonymously." His eyes light with his *ingenious* idea. "In little white boxes with a note of your choosing in each, addressed to Miss Liberty. Items should be here in two days."

I stare at him in disbelief. "Why in the hell would I do that?"

"It's not that she doesn't remember you, *Lucas*." His voice drops as he arches a brow and emphasizes, "She didn't recognize you, *Sergeant Tanner*. It was a stressful night. There is not a woman on earth that doesn't remember her first love, no matter the age. Trust me on this."

"Why can't I just tell her who I am?" Then voice my biggest concern aloud, "What if this spooks her?"

He looks to Reece, rolls his eyes and shakes his head. "And he's the one who called me dumbass in the parking lot."

"Still not getting it, Roger," I admit, though I do snatch a pen and pad of paper off the counter.

"A little like an appetizer a day," Reece answers for him. "Ease her into it. I think they call it food for thought."

"Yeah, well," Roger says pointing to the menu in Reece's hand, "I need food for my belly right now. Hurry up and order."

"Why the extra fortune cookies?" I inquire.

"Confucious was a wise man." He shrugs. "May give us a little inspiration."

I shoot him a wry look. "You know that shit is factory-produced, don't you?"

His phone pings with a message and he smirks after reading it. "Would you rather we ask for Wiley's advice? He's on his way up for a few beers and dinner."

I whirl my head toward Reece and scowl. "Order the fortune cookies."

When dinner is over and the story has been repeated for the benefit of one more set of ears – a short version, no vast details as Wiley said if and when I ever wanted to open up, his ears are available – we crack the last fortune cookie.

"The game can only be won if you play"

"Which means no participation trophies in this game," Wiley announces. He pulls out his wallet and slaps a hundred dollar bill on the coffee table. "You gotta win. My bet's on

Tanner. Who's in?"

Roger looks at the money on the table and snorts. "New retirement plan, Wiley?"

"Ha! This is child's play," Wiley retorts before he looks to me and squirrels his face. "No pun intended, Tanner. She'll remember who you are."

Chapter 17

Liberty

"Liberty!" Liz holds out a small box and a single pink rose in a crystal vase. "These were delivered for you a little while ago. I was waiting for you to take your break to give them to you. You've been bouncing from room to room."

"What is this?" I wrinkle my nose as I take the items from her hands. The tag with the flower only reads 'Liberty Collins' and the box is wrapped in simple white tissue paper with my name written across the top. "Who delivered them?"

"Courier, I guess," she answers with a shrug. "I was so busy checking in patients, I didn't pay much attention, sweetie. What's in it?"

I resist rolling my eyes or throwing the box back on the counter. It's probably another ploy of Michael's. God knows he's tried everything else, though nothing since his apology in the emergency room.

As I don't have an office and I can't very well store a vase in my locker, I leave the rose with Liz at the desk, tell her to 'enjoy it', and tuck the box in my pocket. I can open it on my dinner break.

So much for the best laid plans.

"Someday," I mutter to myself on the way back to the ER, "I'm going to get through a meal before I get paged. I hope Mallory has leftovers when I get home." Through a meal. Ha! I hadn't even gotten sat down at the table before my beeper went off. I was already two hours late for my break. The little white box is nestled in the deep pocket of my lab coat. It'll wait.

Three hours, multiple sutures, a case of cellulitis, an infant's ear infection, a UTI, and a wedged dildo later I'm ready to go home. I'm grouchy, tired, and hangry. Standing in front of my locker, I am willing to admit maybe it is a good thing I missed dinner. I've seen a multitude of cases in my time, but removing a foreign object from a man's rearend while he's screaming like a child? That was a new one. I was so tempted to leave him with a parting remark – something akin to getting a taste of knowing what ladies go through with labor – but instead it was the usual distribution of pamphlets and follow up treatment recommendations. It wasn't like I could hand him a prize in the end and no one in the room volunteered to wash it and send it home with him. Funny thing, he didn't ask for it either.

As I remove my lab coat, I note the extra weight on the right side containing the little white box that had slipped my mind. My initial inclination is to toss it into my purse and take it home, but for some reason I take a seat on the bench and peel the wrap off and open the lid. Inside sit two tiger eye marbles – one light blue and one an iridescent light green – on a cushioned inset pad so they don't roll around inside the box. There's a small folded up note, handwritten in bold black letters, that accompanies them.

"I never could choose a favorite"

Goosebumps envelop my arms as the hair on the back of my neck rises, but before I have time to process . . .

"Hey, Liberty!" Kelsey greets me as she pushes open the door to the locker room. "Wanna join us for drinks? Quinn and Mack are gathering a few of the others as we speak. They've got our favorite strippers at The Tempest tonight." Her eyes flash as she grins mischievously. "Those of the male variety. Figured after pulling the dildo outta that ass, you might want a frontal view. Hank the Hung is on display tonight."

Hank the Hung. Talk of the hospital. Thirteen inches long, slight curve, and . . .

I shiver at the mere thought. "I've never seen it myself, no desire to do so. "No thanks. I'm headed home." I slam my locker door closed after sliding the white box into my purse. "Long day. The only thing I want to see is the inside of my eyelids as I sleep."

"Your loss," she singsongs.

No, it's not, I think to myself, picturing an appendage that would most likely shove my uterus up into my chest cavity.

As I'm leaving via the employee's exit that leads to the parking area designated for us, Sean, the security officer steps toward me. "Hey, Liberty, there's a guy over here that would like to speak with you. He's shown ID. Sergeant Carson with the Phoenix PD."

"I don't know any Sergeant Carson."

"Liberty." The low familiar voice from three nights ago sounds from my left and I turn to see Sergeant Tanner. It's well after dark and while the parking lot does offer a fair amount of lighting, it's the way he says my name that seems more familiar.

"I thought your name was Sergeant Tanner." My voice is harsher than I mean for it to be, but again, I need for this day to be over.

"It's Tanner Carson," he says, seemingly reluctant. "I gave Adam my first name."

"Oh." I turn back to the guard and nod. "It's okay, Sean." He nods as well and steps back, but doesn't leave, eyeing the situation cautiously. "What can I do for you, Sergeant?" I want to call him Tanner, but for some odd reason, it doesn't feel right. It's like a heavy overcoat on a summer day; weighty and ill-fitting. He said he hated it, didn't he? He's not in uniform tonight. He's in faded blue jeans that hug thick thighs, and a navy blue T-shirt emblazoned with PPD on the front with sleeves that wrap tight on bulging biceps. *Yes, I notice. I'm not dead . . . or blind.* He's also of the gorgeous variety. Sun-kissed light brown hair, sharp features, well-trimmed, thick facial hair, and those amber eyes that remind me of . . .

"I . . . uh, wanted to thank you for the way you handled Adam the other night." He grasps the back of his neck as if it's a nervous habit. "He really needed that."

"I was just doing my job."

"You do it well, Liberty."

The low timbre of his voice and tentative way he says my name is shiver inducing. It's as if he's testing it to see how it feels on his tongue; seemingly enjoying it if the soft smile that follows is any indication.

"How do you know my name?"

"Liz at the front desk mentioned it the night I was here." He chuckles nervously. "It's unusual."

"Did you find Jessie?"

His eyes sparkle as his obvious pleasure shows in his answer. "Yeah. She was able to see him yesterday. Signed his cast and everything." He hesitates as if waiting for me to react, but then continues. "Adam has an aunt who's taking him in. She lives in Scottsdale, so Jessie's parents and she are making arrangements so the kids can see each other on some type of regular basis."

The mention of the signed cast nearly shreds my heart. Lucas had one that I had signed; said he would never throw it away. He kept it like a trophy on his shelf. Tanner promised Adam he would call and he followed through. How many cops would actually do that? Did Lucas ever ask for me? Did someone promise him, and not follow through? A sob bursts from my chest without warning as both hands fly to my face to shield it. I'm so happy for Adam, but at the same time the only face I can picture is the one staring back at me from the rear of the police car as I chased it down the street. Adam's case affected me more than I was willing to admit. More than it was supposed to. More than what is professionally acceptable.

"Liberty," Tanner's soft whisper is joined by his gentle touch on my shoulders. "He's going to be okay. He's resilient."

There's something in his touch that is far beyond comforting – it's overwhelming – and I relish it as I lean my forehead on his chest in my moment of weakness, and he props his chin on my head and wraps his arms around my shoulders as I cry.

This is so wrong. I don't take comfort in the arms of strangers. I'm the very definition of antisocial; more so in the last two months than in the last 18 years. I take care of people, they don't take care of me.

Swiping at my cheeks as I pull back from his arms, I feel a strange emptiness. Without another glance up at him, my chin halfway to my chest, I extend my gratitude. "Thank you for what you did for him, Sergeant Tanner. I need to go." I spin on a fast heel and head for my car without looking back, ignoring the pained whisper in his voice behind me as he calls my name.

Mallory is asleep by the time I get home. Pretty sure she has an early morning in surgery tomorrow. These last couple months have taken a bit of adjustment with shift changes. I work more nights than I used to and I miss her constant companionship.

Searching the fridge for something to eat, I hear the pad of her footsteps as she makes her way from her bedroom across the living room.

"Late night?" she asks with a yawn.

"Long night," I reply. "Did I wake you?"

"Nope." She stretches as if working out some sore, stiff muscles and yawns again. "There's steak salad in there for you. Greens are in the bowl, steak is in the glass container. You already know where to find the toppings. Pour me a red, will you?"

"Don't you have to work in the morning?"

"Huh-uh," she answers and shakes her head. "I got called in late today and Natalie's on for tomorrow. I would have stopped in to see you but you were in the middle of," she grins and tilts her head back and forth, "rectus extractus."

I scowl. "That is not a medical term."

She giggles. "So, did the anal retentive patient learn his lesson? Did you coach him on breathing and relaxation techniques, maybe string attachments next time, as you removed his. . ." she clears her throat, "painfully deep wedgie?"

"Are you finished?" I snap harshly yet am kind enough to pour her glass of red, though tempted to throw it at her. "I haven't eaten since breakfast."

She blinks fast, probably trying to clear her eyes of the crusty sleep in the corners. "You didn't get dinner?"

"No! Mr. Butt Plug was brought in prone on a gurney and Dr. Zimmerman was," I use air quotes, "too busy to tend to him."

She laughs so hard her head rears back. "They brought him in by ambulance? Do you think his neighbors saw?"

"I didn't ask and I didn't care." I press my fingertips to my temples before I drop my head and groan. "I want to eat, take a hot bath, and bleach my retinae." My head rises and I glare, recalling the godawful vibrant shade of violet. "Oh, and I have to go buy a new toy. Purple is now my least favorite color."

What I don't mention is the two marbles in the little box in the bottom of my purse. Moreover, the note that accompanied them. Michael wouldn't have done that. He described sapphires and emeralds. Not even close. My eyes are both light in hue; more like aquamarine and peridot – the color of the marbles. It's why it takes people a while to figure out what the imbalance is.

No, what's in this box is more like a teaser, a puzzle. I'm too tired to figure it out tonight. My only hope is it doesn't set me back into a tailspin of wishes and dreams that never come true.

Chapter 18

Lucas

She was in my arms, and nothing has ever felt so good. Liberty Collins fits me just like she used to: perfectly. Her pain was mine. I knew her tears weren't just joy for Adam and Jessie. Mentioning the signing of his cast brought back the picture of Liberty holding the marker in her fingers, her pink tongue edged between her teeth as she perfected the swirly L and slowly filled in each letter; topping the I with a little heart. The tears were pain from the memory of us from so many years ago, too.

Why didn't I just tell her?

Had she opened the box yet? Had she read the words I used

to say all the time? That I could never choose a favorite? I'd spent two hours in that damn collector's store searching for the perfect color of marbles to match her eyes. I'd owned a pair as a kid, so I knew they existed, but that house had been seized and with it went all my possessions.

We were mature for twelve year-olds. Not in the *you-show-me-yours-and-I'll-show-you-mine* kind of way. She felt like my other half, the better part of me. We were inseparable . . . until we weren't. The powers that be forced us apart. That's not to say we would be married with kids by now. That was age 32. *Kidding.* I'm not crazy. Who knows what may have happened? What I do know is now that I've found her, now that I've seen her, now that I've touched her, I need to be sure.

No, idiot. You couldn't be any surer. You simply need to convince her.

The obnoxious pounding on my door sounds like broken bongo drums, not to mention the worst sense of rhythm I've ever heard, which indicates Wiley is in the group of knockers. One could swear it's intentionally offbeat but nope, that's just Wiley. The guy claps out of time, sings out of tune, can't dance for shit, but he can fart every fucking letter of the alphabet song without missing a beat. And no, we do not wonder why he's been married, and divorced, three times. He's a self-admitted shit husband. He'd make a wretched roommate. But he's a helluva friend.

I whip open my door to three grinning morons; two of whom bend to grab six packs off the floor, and the other who picks up two boxes of pizza.

Guess they needed their hands free to perform the shittiest rendition of "Wipeout" I've ever heard.

"Well?" Roger inquires expectantly, shoving the six packs into my hands, snatching a bottle from one, and moving forward to grab the remote.

"Well what?"

"What did she think of gift number one?" Reece follows, though he does carry his six packs to the kitchen counter and sets them down.

Wiley moves past me to set the pizzas on the counter and pops the lid open, grabbing the first slice and stuffing a bite in his mouth. He speaks and breathes hard around it. "Ow, ow, ow. Damn, that's hot!"

Three wives, folks.

Reece pops the top on a beer and hands it to him, then closes the lid on the pizza box and slides his finger across the warning label. "There is a reason it says, 'Caution: contents may be hot', dumbass." He tips his chin at me. "So, talk."

I set the six packs on the counter and shrug. "Not sure she'd opened it yet. I only talked to her for a little bit and she cried."

All three heads turn in my direction. "She what?" Roger chokes on his beer. "What the hell did you do to make her cry, Tanner?"

"She was happy about the kids." I shrug again. "I think."

"You think?" Reece hollers. "Tanner, the only thing a man should ever do that makes a woman cry is propose or make her come so hard she weeps tears of ecstasy!"

Roger snort-laughs. "Or in Wiley's case, disappointment."

Wiley flips him off. "Fuck you! I have rhythm where it matters."

Reece scrubs his hands down his face and groans. "God, I hope so, Wiley. Otherwise, your Christmas present is gonna be a metronome." He turns to him and grins. "Glued to your headboard for the ladies' benefit. You can't keep time for shit."

"I thought we were supposed to be doing a Taylor Swift song!" he shrieks defensively.

All three of us stare at him in mortification before Roger asks, "Who the fuck is Taylor Swift?"

Wiley's face turns a particular shade of red only seen the moment a weightlifter realizes he's about to fart and the 200-pound barbell is still raised above his head in a gym full of females.

"She's...she's with that football player on the Chief's team," he stammers.

"And she sings?" Reece asks, brow lifted, barely able to contain his laughter.

"Yeah!" Wiley snaps.

"Is she any good?" Roger inquires as if truly interested, pinching his upper lip to hide his grin.

"I think so!" Wiley crosses his arms over his chest and juts his chin in defense.

Joining the fun, because, well – Wiley is just too damn easy and somebody needs to end his misery, I ask, "Does she sing better than Kelce plays football?"

Realizing he hadn't told us which Chief's player she's *with*, he scowls at all three of us. "You guys are all assholes!"

Roger holds up a finger. "I just have one question. Do you have a poster of her tacked up on the ceiling above your bed?"

Wiley flips open the pizza box and grabs another slice. "Nope, it's on the wall."

We stare at him in disbelief as he chows on the piece of pepperoni and sausage. "You're not serious?" I ask him.

"You guys are so fucking easy." He chuckles. "The only things tacked up in my bedroom are pictures of my exes pasted on corkboard. I use them as targets for throwing darts. I ain't a pervert."

He tosses two more slices on a plate, grabs a beer, and takes a seat on the couch. "I'm well aware you idiots were trying to do *"Wipeout"* on the door." He smirks as he makes himself comfortable and eloquently explains, "You boys gotta learn to slow down. If you're trying to pump your women as fast as you were trying to do that drum roll, you ain't ever gonna learn the art of good sex. Edge 'em first."

We exchange wary glances before Reece scratches the back of his head and wrinkles his nose. "Uh, yeah. Can we get back to Tanner's situation?"

"Sounds good to me," Roger says hurriedly as he loads his plate with pizza and snatches two beers, heading for his usual spot in the recliner.

"I could give you a few more pointers if you want," Wiley offers with a shrug.

In unison we answer, "No!"

As I move the empty pizza box off the top and open the new one, Reece tells me, "She's working the next two nights. She's got three off after that. If you're going to make your move, you might want to do two in a row. Otherwise, you're going to be waiting for a while."

"How do you know this?"

His mouth twitches and he whispers, "A little birdie told me."

"What little birdie?" I demand. "This was all supposed to be done *anonymously,* Reece."

"And it still is," he reassures me. "Don't get your boxers in a wringer. We got your back. Trust us."

"Who is the birdie?" I grind out slowly.

He sighs so deeply, a low groan rumbles in his throat. "Liz is helping us. She doesn't know any details or who the giver is. However, she is a hopeless romantic. And . . ." he drawls, "seems Liz is anxious to help out as your Liberty has just suffered a pretty shitty breakup with a fiancé. Word has it the good doctor couldn't keep his dick in his pants and she caught him in the act." He smiles slyly. "I say when it's over we hunt him down and cut his bits off."

My face fills with mortification. Who would be so stupid as to cheat on the woman of my dreams? Oh wait! I should send the dumbass a thank you card, after I write him half a dozen or more traffic tickets. Then we'll cut his bits off.

"Wait a minute," I utter low as my stomach flips. "She was engaged?"

"Eighteen years, Tanner," Reece reminds me, narrowing his eyes. "You're damn lucky someone hasn't snatched that woman up. Now, you will be waiting outside the ER entrance when Liberty's shift ends and she opens the last gift at the front desk, upon Liz's insistence."

"What if she doesn't come out?"

He rolls his eyes and shakes his head. "It's Liz! Do you think she'd let anything go off script? Besides, we plan on being there to watch."

"What?!" My stomach churns at the thought of an intrusion on a very private moment. "Don't you guys have to work?"

"We swapped with Boonie and Vic for a night," Roger informs me from the other side of the room where he's been keenly listening. "You think we'd miss this after all the work we've put in? We won't intrude, Tanner. We'll keep our distance."

"This ain't a fucking movie, guys!" I yell in frustration.

"It will be when I get done," Wiley says easily before washing down another bite of pizza. "I'm filming it."

"You're what?!"

"How the hell else are you gonna tell your grandkids the story?" He shrugs – a beer in one hand, the remains of a slice of pizza in the other. "Visuals."

"Grandkids!" I protest. "Guys, she was my best friend. My . . . my . . . I . . ."

Reece slaps my back. "Sagest advice my dad ever gave me was to marry my best friend." He waves his hand around the room from each of us to the other. "As of yet, you guys are my only choice. Sorry, you're not my type. I'm still into rescuing kitties from trees . . . or bar stools."

Roger stifles a laugh with a snort. "And Mallory's pussy from a burning desire that only he seems to think she has."

"She does." Reece scowls before slapping a few slices onto his own plate. "She just hasn't figured out it's me yet."

"You could offer to let her call you *daddy,*" I grumble as I toss a couple slices of pizza onto a plate and grab a beer, recalling her cocky comment in the ER.

"I could what?" He turns so fast he nearly drops his plate and spills his beer. Inquisitive brows rise as he asks, "Do you know something I don't?"

"I'm sure by now we all know what a smartass she is," I retort with a wry grin. "Can we get back to the subject at hand? You guys promise you'll stay away?"

Two loud reassurances come from Roger and Wiley. Three heads turn toward Reece and wait for his response. "Yeah, yeah, yeah, I promise," he says with a wave of his hand before he looks to me and lifts a curious brow. "Daddy, huh?"

Chapter 19

Liberty

"Liberty!" Liz rushes down the hall behind me as I make my way toward the employee exit to the parking lot. She's breathless as she holds out another little white box and a crystal vase with two pink roses in it. "I almost missed you. I'm going to make it a requirement for you to stop by the front before you leave if this keeps up. You must have an admirer somewhere, sweetie. Guess you can take the flowers with you tonight." She leans in a little closer and whispers, "You never did tell me what was in the last one."

Staring at the vase and package I have yet to take from her hands, I shake my head as a chill rushes up my spine. "Just a gag gift."

She looks as if I've slapped her. "A gag gift? With roses? That's . . . unusual." Her mouth twists in contemplation as she studies the objects in her hands. Her nose crinkles with concern. "You sure you want these? Was it a good gag gift? If this is going to upset you, I don't want to . . ."

"It's fine, Liz." I appreciate her concern. Liz is a bit of a mother hen to the younger staff. She's observant, caring, good with people. Never a harsh word and the first to offer a compliment. However, it's my understanding she's like a human shield and a fierce warrior on behalf of those she is fond of. Like Gabby without the bayou accent, and ten years more experience.

"If you're sure." She hesitates before handing them over. "You seem edgy, Liberty. It's discomforting. I won't be party to anything that causes you pain."

"Pain?" I draw back in surprise. "What do you mean be party to?"

She stammers as her cheeks flush, "I-I mean be the deliverer. I can just throw them away as they come in."

"Who dropped them off this time?" I ask for the second time in as many days.

She rolls her eyes and shakes her head. "I wish I could tell you. That front desk gets so busy sometimes."

"Liz," I reassure her with a smile and take the flowers and box from her hands. "It's fine. I'll just take my cache and go. It's time for you to go home too, isn't it?"

"Just about," she says with a sigh. "Gotta sign off on a registration and then I'm outta here."

"Okay, see you tomorrow." I wave goodbye and turn for the exit.

"I'm off tomorrow," she replies. "But you never know.

Goodnight, Liberty."

Once in my car I set the vase in the cup holder and stare at the little box in my hand. It's heavier than the last one. Do I open it now, or wait until I get home? Giving in to curiosity, I turn on the interior lights and tear open the pretty white wrapping and lift the lid to find a refrigerator magnet. A replica of the Liberty Bell. Pennsylvania's own. Moreover, the nickname Lucas gave me so many years ago. We always said we'd someday go together to see it. A road trip, in a convertible, so we could soak up the sun by day and see the stars at night.

Underneath sits a handwritten note in bold black letters, same as the last package.

"You up for a road trip?"

Gag gift, my ass. The marbles were confusing enough. This? This is too much. I throw open my door and head back into the hospital. By the time I reach the front check-in, the only person I see is Ariel and all is quiet. A few chairs are occupied with waiting patients, but nothing urgent.

"Is Liz still here?"

"No," Ariel answers as she glances out the front doors. "Her husband just picked her up. She hates to drive at this time of night." She sighs wistfully then scowls. "I can't even find a boyfriend who doesn't want me to drive my car for dates so he can drink all he wants. Must be nice."

I stare at her in disbelief. *I've got nothing.*

"Goodnight, Ariel."

Liz and her husband have raised four boys, put all of them through college, worked for decades, and are finally nearing retirement. Four boys! Did I mention Ariel was filing her nails when I reached the front desk? Big no-no.

Mal is still up when I get home, the condo smells like Italian food, and she's sitting in front of the TV with a plate of lasagna and garlic bread. It's late and I'm surprised to see her eating at this time of night.

"You fixed Italian?" I ask as I inhale a deep nose full of Sicilian dreams.

She turns her head slowly and carefully, balancing her plate in her hands. "You didn't order it?"

"Uh, no?"

"Whoops," she says humorously. "Wonder which neighbor is still waiting for dinner to arrive."

"Mallory! You're eating someone else's food?"

She bites off a piece of garlic bread and speaks around it, "I thought maybe you ordered it. Who was I to turn it down?" She finishes chewing and finally swallows. "Grab a plate and eat. You never know who might come knocking. If it's the hot guy from the ninth floor, we could share. If it's the lawyer bitch from the eleventh, tell her to come get it so I can throw it in her face." She turns to me, her eyes filled with heat. "I was still in my scrubs when I got home today and she stepped on the elevator at the same time. That stuffy bitch had to nerve to tell me the janitorial staff was supposed to ride the service elevators."

"No!!" My gasp is low and throaty, my jaw unhinged. "What did you do?"

She smirks. "Told her that might be true, but I would be more than happy riding with service personnel because they're polite and nonjudgmental. *And* since I was actually an anesthetist, she might want to watch her manners and her mouth because I could slap a mask over it and she'd be dead in 30 seconds or less."

I snicker. "How did she take it?"

"I've had patients on the table turn paler than she did." She winks. "Told her she might want to sleep with one eye open as well because I knew which condo she lived in and I was friends with all the *janitorial staff*."

"Maybe now she'll move," I say with a touch of hope.

"Or, Miranda Nelson will never sleep peacefully again." She grins cockily and tips her chin. "Never let it be said I am not goal oriented."

Checking the label on the box that sits on the counter, I call the restaurant to report the error and ensure that the unfortunate, and probably hungry and upset customer, is taken care of. Turns out it wasn't an error after all. Also turns out they'd already had a call . . . from Mallory!

"Anonymous?"

"Yup," she answers, stuffing another bite in her mouth. "But it was the usual delivery guy so I knew it was safe. Eat up."

"Why didn't you tell me before I called?"

She shrugs. "Wanted to know if they told you the same thing they told me."

"And?"

"Nope," she replies cockily. "But then I have an in with one of the staff. Reece sent it. He's trying to coerce me."

"Reece? The firefighter that you hate?"

"That would be the one," she confirms. "He wants to meet me tomorrow night outside the hospital. Swears it has nothing to do with sex and I can wear scrubs or sweats if I want."

"Maybe he wants to play doctor?" I tease. "Possibly get *sweaty* with you."

She shoots me a stern look. "Would you fix a plate and come and sit down?"

"I've got something I want you to look at first and give me an opinion." I reach into my bag and pull out the two white boxes and take a seat next to her, handing over the first after she sets her plate on the coffee table.

She stares at the two marbles in the box then reads the note. "What is this?"

Before answering, I hand her the second box and wait. She repeats the process and hands the boxes back. "You want my thoughts?" I nod.

"Cheap asshole. He tells you sapphires and emeralds and sends you marbles of a different color. That, and he still can't get far enough away to keep from answering his damn phone. Pennsylvania," she grunts, then scowls. "What the hell is Michael up to now?" She shakes her head and rolls her eyes. "Go grab some food before it gets cold. Maybe I will see Reece tomorrow and have him set you up with that hot cop."

Chapter 20

Liberty

Have you ever had a day where all you want is for it to end? The day, not the world. Then again . . .

I have three hours left on my shift and I've been puked on – that which required a fast shower in the locker room – spat on, screamed at, had my ass pinched, my boob grabbed, and my hair pulled. All in a matter of the nine hours prior to the three I have left.

"Three days off, three days off," I chant to myself as I pour a quick cup of coffee and wolf down a protein bar in the break room. After today, I'll probably waste half of it by sleeping the first 36 hours. I peek into the cup I'm holding and scrunch my

nose at the godawful brown liquid inside. "And you," I grumble to the current life sustaining goo, "will be replaced with wine."

"Hey there," Eric says quietly as he enters. "I've been looking for you."

"Right here, Dr. Hanson," I address him formally while I throw the half-eaten protein bar and unfinished coffee into the trash. "And now, I'm on my way out." There is only one reason the head of radiology would be looking for me: Michael. And quite frankly, I'm tired of hearing the pleas on his behalf.

"Liberty," he pleads as he blocks my pathway to leave. "He's broken."

I glare at the man in front of me. How dare he. I didn't inflict the wounds, and there comes a time in life when being the recipient of them gets old. I will not be held accountable for pain I didn't cause. "He wouldn't know broken if someone ripped his heart out, because you have to have one in order for that to happen. Now, get out of my way."

He heaves a sigh before stepping to the side. I stop next to him before stepping out. "A conscience wouldn't hurt either, Dr. Hanson."

Maybe I wouldn't be so angry if I hadn't seen it, the graphic display. But I did. And it's all I've seen every time I think of him. I don't remember his proposal. I don't remember the good times. I don't remember his kisses, the whispers in the dark, the tender moments. I. Just. Don't.

The rest of the day comes to a close without major incidents. Thank God! I am so ready to go home, take a hot bath, drown my sorrows, and sleep for a year.

I wish it would rain. It would match my mood. A monsoon maybe. In the rain is the best time for walks; my favorite time.

It mixes so well with my tears and no one can see them.

"Liberty!" Liz's shriek can be heard throughout the hallways as she runs toward me. I'm seconds from pushing the exit door open to make my way home. I was so close. My hours have been odd this week – starting early and leaving earlier than usual. We split the shifts to cover for vacations. It's seven o'clock and I want to go home. I might even be able to last through a Netflix or two.

Taking a deep breath and remembering not to take my frustration out on the wrong person, I turn. "Weren't you supposed to be off today?"

"I had something to do," she explains, then smiles. "We need you at the front for a minute."

At least her hands are empty today. "For what?"

She shrugs, a goofy grin on her face. "I'm just the messenger."

Traipsing back down the hall and around a few corners, Liz by my side with a whole lot more bounce in her step than I feel, we reach the front desk. God, I hope I have her energy when I hit sixty. She leans over the counter and pulls up another crystal vase with three pink roses in it this time along with . . . yup, you guessed it, a small white box.

"Another one?" I snap, harsher than I mean to, but she made me make the trip back for this. The last two had thrown me, but after Eric's confrontation in the breakroom, I'm now convinced Michael is behind this.

She holds up a finger. "With a caveat. You have to open this one in front of me."

"Did Michael put you up to this?" I whisper angrily.

"What?" she whispers back in shock. "No! I wouldn't spit on him if he were on fire after what he did to you." Her mouth twists as she furrows her brow. "Well, unless it was gasoline in my mouth."

Pressing my fingers to my temple, I don't know whether to laugh or scream. Liz is funny, but I don't think she realizes what these little boxes are doing to me. How could she?

She holds the box out, coaxing me. "Go on, sweetheart. Open it."

"I'll just take it home and ..."

"You can't." She shakes her head and holds firm when I try to take the box from her hand. "Trust me?"

Between the determination and pleading in her eyes, I finally concede and take the box, tearing the paper off in front of her. As soon as I do, a particular scent fills my nostrils and I'm taken back to a time that brings tears to my eyes. I lift the lid with trembling hands to find two pieces of nostalgia – one blueberry and one tutti-frutti – over the note that reads:

I believe you owe me something, Liberty Bell. (X) I'm here to collect. Meet me outside.

I lose the capacity to breathe as my entire body starts to shake. Liz peels my bag off my shoulder and takes the box from my hand.

"I'll hold your things, sweetie," she reassures me. "Something tells me you may need your arms. I believe you'll find what you're looking for out front."

Pointing toward the entrance doors of the hospital, my shocked whisper is barely audible. "Out there?" She only nods and smiles. I run to the doors on wobbly legs, grateful there are no patients entering. The whoosh as they open is a mere match to the blood rushing in my ears and the pounding of my heart as I make my way through. My eyes scan the area frantically searching for a familiar face – the boy from my childhood – though what exactly am I looking for?

People pass by on the sidewalk out front on their way to the parkade or the parking lot ahead, some sit on the benches as they wait for their rides or for taxis. They chat with each other as if it were a normal day; as if their worlds weren't about to implode. As if the opportunity to change the ending to the movie reel that has run through their minds for the past eighteen years hasn't finally presented itself.

Where are you, Lucas!?

A short distance ahead, off to the edge of the wide sidewalk, I see Sergeant Tanner, out of uniform . . . again, standing and waiting, hands tucked in his pockets.

"Sergeant Tanner," I ask breathlessly, "have you seen . . ." The words get stuck in my throat as the dimple in his right cheek I remember so well appears and dawning washes over me. I stare in wonderment at the man he's become, my heart pounding so hard it feels like it's going to jump from my chest. I recognize it now; the sparkle in his eyes, the way his smile tips more on the right side than the left making the dimple more prominent, the way he looks at me, the slight tilt of his head as he waits.

I'm afraid to speak his name for fear he'll disappear – that this is all a dream – but God wouldn't be that cruel, would He?

"Lucas?" I finally utter.

"Hey, Libby," he says softly, the way only he could. "It's been a long time."

Don't ask me how I do it, how I get to him, what eternity feels like until I reach him, because all I can tell you is nothing has ever felt so good as Lucas' arms wrapped tightly around me; my feet off the ground, as I bury my face in his neck and sob.

"You-you're h-here," I sob into the crook of his shoulder, breathing in a scent that is new, but feels like home. It's woodsy, spicy, and all man. My best friend all grown up.

"I'm here," he whispers, "and I'm not going away."

"Wh-where, h-how . . ."

"Uh, uh. First things first," he says with that impish grin I've missed so much as he sets me on my feet and gently palms my cheeks. He brushes his nose against the side of mine and murmurs against my mouth, "I've waited eighteen years for my tomorrow. A promise is a promise, Liberty Bell."

It starts as a gentle caress of my lips, an exploration of sorts, a taste, a tease . . . until the explosion. I've never been kissed like this. I doubt it would have been the same back then. This is eighteen years of fantasized osculation come true. Nightmares washed away and dreams made reality. The final scene rewritten. My heart is whole again. Nothing held back, nothing tucked away. No nonrefundable portion, because the owner has finally come home and I can give it freely.

When the kiss ends, Lucas leans his forehead on mine and closes his eyes. "Pink," he whispers. "I knew it had a flavor."

My giggle is mixed with a half sob. "You mean tutti-frutti."

"No." He chuckles. "I mean Liberty Collins. I've missed you so damn much."

"I've missed you, too. Where have you been, Lucas? I've looked for you."

"I could ask you the same, Libby." He dips his chin. "I've looked for you too. I came back for you. You were gone."

"Y-you what?" Tears spring to my eyes again as I recall trying to convince my mom not to move; that Lucas wouldn't be able to find me if we left. I knew he would return . . . someday.

He kisses my forehead, holding his lips to my skin as he murmurs, "We have a lot to talk about. You up to it?"

"Yeah," I agree, as if I hadn't just worked a 12-hour shift and am running on adrenaline. "I have the next three days off. I'm all yours."

He brushes a fallen tendril away from my face with a gentle

finger and swipes a tear from my cheek with his thumb. "I've always been yours."

Chapter 21

Lucas

I can see it in her eyes the moment she realizes who I am. But then, I've always seen everything in and through Liberty's eyes – my two favorite colors. How to see, how to feel, how to function. Right from wrong. Truth from lies. Genuine from imitation. Seeing her now, the way she looks at me only proves she was, and still is, the best thing that's ever happened to me. It's like time has stood still and waited for us, knowing eventually we would find our way back to each other.

Hearing her say my name is the best sound to touch my ears since the last time she spoke it – not screamed it. It's not just a melody, it's the whole fucking song.

Holding her in my arms fills the void and seeps through the wall that no one else has ever been able to permeate. It lights a fire I led myself to believe I didn't have; so far beyond the physical. And now I know why. It's my heart . . . beating again.

And pink? Maybe it's not so much a flavor as it is a feeling.

Applause breaks out as the group of misfits approach. Reece somehow talked Liberty's friend into joining them.

Liberty looks aghast as she stares at her friend. "You knew about this?!"

"Not 'til now." Mallory shakes her head and makes her way toward us. She gives me a quick scrutinizing once over with narrowed eyes. "Well, so much for the beer belly and a transmission in the bathtub in Kentucky." She lifts an inquisitive brow and asks, "You got seven kids and a wife?"

My face scrunches in confusion before Reece holds up a hand, flashing a full palm of five digits then switches to two behind her and mouths "five and two".

Playing along and feeling a little retribution for her cockiness in the ER is in order, I deadpan, "Five kids and two ex-wives. Is that a problem?"

"How many?!" Mallory shrieks as the three grinning idiots behind her burst into laughter. She turns to them and scowls. "You assholes!"

"Aw, come on, kitten," Reece pleads as he wraps his arms around her shoulders from behind and nuzzles his face in her neck. "You know we were just teasing." He whispers something close to her ear, inaudible to the rest of us.

She elbows him hard in the ribs and sputters, "I would sooner squash your balls! I don't have a daddy kink! What the hell is wrong with you?!"

I pinch the bridge of my nose with one hand while keeping my other arm wrapped tightly around Libby and sigh heavily.

"Reece, it was a joke."

Reece raises his head in shock, rendering Mallory an advantage and the open space to deliver one more vicious elbow to his ribs, before she storms off toward the parking lot.

"I thought you said she . . ." he rages.

Roger slaps him on the back of the head. "What he said is she's a smartass. I told you to just ask the lady out. Daddy kink," he grumbles. "You are such a dumbass. Go chase her and start groveling. Get on your knees if you have to."

Reece's face lights in a devilish grin. "I could do that. I've been told I'm good on my knees." He takes off at a dead run in the same direction Mallory did.

"Should I follow them or stay here?" Wiley asks as he holds his phone in the air.

"Wiley," I huff. "Why are you still recording?"

He shrugs. "Blackmail?"

I scowl. "*Another* retirement plan?"

He chuckles. "This is only supplemental income."

Roger grasps the back of Wiley's neck and threatens, "You ain't going to make it to retirement if you don't pocket that phone."

Liberty's perfect giggle is music to my ears and makes her body quiver in my arms, because I haven't let go of her and have no intention of doing so unless I have to. "Are they always like this?"

"Give 'em time, it only gets worse," I mumble.

Roger steps forward, his hand held out, and winks. "Hello there, you must be the long lost Liberty. I'm Cupid."

Liberty extends her hand over my forearm that refuses to move, glancing up at me first before she grins at Roger. "Hi, Cupid."

"It's actually stupid," I correct as Roger flashes me a wicked grin and lifts Liberty's hand to kiss her knuckles. "And if he doesn't knock it off, it's going to be prisoner number 69," I narrow my eyes and warn, "with a cellmate named Bubba."

Roger and Wiley burst into spontaneous laughter as Wiley shoves Roger to the side and moves forward to shake Liberty's hand. "I'm Wiley, Tanner's advisor. Taught him everything he knows, but not everything I know so if you want someone with experience to . . ."

"What the hell is the matter with you!" Roger hollers as his slap reaches the back of Wiley's head. "You're old enough to be her father."

"I was gonna offer her financial advice!" Wiley exclaims indignantly.

Roger digs the heel of his palm into his forehead and grimaces. "Jesus, Wiley. I can't take you anywhere. It's no wonder they dumped your ass."

Why are we still standing here? I tasted pink for the first time in my life tonight and I want more. My dream girl is in my arms and I'm listening to these idiots argue. Mind you, I owe them. They did help me reach my goal, but I can hear this palaver – and usually do – any day of the week.

As I wrap my hand in Liberty's hair, the messy bun nearly falls out of its confines and I drop a kiss to her temple. "No ex-wives and definitely no kids. Can we get out of here?"

"Yeah." Her breath is warm against my neck as she chuckles, a new sensation I hadn't anticipated that sends a rush up my spine. "I have to grab my bag from Liz."

Turning her shoulders as I shoot a sincere smile to the woman standing just feet away, I tell her, "Don't think you have far to go."

Liz holds out her bag and takes Libby's hand in hers. "I put the box inside. Someday you kids are going to have to tell me the story behind this. He's one of the good ones, Liberty." She smiles sweetly then winks at me. "Guess it's a good thing you came back in to check on that little guy, huh?"

Pondering the odds of the particular situation that brought us together again gives me chills. Only Liberty and I could have those odds stacked so high against us and the fact that we're here seems literally impossible. Which leads me to believe it was meant to be. How could it not?

With that thought, I take the bag from Libby to carry it for her and place my other arm around her shoulder. "I guess so. Thanks, Liz."

"I need to get my car," Liberty says as if suddenly remembering where we are. "I can meet you somewhere."

"Gotcha covered," Roger reassures her from behind us as he texts a message. "Poor Tanner would have a coronary if you got separated and we're not on duty tonight. Give me your keys and tell me which one it is. Reece and I rode together, Mallory hasn't killed him yet, and this way . . ." his voice is playful as he finishes, "he can find out where you live when he has to pick me up after I deliver it."

She eyes him skeptically. "Didn't he have dinner delivered to us last night?"

He laughs heartily. "He could only do it because of her name. The restaurant wouldn't give him the address. Seems you two are regulars."

Liberty nods in agreement. "She does like Italian."

He winks once more. "Yeah, well, Reece is hoping to sway her tastes toward the Texas born, cattle ranch, steak-eating type."

Liberty giggles as she reaches into her purse and pulls out a set of keys, tosses them to Roger, and informs him where to find her vehicle. "Don't tell her I told you this, but she does have a thing for cowboys. Better warn Reece to saddle up tight.

She's not an easy ride."

"Goodnight, gentlemen," I bid them adieu with a roll of my eyes as I wrap my arm tighter around Liberty and lead her toward the parking lot. Glancing back one more time, I smirk. "And I use that term loosely."

"You drive a Jeep, too?" Libby asks as I open the passenger side for her and wait for her to climb in, apparently surprised by my choice in transportation.

"I've always had something I could take the top off of." I wink as I lean in and pull the seatbelt over her shoulder to fasten it for her. "We need a convertible for our trip to see the Liberty Bell."

Her eyes rim with tears as she gazes into mine, reaching for my cheek that is now covered with facial hair, and runs her fingers through it as if discovering something new. Damn, it feels good. "You haven't forgotten a thing, have you?"

"How could I?" I reach for my wallet and pull out the picture of the two of us by the pool. "Someone was determined I didn't."

She takes the picture from me with shaky hands and stares at it. "Y-you've had this all along?"

"As well as the note, bracelet, and bubblegum. Officer Sullivan gave it to me when I ran away and came back looking for you." I collect the picture and tuck it back in my wallet. Tipping her chin up, I whisper, "I didn't need it to remember you, Libby. You were the reason I woke up every day. But you have no idea how much it helped to know you wouldn't forget me."

She unbuckles her seatbelt in a rush and throws herself forward to catch me in a tight hug. "I thought you hated me," she sobs. "It was my fault."

"What?" I gasp and pull back, taking her cheeks in my

palms. "What are you talking about?"

"I-I'm the one who made mom and dad call the police," she stammers. "If I hadn't run inside and told them . . ."

"Oh shit," I mutter, pulling her to me once again. "No, Libby. Mom had already called them. That's what set the old man off. He went into a rage and there was no stopping him. It wouldn't have mattered who called them. Liberty, it wasn't you." I pull her out of the Jeep – the awkward embrace we're in not enough – and simply hold her, putting full effort into squeezing the demon out of her as she sobs against my chest.

Way to go, old man. Your outreach was wider spread than I gave you credit. Makes me hate you even more than I already did. You hurt my Libby too. Even if she were the one to call the police first, it would have made no difference. You were an evil sonofabitch. That night wasn't the first time you went off the rails.

I don't want to share her with a restaurant full of people. I don't want to take her home to prepare to go out; that's just lost time. Ten to one says Reece is groveling outside the window . . . on his knees, I'm sure. Unless he's talked his squadron mates into bringing a truck and a ladder to hoist him up if need be. I sure as hell don't plan on letting her go. I'm more than willing to wine and dine her in the scrubs she's in. At. My. Home. I've never seen scrubs look sexier. No, I don't want to share her . . . with anyone.

"Hey," I whisper, "how about we order in? I can give you some sweats to get comfy in and I'm pretty sure I have access to wine."

She nods heavily against my chest. "I might fall asleep mid sip."

I chuckle lightly as I kiss the top of her head, breathing in a soft scent of vanilla and coconut; like sunshine on the darkest of days. Just like Libby. "Did I mention I have pillows and a bed, too?" I pull back and dip my chin. "So long as I get to see my two favorite colors when you wake up."

"I've missed you, Lucas." She squeezes around my middle tighter. "I was never the same after that night."

"Neither was I." I tip her chin up and gaze into the eyes I've only been able to see in my sleep with every dream. "It's what happens when someone takes away the best part of you."

Stealing one more kiss because I can't help myself, I tuck her back into her seat and buckle the belt. There will be time. I've finally found my other half.

Chapter 22

Liberty

"Tell me what you like to eat," Lucas says as he starts the vehicle that is a virtual twin to my own; mine being red, his being black. It's almost laughable. Same trim package, same interior color, same stereo.

Dinner isn't the only thing I haven't had, and it's not first on my agenda either. I need a shower, despite the fact I had one four hours ago, taken in a matter of seconds in order to wash off bodily fluids that soaked through my first set of scrubs. I love my job, but I don't want to smell like my job. I also need wine. So much wine. But I don't want to fall asleep. I want to hear every word. I want to savor every moment. I want to know where he's been, what he's been doing, why his name isn't Lucas anymore.

"We're going to your place?" I inquire once the thoughts in my head unscramble enough to separate person, place, and thing over to current time and circumstance.

He glances at me before pulling out of the parking lot and arches a brow. "You and Mallory are roommates, right?" I nod. "Did you want to try and have a conversation around Reece pleading outside the window? Possibly serenading her?"

"We live on the tenth floor." I chuckle at what would be futile attempts by the pursuer, or the bucket of water Mallory might be tempted to dump on him should he try. "Good luck with that."

"Did you forget he's a firefighter?" He smirks. "With resources and access to trucks and ladders."

"Your place it is."

He reaches over the console and squeezes my knee. "I'll take you home whenever you want. But I'm really hoping the three days you have off will be spent with me, Libby. I think we have a lot of catching up to do."

Placing my hand on top of his, I voice agreement. "Me too. But I will need to get some things from home."

"Not tonight though, right?" he asks, his tone hopeful that he can continue in the direction he's headed.

"Not tonight." I shake my head as we stop at a red light. "You promised me dinner, sweats, and wine."

He laughs, the sound of which fills that corner of my heart that's been empty for years then turns to me as the light turns green, squeezes my knee once more, and winks. "Can't wait to see you in my clothes, Libby."

I like this grownup version of him. It's easy, comfortable, confident. And sexy as hell. If this is a dream, I don't want to ever wake up.

"My humble abode," Lucas announces after closing the door behind us, then slides the bag off my shoulder to place it on the counter. It's a beautiful condo, furnished and decorated for the typical bachelor. Masculine furniture in dark colors, built to hold figures of the larger variety, i.e. men. Two recliners, a deep sofa, an enormous TV hung above the fireplace, coffee table, end tables, and a few pictures on the wall of various cityscapes. The kitchen is all stainless steel appliances, sleek, with a breakfast bar accommodating two bar chairs, though room for four if he wanted. It's clean, organized, well kempt.

"Nice place," I comment with a smile. "Did you clean for me?"

His mouth twitches on one side. "Would you believe me if I said yes?"

"I'd believe anything you tell me, Lucas." My voice drops to a whisper. "You're one of the few people in my life who never lied to me."

A slow grin spreads across his mouth as the backs of his knuckles skim my cheek. "Then I'd better confess my housekeeper cleaned her ass off."

I burst into a fit of giggles but stop when I see him staring at me. "It hasn't changed," he whispers in astonishment, tracing a finger from my forehead to my chin. "I've often wondered if the giggle I remembered and heard in my dreams was still the same." He takes one step closer, our bodies mere inches apart. His hand moves into my fallen locks and he murmurs against my mouth, "I much prefer the live version though."

Somewhere deep in my heart, I wish we'd learned to kiss together, but admittedly as a second act, we're not too shabby. We're like dance partners who've performed the Tango for years together.

"Libby," he breathes the nickname I only ever allowed him to use as he breaks the kiss and leans his forehead on mine, one hand in my hair, the other squeezing my hip. "Dinner, comfy clothes, conversation, before I get carried away."

Oh good! It wasn't just me.

"Don't forget the wine," I remind him, fighting an odd sense of rejection though I know it's not. We're virtual strangers. It was a lifetime ago. An eternity that always felt like only yesterday because the memories were so clear.

He brushes the side of my nose with his and drops a soft kiss on the corner of my mouth. "Red or white?"

"White."

He lingers and repeats the action, squeezing my hip a little firmer. For a man who didn't want to get carried away moments ago, he's having a hard time resisting temptation. "Chardonnay or Pinot?"

"Sauvignon Blanc," I tease, enjoying his touch. I couldn't care less what kind of wine it is. In my college days I poured wine from a spout on the box in the fridge. Anything fruity would do. I wasn't a snob then, not a snob now.

He releases a low throaty growl. "God, I love the way you say that. Sounds sexy as hell." He drops another kiss to my jaw. "Brand name?"

"Are you stalling, Lucas?"

"Maybe," he hums against my skin, the vibrations causing delightful sensations I haven't felt since . . . well, ever. "It's hard to let go. This feels so right, Liberty. My world fell apart after losing you. Nothing felt the same after that night. No one has called me Lucas since you."

"Do I have to call you Tanner now, like everyone else does?"

He pulls back slightly and grimaces. "We'll figure something out, okay?"

There have to be reasons; I simply don't know them yet. He'll explain when the time is right. Offering a smile of understanding, because I've always trusted Lucas implicitly, I proffer, "Maybe I'll call you Lucas when it's just the two of us?"

His eyes mist over as he gazes into mine and he places a hand on my cheek. "How in the hell did I ever survive without you?"

I place my own hand on his cheek as well and run my fingers through the thick, finely trimmed, short beard. "You had to," I utter softly, "so you could come back to me."

"Did you ever think it would happen?"

"*If it were not for hopes, the heart would break*." I borrow the quote to explain the wish I've held onto for years, the chance that someday I would find my best friend again – the yin to my yang, the light to my dark; be given an opportunity to apologize. Instead, finding out as an adult I had nothing to apologize for and the feelings he's stirred are so much more.

"Thomas Fuller," he says with a knowing smile. "Got one for you. *You never forget your first love*."

"Wendelin Van Draanen," I say with a chuckle.

He twirls a tendril between his fingers. "She was right. I've never forgotten you, Liberty. But after so many years, I think I had given up hope. That's why I clung to that picture you left for me. The only proof I was once happy was that picture, the two of us together. The last thing I remembered was this sweet innocent blonde girl running behind the car I was trapped in, screaming my name, begging me not to go. I felt your pain because it was the same as mine, and I couldn't take yours away."

He still has that tendril of hair wrapped around his finger as he stares at it and mentally takes a trip back in time. "The authorities took everything from the house. I got none of my stuff back. No pictures, no toys." He smiles sadly and acquiesces, "No baseball glove or arm cast with your signature on it. I don't remember much about that night, just bits and pieces. I think the trauma made me block a lot of it out. I barely remember my folks, Libby. But you . . ." his words trail.

He studies my face again and while I see a touch of guilt in his eyes – probably on behalf of his mom as they had a pretty good relationship – I also see gratitude. "Your face being the last one I saw was a helluva lot better than anything I could have seen in that house. As painful as it was to see you cry, I knew from your scream you would miss me, that I was wanted by someone, that . . ."

"You were loved," I finish for him through a choked sob before I pull him into a hug so tight there is not a millimeter between us. "I have missed you, so much, Lucas."

"It was always you, Libby. I've missed you more than any of them," he confesses as he buries his face in my neck. "And I can't bring myself to feel guilty about it."

"You don't really mean that," I say softly against the crook of his neck. "You loved your mom."

"She should have turned him in long before she did. It never had to happen that way." He squeezes my middle tighter as if pulling strength from his hold on me. "Your mom and dad made me feel more comfortable than my own did."

"I'm sorry." The words spill from my mouth as if on autopilot, having learned to express them over the years on multiple occasions under various circumstances. Two words that neither of us have ever had to exchange amongst ourselves, because we never inflicted pain on one another. We worked to soothe it if the other felt it. We were never the cause; only the cure.

"Don't be," he murmurs before he pulls back from the embrace. "It was a lifetime ago. And I am so sorry about your dad. I wish I had been there for you."

"Like you said, it was a lifetime ago." It's an honest statement. My dad's been gone for sixteen years. I miss him, but Tom makes my mom happy and he's made the loss much more bearable. A bonus neither one of us expected.

"I suppose we both have some blanks to fill in, but I promised you dinner." He drops a kiss to my nose and chuckles. "And wine."

"Mind if I get a shower first?"

"Promise not to wash your hair?"

"What?!"

He drops another kiss – to my forehead this time – and draws in a deep breath. "I love the scent of your hair and I don't want you smelling like my shampoo. I suppose I can tolerate my body wash for one evening, but don't wash the hair, please."

I giggle and push at his chest and am met with rock hard pecs. "You're weird."

He winks and smiles, my favorite dimple making a star studded appearance in his right cheek. "Just like old times, huh? Come on, I'll get you some sweats."

Funny, I don't remember old times giving me goosebumps, or chills, or a sensation that starts low in my belly and travels between . . .

Shower! Now!

Chapter 23

Lucas

Roger: Has the lovely Liberty shared her address with you?

The text arrives shortly after I leave the bedroom so Libby can get her shower. She chose a well-worn T-shirt with the PPD logo on it and the smallest pair of jersey sweatpants I had available. Newsflash: she'll be rolling them at the waist, probably four times.

Me: Is there a reason she should?

Roger: 10786 Atticus Parkway Condos

Me: Is this a joke?

Roger: I'm not laughing, bro. I'll give you three guesses who I saw entering the building as I was leaving. It's all good, kept my crotch covered. She's been out to bust my balls ever since I threw her out of your condo.

Not wasting any time, I push the button to call him.

"Is she sitting beside you?" he answers in a hushed voice sans a hello.

"Are you kidding me?" I snap through a harsh whisper, ignoring his inquiry.

"You took her home already? She didn't dump your sappy ass, did she?" he teases, the sound of glass tinkling and low voices in the background. Apparently they've stopped for a much needed drink.

"No, dumbass," I growl, heading for the kitchen to grab the glasses and a bottle of wine. "She's in the shower. You're serious? Miranda lives in her building? I'll never be able to show up at Liberty's place. That's like putting a match to gasoline."

"Guess it's a good thing you have friends who are firefighters," he says confidently as Reece backs his statement with a hearty chuckle. Apparently I'm on speaker phone as they sit at the bar.

"She's been relentless, guys," I remind them. "Nudie texts, voicemails from unknown numbers, asking for me at the station. She sent me a fucking pair of dirty panties in the mail, for God's sake! She's psycho!"

Reece's laughter mixes with the low chatter of voices at whatever bar they're patronizing as he adds to our conversation, "That's what having a ten-pound dick will get you."

"Aw shit!" I sputter, recalling the mention of floor level. "Liberty said they live on the tenth floor. Miranda's on the eleventh. Could this get much worse?"

Roger snort-laughs. "Could work to your advantage. That's one more story to fall when somebody tosses her out the window."

"This isn't funny, assholes," I grind through a clenched jaw and shoot a glance at my bedroom door to ensure Libby can't hear.

"Hey!" Roger chides. "Liberty was engaged to a cheating dick. Everybody has a history. I'm just giving you a heads up."

"I doubt her former fiancé has green skin, wears a pointed hat, flies around on a broom, and collected a used condom with my cum in it." I scrub my face with my hand and groan. "That is one association I would prefer to omit . . . and forget."

"Got a few of those myself, Tanner." He chuckles. "Might want to shave your head or wear a cap if you're going to be visiting."

"Or carry holy water to see if she melts when I throw it on her," I grumble. "Thanks for the heads up."

"Hang on," Roger says before I disconnect. "Mallory packed a bag for Liberty with a few days' things in it. She figured you two could use some time together without having to go back and forth. I can drop it outside your door when we get back. You know, knock twice and make ourselves scarce. Unless, you want another round of *Wipeout*."

"We could bring Wiley and have him do a Taylor Swift song for you," Reece offers cockily.

"Two knocks," I warn him, "or you will both have traffic violations on the daily for the next two weeks."

"The good news is Mallory didn't castrate Reece and now he knows where she lives."

"Has he forgotten she can *desuscitate* him?" I snidely remind them.

Reece howls with laughter. "As long as it's with her kitten

on my face, I'll die a happy man, Tanner."

"I'd get her declawed first, Reece," I warn him – jokingly – sort of. "Goodnight, guys. Thanks again for the warning." I disconnect and toss my phone on the counter.

"Who would you get declawed?" The sound of her voice is an instant relaxant to the tightness in my muscles. I spin to see her standing in my T-shirt and a pair of sweats that literally swallow her whole, and the tightness returns. She's braless. Just kill me now. I'll bet she has no panties on under the sweats either. *Concentrate, Lucas. Put your dick away. This is Liberty, and you are not Tanner. You have waited a literal lifetime for her. The moment you saw her, every woman you have ever entertained became a blur.* She's barefoot; pretty pink colored toenails peek out from the loose hem of the pants. Her hair is no longer in the messy bun – a little damp from the steam – and falls softly around her shoulders. Her face is free of makeup; such a change from any of the other women I've been with over the years. Comfortable in her own skin. That's my Liberty. Confident, real. Porcelain complexion with a few tiny freckles scattered across her nose.

And those eyes. My favorite colors of blue and green. The eyes that could always see right through me. But I was always willing to let her. I never had reason to hide from Liberty. I was an open book, willing to let her read every page, hoping someday we'd write our own epilogue.

"You look good in my clothes." I take the necessary steps it takes to reach her and place my hands on her hips, satisfying the need to touch her.

She tilts her head and arches a brow playfully and . . . expectantly. She hasn't changed a bit. She doesn't need to repeat the question. She knows I know, and I know she knows I know. She doesn't narrow her eyes, no threatening glare, no *or else* in her expectant gaze.

It's our shared *'you can tell me anything'* promise.

Our *'I've got your back no matter what'* agreement.

Our *'tell me your secrets and I'll tell you no lies'* trust.

"Mallory." I cringe with my response. "It's kind of a private joke with Reece. She told him once she could *desuscitate* him faster than he could resuscitate her." I resist laughing but fail miserably. "He's hoping it's with a certain body part versus suffocating him with a gas mask. Hence the reason he calls her kitten. Need I say more?"

She drops her forehead onto my chest and groans. "They deserve each other."

"She is a bit of a smartass," I mutter as I rest my chin on the crown of her head.

"She rescued me when no one else could," she whispers against my chest. "We've been attached at the hip since we were fifteen years old. Introduced herself the first day of high school as hetero too." She lifts her face, points to her eyes, and grins. "Sex, not the eyes; she was all about the penis. Then told me she doesn't like vanilla, shakes or sex, and we went to the beach and had hamburgers."

Lifting a high brow and dipping my chin, I inquire, "Your very first conversation was about sex?"

"No." She smiles and shakes her head. "It was her way of breaking the ice. She read me like a street sign. I always thought mine read STOP. She said it read: Proceed with caution. She likes a challenge. She's the only one I've ever told about you."

"Déjà vu," I utter before I can stop myself.

"What?"

"The night we brought Adam in," I explain. "When she came charging into the room worried about you, she made the remark about déjà vu. It gave me some hope you hadn't forgotten."

"You knew who I was?" she asks, incredulous. "Why didn't you say something?"

"Libby," I breathe her name like a prayer and brush a wayward strand away from her face. "It took everything in me not to drop to my knees. You didn't recognize me."

"For a moment I thought I did," she confesses through a single tear that falls, soon followed by another. "I swore I saw it in your eyes, but then Adam called you Sergeant Tanner and my heart literally sank. I convinced myself I was looking for something that wasn't there. Just one more shattered dream."

"And in the parking lot a few nights later?"

"I had just opened the first package with the marbles. I was upset and convinced it was my ex fian..." She stops short and shakes her head. "Never mind. Anyway, it had been a really bad day with a godawful, purple dildo and then you hugged me and I felt all these things and . . ."

"Yeah." I wrap her in my arms and hold her closer. "I felt all the things too." *Wait a minute!* I pull back from the hug and dip my chin, my brow furrowed in puzzlement. "A purple dildo?"

"Oh God," she groans once more and buries her face into my chest again. "Don't ask. Please."

Some things must – or should – remain a mystery. At least for now. Inquiries regarding a dildo in the ER can wait – possibly forever. Sounds like a story for game night, lots of drinks, and oh! I know. Ava, chapter: 21, paragraph: 33. Not that I'll ever read it but it could make good fodder for the pages.

"Have you decided what you would like to eat yet?"

"Food," she utters.

I hold her head to my chest and kiss the top, breathing in the scent. *I am home.* "You're tired, aren't you?"

"I don't want to sleep," she whispers. "I want to hear your story."

"And I want to hear yours," I whisper back.

Two light taps on the door indicate her bag has been left outside. She pulls away and questions, "Did you order dinner already?"

"That should be your bag." I move for the door and toss back, "Mallory packed it for you and Roger was going to drop it off."

"Mal packed a bag for me?"

Opening the door, I find the bag and a note on top that reads: *For the Lost Then Found. Congrats.*

Setting her bag in the foyer, I show her the note. "Boy, they got that right, didn't they?"

She stares at the words, her eyes brimming with tears once again, before she looks up and sniffles. "I like the found part best. I never felt more seen than when I was with you. We were so young, Lucas." Her forehead creases and her mouth takes on a funny little twist. "Are we crazy?"

"Yes," I say without hesitation, my mouth helplessly twitching on one side. My palm finds its way to her cheek, my fingers edging into the silky locks that frame her face. "Probably certifiable. But we never did do anything halfway, did we?"

She smiles sweetly and as she does, a lone tear falls from her blue eye; the side my palm is on so I brush it away with my thumb. "No, we didn't," she whispers.

"Go crazy with me, Liberty. Give us a chance." I drop a light kiss to the perfect pink bow of her upper lip and pepper more to the corners as I explain, "No rush," *kiss* "explore," *kiss* "discover," *kiss* "start over, continue," *kiss* "whatever you want to call it. I don't want to fuck this up. All I know is I want you in my life because for the first time since I lost you, I finally know what it feels like to breathe." I take both cheeks in my palms and concentrate my gaze on my favorite two colors. "I have every item you left in that box. I've read that note thousands of times. I didn't throw them away, Libby. How could I fall in love without you?"

"*In* love," she emphasizes as her chin trembles. "That's the whole difference."

I capture her breath with the next kiss. It's a mix of tongues and teeth, pants and gasps. Yet never have my lungs felt so full. I want to take away the pain that asshole fiancé caused her and make her forget he ever existed. I want to make up for eighteen years of absence and emptiness. Yes, that's a lot more time apart than we were ever together. But that time together was priceless and unforgettable.

You can love all sorts of people throughout a lifetime. So many different kinds of love. But how many do you fall *in* love with? I know my number, and she's standing in front of me. My one and only Liberty.

We'd been inked, timestamped on each other's hearts with no expiration, waiting for the world to get out of our way and for the path to open up so we could find our way back to each other.

No, we are not crazy. We are indelible.

Chapter 24

Liberty

It's nearing one o'clock in the morning. Half of my Chinese dinner sits cold and uneaten. I did manage two glasses of wine, followed by two glasses of water. A few hours has hardly made a dent in our histories, but as Lucas put it: "We can cover the details later. What counts is we've found each other."

So here we sit, my head on his shoulder, eyelids heavy, his fingertips softly brushing my skin while he occasionally drops a kiss to the top of my head. Comfortable, wordless silence as we soak in the information we've both fed each other. No chronological order to the time spent apart.

He wrote me letters that went undelivered – probably

intercepted and never left the point of origin – due to safety reasons.

I wrote him letters that were never sent because I had nowhere to send them. They were therapy for me. Written apologies begging forgiveness. Pleas of a young girl asking for another chance. Wishful thinking transferred from my brain onto the pages as if it might someday come true. The final scene of the movie I wanted to play out the way my fantasy had created. The happy ending.

If my parents knew the whole story, they didn't divulge it.

His aunt and uncle could have found a way to open communication for us, but probably thought it best to leave the past behind. For safety reasons. They had two other children to protect.

"They were parents doing their jobs." I finally break the silence.

His chin moves against my head as he reluctantly agrees. "Yeah."

"You're lucky you had them, Lucas. I'd love to meet them someday." I lift my head from his shoulder. "The people who gave you everything they possibly could when you needed them most."

He frowns, acquiescing, and brushes a loose tendril away from my forehead. "Everything but you."

Knowing there is so much we don't know about each other yet it feels like we've picked up right where we left off – hearts don't change – I feel at ease reassuring him, "You've got me now."

"Do I?" He lifts a brow in question. "Are you over him, Liberty? I would really suck at sharing and I sure as hell don't want to be a rebound."

I let out a pitiful huff and sit up straight. "You want to hear something sad?"

He sits up straight as well and rounds his neck to loosen it and clenches and unclenches his fists once. "Am I going to want to kill him?"

Dropping my chin to my chest and chuckling softly, I shake my head. "No, let the good doctor live. Too many people depend on him."

"So what is it?"

I lift my gaze to meet his. "I haven't even cried. Two months and I haven't shed a tear over it. I walked in on the man having sex with another woman and I've felt nothing. I have this habit I developed many years ago of comparing any pain to one I felt when I lost my best friend. There is only one that has ever compared. That's when I lost dad. I cried buckets for days; wasn't sure I'd ever stop. Nothing has even come close since then."

"Liberty," he breathes on a soft sigh.

Holding my hand up I stop him and continue, "No, I'm not done. I'm not generally a crier. That night in the parking lot when I broke down, it was because Adam's case was so similar to yours. But you were so good with him. You followed through with your promise. You found his best friend. All I could think about was him asking for Jessie and wondered if Lucas ever asked for me. It was selfish."

I try to bury my face in my hands, but Lucas catches them before I can and pulls me to him. "Libby, I begged for you. I kicked and screamed until they sedated me because they were afraid I would hurt myself." He tangles his fingers in my hair and holds my head to his chest. "Oh baby, I would have done anything to have you with me. You were the only thing that mattered. You always have been, always will be."

He adjusts himself on the sofa and pulls me with him as he lays back on a throw pillow, tucking me next to him between the cushions and his warm body. I take comfort in the shelter of his arms, my head on his chest, his heart beating steady in a rhythm that lulls me into a peaceful, dreamless slumber.

The smell of coffee partnered with bacon and eggs wafts through the air and stimulates my senses so strongly my eyes not only open, but they roll to the back of my head once. Mallory doesn't cook eggs and . . .

Oh! I'm not at home. And this is not my bed. The T-shirt clad chest I fell asleep on last night is now bare and front and center at the stove as he turns bacon. Holy Moses! Lucas is most definitely all grown up. Broad shoulders, ripped muscles, golden tanned skin, a few tats that I'll have to admire close-up once given the opportunity, and low slung sweat pants. His hair is wet from an obvious shower, mussed in a way that makes my fingers curl. And what is it about finely trimmed facial hair?

He turns to catch me peeking over the arm of the sofa and smiles so brightly the corners of his eyes crease. "There are my two favorite colors. Good morning, sunshine. Breakfast in bed or do you want to join me at the bar?"

I blink slowly, twice. It's that or pinch myself to assure I'm not dreaming. "I have never had breakfast in bed."

He holds up one finger. "Not true, Libby. I brought you breakfast in bed after your tonsillectomy. Popsicle and Jell-O. Have you forgotten?" He places a hand over his heart and pouts. "I'm wounded. I even snuck you a puddin' cup, too. It wasn't my fault it gunked up your throat and made you gag." He shakes his head and grimaces. "Your mom was so pissed at me. If I hadn't cried out of guilt, I think she would have taken away my visiting privileges."

The man is eidetic, I swear. I did gag. The pudding coated my throat, causing me to choke. Lucas feared he had killed me. Mom had to calm him as much or more than me that day. We were ten, and Lucas ended up camping out that night in a sleeping bag on the floor of my bedroom *just in case I stopped breathing.* The door was left open and every time I moved or moaned, he jumped up and asked if he should go get my mom. He was the best ten-year-old nurse ever.

My hand flies to my mouth as I try to cover yet another sob. For a woman who is generally not a crier, I sure have found my water reserves. All those bottled up memories are coming back as if it were yesterday.

Lucas slides the pan off the burner and rushes to my side. "Hey," he whispers, dropping to his knees in front of the sofa, taking my hands in his. "Libby, it's a good memory for me." His brows lift as his mouth tips in a crooked grin. "Now that I can laugh about it. You lived."

As always, in true Lucas form, he manages to take away the tears and replace them with laughter . . . or giggles. "My mom had to give you a paper bag to breathe."

"I did kinda panic." His forehead creases as he swipes an errant tear from my cheek and murmurs, "I was afraid I'd hurt you."

"Never," I reassure him of the trust I feel all the way to my bones. How I can feel what I do after all this time away from him is beyond me, but I do. It's not a childhood trauma that I couldn't get past. Even when I was with Michael, I didn't stop intermittent searches for Lucas. This is not a project that I needed to put finishing touches on. It's not an ending that needs rewritten. I don't want an end, I want a new beginning. I want all the in-betweens too.

"Go crazy with me, Liberty. Give us a chance."

As Lucas stands and tugs on my hands to help me to my feet, the lone tattoo on his chest over his heart nearly takes my breath away. *The Liberty Bell.* I rise to my feet but my eyes are glued to his chest as I study the magnificent piece of art inked in his skin. He doesn't move, his breaths slow and steady as he waits. My finger traces the outline of the replica of Pennsylvania's monument and Lucas' nickname for me.

My eyes flit to his and a soft smile forms as he whispers, "Look closer."

The crack in the bell is defined and wide, a bit longer than on the original, and hidden between the crooked lines from top to bottom are the letters, L-I-B-E-R-T-Y.

"I have carried you with me every day since my eighteenth birthday and it was legal to get you stamped over my heart." He lifts my chin with two gentle fingers. His eyes hide nothing; they never did. "It's always been you, Libby."

We weren't typical. We weren't normal. We were classic, unbreakable, timeless.

His mouth on mine is the best sensation in the world. Every kiss is like the first one; the best one. The one I'd waited for since the day I let him ride away on that bicycle with the promise of tomorrow.

"Ooh," I protest, popping our mouths apart and quickly turning my head. "I haven't brushed my teeth yet. J-just hold that thought."

Lucas wraps his hand in my hair and turns my face so we're breathing each other's air – his minty fresh, mine probably wet hair of the dog – narrowing his eyes. "Don't ever do that again." He seals his mouth over mine and coaxes my lips open with his tongue, gaining entry with my concession. Ah hell, who needs a toothbrush? When the kiss is over, he leans his forehead on mine and sighs deeply. "I don't care if you've been asleep for four hours or four days. I don't care if we ate garlic and onions for dinner. Eighteen years of tomorrows is a lot to make up for, Liberty. Better stock up on Chapstick. I'm gonna be chewing that shit off like cotton candy. You may not have been my first kiss, but you can bet your sweet little ass you are my best kiss and you will be my last kiss."

"I like the sound of that," I whisper against his chin as I try my best not to breathe toward his senses.

"Breakfast?" he proposes.

I glance up, my brows raised, and flash him puppy dog eyes as I bat my lashes. "Can I go brush my teeth first?"

He palms my cheeks tightly as he slides his tongue in my mouth once more, delivering a moan worthy kiss before ending it with a loud pop. "If you must."

"Liberty," he calls out as I head for the bedroom toward the master bath. I turn and wait. He winks and grins. "Still pink."

Rifling through the bag Mallory packed for me, I find a veritable potpourri of items to include a few pairs of shorts, tops, undies, bras – a few naughty underthings that really shouldn't have been packed, as well an envelope stashed inside addressed to "Liberty's Vagina".

"Sorry. I didn't pack your little buddy. No reason for it. If I had a childhood sweetheart that looked like that, I'd be on my way back to NC. You've spent a lifetime looking for him. If you come back anything less than bow-legged and whimpering, I will kick your ass! The icepacks for your crotch will be in the freezer."

Leave it to Mal to make it all about sex. It's her way of saying 'don't let what Michael did get in your way'. It's also her hidden way of saying 'don't let *us* get in the way'. She can afford our condo on her own – not that I would ever let that happen. I think she knew all along Michael and I were not going to happen. That, or she was going to be damn sure he was worthy before we did. Therefore, I feel it my duty to do the same for her. And by all standards, Eric Hanson has failed miserably.

Standing in front of the bathroom mirror, I see the reflection of a woman I barely recognize. Her cheeks are slightly flushed, her eyes are brighter – nearly translucent – her smile is immovable as if permanently etched on her face. She's happy. So damned happy. How long has it been? All these years

I've been . . . just okay. Confident in my skills, fulfilled with my job, secure in my friendship with Mal and a few others, but when was the last time I could truly say I was happy? Two years with Michael Knight and I couldn't choose a date. I know now he wasn't my happiness.

I'm also pretty sure he wouldn't have kissed me before I brushed my teeth.

Leaving the bathroom, I press my lips together in an effort to hide the giddy grin that thought brought to mind. My face is washed, my hair is brushed, and my mouth is minty fresh. It may not make a difference to Lucas, but it does to me.

Arriving to the kitchen area I see Lucas, still shirtless, setting two plates of bacon, eggs, and toast on the breakfast bar next to two glasses of orange juice. As he pours two cups of steamy brew, he looks up. "Have a seat. Cream and sugar?"

I tap my lips with my index finger. "Don't you want a fresh minty kiss?"

He sets the pot back on the warmer and looks at me thoughtfully. He rolls his tongue around in his mouth before smacking his lips loudly twice and squints as if mulling it over. "I was kinda enjoying that leftover General Tso's chicken."

My jaw hangs agape as I stare at him and huff. He rounds the counter and stands in front of me, forcing me to lift my gaze to meet his. "You don't have to ask me *if* I want a kiss, Liberty. You never have to ask *when* I want a kiss. The answers are always yes and right now. Can you remember that?"

"Yeah," I answer with a nod and turn toward the breakfast bar.

He chuckles and snatches me around the waist, pulling me back to him. "Damn," he utters against my mouth, "you've got a short memory."

Chapter 25

Lucas

Liberty's phone rings as I set the last plate in the dishwasher from breakfast. She dries her hands quickly with the dishtowel and rushes for the coffee table where her phone sits as she calls out excitedly, "That's my mom. She Facetimes me on my long shifts off. I email her my schedules once a month."

Mrs. Collins. Talk about a sentimental journey and a blast from the past.

"Hey mom," Liberty answers the lit screen in front of her with a bright smile.

"Hi, sweetheart," Mrs. Collins returns in a voice I remember from years ago. Some things never change. "You look chipper. Wait a minute, that background isn't your place. Where are you?"

Still the same Mrs. Collins. Eagle eyes, always aware, two steps ahead of us no matter where we were. The ability to whistle so loud you could hear her from three blocks away and you'd better come running, or riding, as soon as you did. Those were the rules. She also taught Libby how to whistle just as loud. Safety measures. I'll place a bet she'll be mothering Libby when she's in her eighties; Libby, not Mrs. Collins. Mrs. C will live to be a hundred with the sole purpose of ensuring her daughter's happiness. Mrs. C rocks. She could hug better than a warm blanket and made the best lemonade and chocolate chip cookies in the world. She and my mom were friends . . . when my dad wasn't home. My old man wasn't friends with anybody.

Those long ago thoughts have taken me away from the conversation taking place in the living room until Libby states, "I have a surprise for you, Mom. I've got somebody I want you to see."

"You're not back with . . ."

"No!" Libby snaps hurriedly as my stomach rolls, strongly suspecting that question was aimed with regard to her former fiancé.

Libby waves to me with one hand to sit beside her while her other holds her phone. She nearly bounces on the sofa cushion as she waits for me to take a seat next to her.

"Liberty," Mrs. C scolds with a laugh. "Sit still. You're making me dizzy."

"Oh, sorry." Libby giggles as she turns the screen to me and says, "Say hi."

Mrs. Collins has aged, but I do my best to hide my shock. Don't get me wrong; she still looks good. Her hair is peppered with a bit of gray. Her eyes remain bright, but creases line the edges. Very few wrinkles, but eighteen years and the pain of losing her spouse show. Truth be told, I believe I would still know her at random on the street.

I smile tentatively as I peer at the screen. "Hi, Mrs. C."

She squints as she studies the screen and tilts her head slightly. "It's actually Mrs. Mason. Nobody has called me Mrs. C since . . ." Her eyes go wide and she gasps before her hand flies to her mouth. "Oh my goodness. Lucas? Is, is that you?" The phone shakes in her hand before it falls with a thud onto whatever surface catches it in front of her – a table maybe?

A worried male voice suddenly echoes through the phone. "Lauren? Honey, are you okay? What's going on?"

The sound of her soft cries tears at my heart a bit as she reassures him she's fine, before the man picks up the phone and looks at the screen, narrows his eyes, and gruffly demands, "Where's Liberty?"

I turn the screen back to Libby and hand her the phone. "Maybe we should have warmed her up first."

"It's okay, Tom," she reassures the man on the screen. "Mom wasn't expecting the surprise. I think I caught her off guard."

Mrs. C – or Mason, I guess – cries from the background. "It's okay, Tom. I want to talk to him. Put Lucas back on."

Phones exchange hands on both ends and Mrs. Mason's face appears before me once again. Tears fill her eyes as she tells me, "Forgive me, please. I can only imagine how Liberty reacted. You turned out so handsome, Lucas. You've still got your mom's smile. You always had her sweet demeanor, too." Her voice cracks as she apologizes for something that, once again, could only be attributed to one asshole, "I am so sorry. My dear boy."

"Thanks," I utter as a sudden memory of my mom and Mrs. C sitting around the Collins' pool in the afternoon, sipping lemonade while Liberty and I swam, enters my mind. I haven't experienced a clear memory of my mom since the night I was taken away.

"We're coming to see you as soon as possible," Liberty's mom rushes to tell me. "Is that okay? We haven't seen Liberty in a couple months, so we're due. This is icing on the cake. It's like having my kids back together again."

Not quite, Mrs. C. We're hardly kids, and the thoughts running through my mind regarding your daughter are hardly chaste. We've moved past bubblegum buddies and are swapping spit now. But we'll save that little tidbit for your visit.

And with that thought, I nod as I reach for Liberty's hand and take it in mine. "That'd be great. I'll hand you back to Libby and let you two work out the details."

"Aww," Mrs. C says sweetly once Liberty has the phone in front of her, "he still calls you Libby. Nobody else got to do that. You have so much to tell me."

"We'll talk more about this when you get here, Mom. In person." Libby looks to me with hopeful eyes. "Can you get time off?"

Yeah, if I weren't on Sully's shitlist I wouldn't be off right now, involuntarily, for another five days. But that's a discussion for another time.

It's automatic reflex – I swear – as I drop a kiss to her temple and promise, "I'll see what I can do. It's not like I work twenty four hour shifts. We'll still have some time together."

"But you need your sleep," she protests. "You need to be alert in case . . ."

Her concern for my welfare is overwhelming. Liberty's eyes always shone a little brighter with her mood changes, a little lighter green and blue when she was on the verge of tears; just as they're doing now. My hand finds its way to the back of her neck where it wraps the pale blonde locks gently in my fingers. "I'll stay alert and I will always find my way home to you."

"Uh . . ." Mrs. Collins stammers through the phone clutched in Liberty's hand, fortunately now aimed at the ceiling. "How about you call me back when you have a schedule figured out? We're pretty open. Make it soon, okay?"

Libby sniffles and brings the phone back into focus. "As soon as we get a schedule figured out, I'll get back to you. I promise. Love you, Mom."

"Love you too, sweetheart," she returns. "And Lucas, take care of my girl."

"Will do, Mrs. Col . . . Mason," I quickly correct. "It was good talking with you."

"Wait!" she calls out, halting the disconnect, and Libby turns the phone toward me once more. "What do you do for a living?"

I draw in a deep breath and let it out slowly. Her question is probably more related to Liberty's concern about *sleep* than it is income. "I'm a cop."

"Oh!" She doesn't hide her surprise, nor her discontent, but finally replies with a tight smile, "Well then, take very good care of my girl. And Lucas?"

"Yes?"

"I was just making sure you weren't a stripper." She arches a brow and shoots me a stern glare. "Do the police in Phoenix usually go shirtless?"

Oh shit! My chin drops as I pinch the bridge of my nose. I had been enjoying the touch of Libby's hands on my bare skin as she traced the outline of the tattoo so much, I'd foregone putting on a T-shirt.

"Bye mom!" Liberty shouts before she disconnects and sets the phone on the coffee table. "That went . . ." she hesitates, "well."

"Shellshock. We probably should have eased her into it."

Narrowing her eyes, she studies the phone as if contemplating. "Sure didn't take her long to recognize you."

Having noticed that myself, yet desperate to veer the direction of the next three days on only the two of us, I tip her chin toward me, and smirk. "She did say I was handsome."

She slaps my chest playfully and giggles. "Any idiot can see that."

I grasp her hand before she can yank it away, meeting her halfway in the pull to me, and kiss the corner of her mouth. "Are you an idiot?"

"Fishing for compliments?"

"Nope," I murmur against her mouth. "Want to be sure you agree that drop dead gorgeous and handsome are a good combination because you," *kiss,* "are," *kiss,* "the most beautiful," *kiss,* "woman I have ever seen in my life."

She straddles my lap as if it were second nature and holds my face in her palms, her eyes on mine; the expectant gaze I know so well only ever wanting the truth. "Do you say that to all the women you've been with?"

I match her gaze, admiring my two favorite colors, and spill the truth. "I have never said that to any woman. Those words have been on reserve for the girl of my dreams. I knew who she was, I knew the colors of her eyes, I knew she would taste like pink. I knew the sound of her giggle. I just didn't know where to find her."

Libby initiates the kiss this time; her lips soft and so full of promise as she teases with the tip of her tongue. The touch of her fingertips at the nape of my neck as she applies firm pressure sends tingles down my spine. Liberty doesn't wear her nails long – due to her job, I'm sure – but the mere sensation ignites a fire I've never felt before. It's like a sensuous massage versus a cat clawing its way out of a box. Her now taut nipples through the thin T-shirt she wears against my bare chest are screaming for me to take one in my mouth, the other between my thumb and finger. The hard-on I'm sporting between us is nearing the point of painful, and her movements against it are only causing unbearable temptation. I'd already tamed the beast in the shower before she woke up – keeping myself in check. Sleeping with her in my arms was a delightful punishment, but this is downright torture.

It's also not at all the way I want things to happen. She needs to be sure. I lost her once. The agony of defeat would be the death of me if I lost her again.

I could take her right now. I could take her for hours on end. But would she be mine in the end? I don't want Liberty for a while. I want Liberty for the rest of my life. Yet, as hard as she's riding the pony and the faster she moves, the weaker my resolve becomes and I relish every movement as she rides out her orgasm through the two layers of sweatpants; my hands on her hips guiding the rhythm and pressure. God, she's beautiful. Her breaths are labored, her thighs tremble against my hips, and the whimper she lets loose is music to my ears as she buries her face in my neck. She held back – what a shame – but my Libby is in there. My sexy little spitfire all grown up.

"Been awhile, huh?" I whisper against her neck as she settles.

She stutters an embarrassed giggle and nods against the crook of my neck. "Yeah. Now what about you?"

"I . . ." I announce exaggeratedly, lifting her off my lap and setting her next to me, "have got a surprise for us."

"You," she matches the exaggeration of my announcement with her own as her eyes flash to my obvious unrelenting hard-on, "seem to have a pre-*dic*-ament."

My head hits the back cushion of the couch as a sudden burst of laughter rolls out of me. She is spectacular. My bold beauty. The light to my darkness. The very summit to my bottom; the metaphor of holding me up whenever I was down. I draw her into my arms and kiss the top of her head. "He'll be fine. We can tend to him later."

"So," she drawls, looking a bit insecure, "not as long for you?"

I wink and grin. "Actually took care of him this morning in the shower. Sleeping with you in my arms was a bit . . . stimulating."

She blinks once, twice, then looks to my crotch again – making my dick pulse – and scrunches her nose. "And he's back again?"

That fiancé must have been an anesthesiologist. Maybe too much exposure to the sleeping gas. Snooze fest. Do not laugh, Lucas. Do not laugh.

Dropping a kiss to the tip of her nose, I reassure her, "He's not going anywhere. No rush. Now let's get ready."

"Where are we going?"

"How would you feel about a bike ride?"

Her face pales as she stares at me for an uncomfortable period of time. "A bike ride? I haven't been on a bike since . . ." Her words trail as she turns away and shakes her head.

"Since us?" I ask tentatively, now unsure if this was a good idea. It was our favorite thing to do; where you could find us every day. Maybe nostalgia wasn't such a good idea.

"Yeah," she whispers so softly it's nearly inaudible. She turns back to face me, her shoulders deflated, a faraway look in her eyes. "I lost all desire to ride after that day. Mom and Dad tried, but I haven't been on a bicycle since the last time we rode together."

I stand from my seat on the couch and hold my hand out for her to take. "I haven't either. I hated looking at the damn things. Won't even ride them at the gym. Thought since I had my bike buddy back, we could give it a whirl. I've rented a tandem for the day. What do you say, partner?"

She's thoughtful for a moment before she eyes me skeptically, a slight twitch edging her lips. "What if I fall and scrape my knees?"

I pull her up off the couch and bring her to my chest, then plant a soft kiss on her mouth and grin. "I'll carry you piggyback. You were supposed to teach me how to apply the Band-Aids correctly. It's why you became a nurse, isn't it?"

She runs her fingers through my scruff, her eyes shining with the memory. "You really haven't forgotten, have you?"

"I remember it all, Libby. You were my port in the storm. I would bury myself in the memories so I wouldn't have to deal with the realities. You were my refuge."

"I should have kissed you that day," she acquiesces on a whisper.

"Nah." I brush my mouth against hers, getting lost in the softness and sensation. "It would have felt like goodbye after that night. I needed something to anticipate, to hold onto, a promise I knew you would never break."

"I'll kiss you whenever you want, Lucas."

"Right now is good."

Chapter 26

Liberty

Lucas rolls his Jeep into the parking lot of a trail riding and hiking shop on the outskirts of the city. I've never been and, quite frankly, didn't know existed. If Mallory knew, I'm sure she would have had us out here long ago. She loves to hike, and we go as often as we can. But this? It's a combination of biking and hiking trails, separated by entrance gates; gear available to rent for both adventures.

Lucas snatches our water bottles and two bike helmets from the back of the Jeep before we head inside, and hands one helmet to me. "It's Ava's. You'll meet her eventually. Erotica writer who lives in my building. I got mine from John, her partner in crime and . . ." he bobs his eyebrows, "grind."

Rolling the helmet in my hands, I crinkle my nose. "A smut writer?"

"You don't read smut?" he teases.

"I didn't say that," I huff indignantly. I mean, really, those writers are the bomb. She may become Mallory's best friend. "Why is she loaning me her helmet?"

He nods at the pink bubble in my hands. "It's that or take a chance of head lice with a rented one."

Without hesitation, I turn the helmet upside down so I can flip the straps out and under my thumbs in order to put it over my head, only to find an inscription inside. *'I give good head'.* Mortification fills my face as I stare at it, then look to Lucas. "Are you aware of what's written inside this?"

He turns the inside of his shiny blue and black helmet toward me and says, "Is it any worse than this?" *'My best head is in my pants'.*

Placing the helmet on my head, forgoing buckling the straps until we're ready to go, I tell him, "Put that on. Thank God they didn't put it on the outside. I just may have been willing to chance the head lice."

"Tandem on reserve for Tanner Carson for four hours," Lucas tells the desk assistant as he shows his ID and presents his credit card. It's so odd to hear him refer to himself as anyone but Lucas. I'd already forgotten. He's been Tanner longer than he'd been Lucas. Is there still danger connected to the Monterrey name? It'll be difficult, and with time I'll adjust. But he will forever be my Lucas.

"Looks to be clear until this evening, but we got some storms moving in tonight," the desk assistant warns him before checking the ID. "Four hours is nothing but be sure to follow the trail and turn back fast if you see any clouds moving in. You're not tourists, are you?"

Lucas chuckles and shakes his head. "Nope."

"Well," the assistant says with a frown, "we're in monsoon season and some of these hotshots ignore all the warning signs. We got better drainage here than on the streets in the city, but you never can tell."

"We'll keep an eye out, thanks," Lucas reassures him.

"You ready to ride, Liberty Bell?" Lucas cups my cheeks and tilts my head up. My helmet isn't buckled yet and my shades are still in my hand. The look in his eyes and the smile on his face is priceless. He's trying so hard to relive some of our best moments – the packages he left at the hospital were proof of that – but he needs to know I have relived those moments so many times over the years that I don't need reminders; I could write the screenplay from memory.

"I'm ready to go anywhere with you." I tip up onto to my toes and plant a soft kiss on his mouth. "Buckle up, big guy. Let's ride."

We're steady, solid and strong as we ride the wide trail. I guess it's true what they say: *It's like riding a bike.* Not sure I would be this steady if I were riding solo, but this feels like I've been doing it for years. After a few miles in, I have a little fun and let Lucas pedal our weight on his own as I let my legs fly out to the sides, giddy as a little girl.

"Do your part, Liberty Bell," he calls back to me.

"It's kinda like a piggy back ride." I giggle.

He laughs. "And you're kinda crazy."

"Yeah," I agree all too quickly. "But I'm your kinda crazy."

He applies pressure to the brake until we come to a complete stop, hops off, drops the kickstand, holds his hand out and waits for me to dismount. Sweat be damned, our helmets bump and our shades shift as he lifts me off the ground until our faces are level and he covers my mouth in a delicious kiss.

"Damn right you are," he whispers against my mouth as the kiss ends. "The best kinda crazy." *Go crazy with me, Liberty.*

The sound of a bicycle bell and a male voice breaks our spell as another rider approaches. "On your left," he cautions us, as is protocol when riding the trails. On his way past, he teasingly warns, "Might want to move that action behind a tall cactus. This sun'll burn your buns. Watch out for thorns."

Lucas only laughs and hollers out, "Thanks for the warning," before we remount the bike and start to ride once again. The wind blows over my skin as the sun beats down on us, distributing warmth I haven't felt in years. We laugh. We whoop and holler as we ride the bumps and surely bruise our butts. It feels like freedom. The burden of worry and wondering is gone.

There's no one to call us in from our venture. No one to spoil our fun. No monster to run from anymore. We're not editing a script from years ago – we're writing a whole new story.

An hour into our trek, miles ahead of us, off in the distance, the sky starts to darken and the clouds are rolling in. I've seen it happen many times over the years. It's monsoon season in Arizona. Literally "when it rains, it pours". We're not graced often with sprinkles. When the sky opens up, you'd better be ready to get wet.

"We're gonna have to turn back, Libby. Looks like the rain is moving in faster than they predicted," Lucas informs me as we slow our pedaling. "We can do it again any time you want."

"I want to do this again. I loved it." We turn the bike around to head back, but my provider instincts niggle at me as I scout the area for the other rider that passed us some time ago. He was probably in his fifties, riding solo, and I haven't noticed any other riders since. "Lucas, do you think that man is okay out here? He should be heading back too. We've got a good hour to go, unless we really push it, and he was farther ahead than we are. I don't see any sign of him."

"People ride this trail all the time, Libby." He obviously sees my concern as he reassures me. "If we haven't seen any sign of him within half an hour of the time we get back, we'll report it. Okay?"

The storm rolls in quickly but Lucas and I are back to the rental store well before it hits, and we watch as people are returning their rentals and virtually running to their vehicles to beat the rain home. Arizona streets are not designed for rain. Roads flood, yards fill with water, cars get stranded. It's a common occurrence in monsoon season.

As soon as we arrived, Lucas reported the other rider to the front desk as well as our concern with his whereabouts and the fact he was a lone rider.

Their concern was rather underwhelming which caused us to wait around until we could see the red-shirted man on the bicycle pull in and be sure he had returned safely. That little niggle in my brain was unrelenting. We waited a bit longer – watching the dark clouds and wall of rain move closer with no rider in sight yet – and Lucas finally flashed his badge at my insistence.

Within five minutes there was a drone in the air followed quickly by two Gator utility vehicles ready to head out on the trail on a rescue mission for the fallen bike rider spotted by the drone, and a pissed off Lucas and me with an employee on one of them. At least they're hi-tech. A drone?

"Have an ambulance here and waiting!" I shout at the front desk assistant on my way out the door.

"Libby," Lucas pleads before we take off on the trail in search of the man on the bike. "I really wish you would go back inside and wait for us."

Flashing a him a snarky grin as I hop onto the back of the Gator and strap myself in, I quip, "Still better at Band-Aids than you are. You may need me out there."

The Gator hits a rather large bump and veers to the right before the driver puts it back on the trail. An angry and impatient Lucas glares at him. "If you can't drive this fucking thing, I will. Do that again and I'll toss you out on your ass and let you walk back. Got it?"

"Sorry, sir," the driver mumbles.

The rain hits like a wall of water ten minutes into the trek. Reddish mud flies from the wheels behind the Gator as the deep tread tires grind their way through the muck and small stones laid in the trail. Hard to believe an hour ago we were riding in the sunshine on solid ground, enjoying a peaceful, blissful day. My hands grip the grab bar as I say a quick prayer for the man who tossed us a cocky remark on his way past. There he was, all alone. And for the first time in so long, I wasn't. I wonder what his story is.

"There they are!" Lucas shouts over the rain that beats down on us as he points to the stopped Gator ahead. As soon as we're stopped, he hops out of the front. I'm already standing the edge of the back, and he reaches for me to help me out. My feet sink slightly into the softened and muddy ground below me, and as soon as I raise one foot to take a step, the mud sticks to my shoe, causing me to pick up a pound or two to carry with me.

Good times. Cool. No leg lifts this week.

The bike rider is laid out on the ground while the workers hover over him. Doesn't look like they're doing much, but I'll give them credit for trying to shield him from the rain. Not that it does a lot of good, but . . . His bicycle is on the ground, a bit bent, the front tire is crunched. Definitely needs repair. Not sure what he hit, but I'd be hard pressed to believe it walked away without injury.

I shove my way through and kneel next to the groaning man on the ground, my knees sinking into the mud almost as deeply as my shoes did. I wave to the workers and Lucas. "Come stand over him. Shield his face as much as you can." I lean down close to him and ask, "Can you tell me where you're hurt?"

He grunts and opens his eyes, blinks a couple times, and chuckles through raspy breaths. "What do I gotta say to get me some mouth-to-mouth?"

"Sir," I scold, "you are not funny."

He releases a deep breath and coughs. "I thought I was."

"Where do you hurt?" I demand this time. "I'm trying to help you." He has a helmet on and his arms and hands bear a few scrapes and scratches.

"My leg." He attempts to raise his right leg at the same time he puts effort into lifting his head, but the pain is too much. He's in khaki pants so any wounds are hidden, but his pantleg is torn and bloodied. Rather hard to estimate blood loss as the rain has soaked it.

"Any of you guys got a pocket knife?" The pants are thick and wet and not easy to tear. An open blade appears from a hand that could belong to any of them. I extend the tear in the pantleg to examine the damage underneath only to find a gaping hole in the man's calf. A pretty deep hole. It's gnarly, rough edges, and bleeding profusely. I quickly cut the pantleg toward the hem and rip it open. I whip off my tank top to tamp the wound and demand from any of the others who might still be standing – as one of them has landed on his knees, retching and losing his cookies somewhere behind us, "Give me a shirt. I need to tie this off."

I have a T-shirt in my hands in no time and a bare-chested Lucas is holding the man's limb in his hands while I tie off his leg above the wound to slow the blood flow. "You're doing great, Libby. Damn, I'm proud of you."

"I need another shirt to tie this tamp down. He's bleeding through my tank. I need more pressure."

Lucas hollers to the others, "Give us another T-shirt!"

Before too long, I have a rolled and stretched wet T-shirt in my hands ready to tie over the tank top I applied to the wound. Lucas applies pressure while I tie. "We need to elevate and immobilize his leg and get him back as soon as possible."

"We'll prop it on the back of the front seat in the Gator to elevate his leg while he sits on the bed in the back," Lucas says as he studies the situation, then looks to the workers. "You guys got a splint? A piece of wood? Anything?" His questions are met with a round of grunts and negative responses.

"Can you ride next to him in the back on his right side and try to keep his leg still?" he asks me. "It's gonna be tight, baby. I'll drive. I think it's our only option. There's no way they can get an ambulance through the mud on this trail. You okay with that?"

"Yeah. Let's do it," I quickly respond.

The rain is relentless and it's hard to hear, but his plan sounds solid. What I also note is my best friend, the yin to my yang, take charge and show a calm and cool side of him that makes me fall so hard, so deeply in love, it makes me question how I ever survived without him.

"Radio in and tell them we're on our way!" Lucas shouts instructions to the workers with such precision, one would think he has a blueprint. "Take his left leg, you two take his upper body. I'll hold his right leg. You're the squatter under his leg in the back. You just became a cushion. And you'd better not puke again. Move it!"

Once loaded on the bed of the Gator, it's tight. The poor kid on his elbows and knees looks ready to vomit, but he's holding steady as a leg rest. I'm holding tightly to the patient's leg to prevent it from rolling.

"What's your name?" I inquire of the man in an attempt to distract him from the discomfort of the ride. I'm leaning over him in an effort to shelter his face from the rain pelting us at a nasty harsh angle. It's quite a test for my contortionist skills, but – hey! – *no yoga this week either*. I also want to keep him as alert as possible. Lucas veers around the pitted tire tracks left by the Gator ahead of us.

"Martin Kiesner," he groans. "What's yours?"

"Liberty."

He snorts. "And justice for all."

Bypassing an eye roll, I shake my head. "Witty. Never heard that one before."

He lifts his brows. "Really?"

"No." I shoot him a wry look. "Want to tell me what happened out there?"

"Hit a deer," he grunts and shifts in pain. "Damned thing ran right in front of me out of nowhere. Thought I was gonna miss him, then I thought I was a goner, then the mean sonofabitch turned around and damn near horned me to death."

If he were in the ER, I would be ordering a full neurological exam for possible head injury as well after that story. Close call, goner, and horning. Got it. This is one for the books.

"Care to elaborate?" I ask in an effort to distract him as I casually check the T-shirt tie-off bandage on his thigh and surreptitiously and slowly work my way toward a crucial area that I can only hope he is oblivious to.

"I only clipped his hind leg and he reared around and horned me in mine," he states matter-of-factly as if reporting a crime. "It was like he wanted revenge and whoa, whoa, whoa!" he shrieks and jolts as he shoves at my hand. "I usually take a woman to dinner before I let her hop on that playground, young lady."

"I'm trying to check your femoral pulse, you idiot!" I scowl and hold his thigh firmly with my right hand and proceed to the checkpoint with my left. "Besides, you'd have to liquor me up first!"

He laughs. Actually laughs. He also coughs, but he calms quickly. "I think I like you."

"The jury is still out on you." I smirk and roll my eyes. "But you have time. Looks like you're going to live."

He squeezes my bicep with a beefy paw. "Thank you, kiddo."

Kiddo. He sounds just like my dad. Do not cry, Liberty. Do. Not. Cry.

Chapter 27

Lucas

I can't hear much, but I hear a little. Navigating the trail is hard enough. I don't have to wonder how she does it; she just does. Pure powerhouse. The guy has a hole in his leg and she still makes him laugh.

The building comes into view through the relentless rain and the closer it gets, the more relief I feel for one matter and the madder I get for another. It's cool; I know the sweetness of revenge.

As we pull under the metal awning at the back of the building, we find the EMTs as well as the usual accompanying firefighters for emergency calls, waiting with a gurney ready for the patient. In our occupations, some we know, some we don't. However, in this particular situation, Reece and Roger, along with a couple others from the station stand waiting, goofy grins on their faces as they take in the scene before them. The guy who radioed in must have let them know it was urgent, but not life threatening.

"Damn!" Cody, a familiar EMT, laughs at the two of us as they approach the Gator. "If you two didn't look like drowned rats I would have recognized you right away." He flashes Libby a sexy smile and winks – my teeth grinding as he eyes her soaking wet sports bra. "I'd have known you anywhere, Liberty, wet or dry." He tips his chin at me. "How ya doing, Tanner?"

"Martin Kiesner." Liberty ignores his obvious flirtation – and drooling that's going to get his ass kicked – instead reporting on the patient. "Deep wound to the right lateral calf and took a fall from his bicycle. I've got no vitals as I had no equipment." They do a quick assessment, then transport him from the Gator onto the gurney. Once the gurney is loaded, Liberty hops off the platform of the Gator and walks beside it. "Says it was a vengeful deer that didn't appreciate a hip clip." She grins at the patient. "Isn't that right, Mr. Kiesner?"

"Sounds about right." He smiles weakly, holding a hand up for her to take, and winks. "If only I were twenty years younger, my dear."

Stepping up beside Liberty, I grin and place one arm around her and take his hand to shake it. "But you're not, and she's mine. Good luck, sir."

Cody's head whips up in surprise as he ties another strap to the patient, securing him for transport. "Yours? Really?"

"Mine." I eye him with a severity that leaves no room for doubt and pull Liberty closer. "Feel free to spread the word."

"Lucky sonofabitch," he utters what should be a silent

thought.

"Don't I know it," I whisper against her temple before leaving a soft kiss. She is mine, always has been. Even when she wasn't with me. And today, after watching her do what she did, she is also my hero.

The crew wheels Mr. Kiesner toward the door and into the lobby to the waiting ambulance out front, and we wave one last time before he's out of sight.

Reece slaps me on the back – my bare back. The sting is sharp and the temptation to elbow him hard is strong. He mutters in my ear, "If this is your idea of *extracurriculars*, I haven't taught you very well. You're making me look bad, Tanner. When I told you to ride them 'til the cows come home, it was all about yippee-I-KY. It had nothing to do with bicycles."

Eye-to-eye, I glare. "Don't you have a kitten to rescue?"

The puckish grin he shoots me indicates he's either scratched his itch with Liberty's friend or is still enjoying the scratches on his back by way of the bar stool warmer he enjoyed before starting his 72-hour rotation.

"You've got the code to my condo," he reminds me with a chuckle – and another slap to my shoulder. "There's a lesson book on the kitchen counter. Feel free to use it."

"Go back to work, Reece."

Roger grabs the back of Reece's neck and pulls him away, uttering what he feels are words of wisdom, aka twit speak, "Don't listen to this moron. He can't hit a clit with a firehose. Though I will admit, Tanner, there are better methods of makin' her wet." He lifts his head and smiles at my girl as he pulls Reece away. "Good job out there today, Liberty. Now go make better use of your time off."

She rolls her eyes. "This wasn't exactly how I planned on spending my day."

Reece isn't slow, I'll give him that. "I have some recommendations."

Roger backhands his stomach and scowls. "Let's go, idiot."

We stomp the mud off our shoes as best we can before stepping into the lobby of the bike rental store. Liberty looks around until she finds what she's looking for. "I need to visit the little girls' room. I'll be back in a bit."

"Take your time." I kiss her forehead. "I've got something I need to take care of. I'll meet you back here."

I watch my little soaked wonder walk away before I step to the front desk. "I want to see the four guys who went out with us. Now."

"Uh," the desk clerk fumbles. "I think they're drying off in the locker room."

"Which would be where?"

She points to a hallway in the opposite direction of where Libby headed.

"It's for employees only," the clerk calls out as I stomp toward the hallway.

"Consider me a temporary hire," I call back. She has no idea. Turning the knob and shoving the door open, I catch the chatter as they laugh and comment about the wonderful adventure they've all just experienced, oblivious to my presence. If only that chatter pertained to the actual rescue. It never fails. An asshole is an asshole. In this case, three of them. Their tongues were catching as much rain as our clothes because the dumbasses couldn't keep them in their mouths. The only one off the hook is the puker. His weak stomach saved him. He's in the back over the throne – groaning.

"Damn, when she whipped her top off, all I could think about was taking a nipple in my mouth. Kinda wish I was the lucky sucker under 'em on the way back."

"I was ready to beg for a full strip tease, man," another laughs.

"When she dropped to her knees in the mud, I wanted to pull my dick out and stick it in her . . ."

"Finish that statement and you'll be pulling your teeth out of the drywall when I smash your face into it," I promise him. Why bother with a threat? I mean every word.

"Uh . . . uh," he stammers, holding one hand up, the other clutching a flimsy towel to his hairless chest, as all three of them shoot shocked wide eyes and dropped jaws my way.

"I want your license plate numbers, make and model, and full names." I nod toward the desk in the far corner of the room. "Write them down. Lie about it and I'll nail your asses for falsifying records. I'm a cop. Think twice before you do something really stupid. I can call your boss and get them from him."

"What do you want those for?" The one who looks like a deer caught in the headlights asks warily.

"Do it, now," I order without obliging the inquiry.

They list each one – spoiled brats by all indications. They're not old enough to afford BMWs or Audis. I hold up the paper. "These your parents' cars?"

"No," they answer in unison.

"You realize all I have to do is run them through the system to verify, don't you?"

"They're gifts from our moms and dads," one mutters. *Nailed it.*

"Hmm," I hum and smirk. "A little warning, boys. One mile over the limit, one taillight out, one crack in your windshield and you won't get a warning, you'll get the ticket. One oops over the yellow line and you'll be blowing into a breathalyzer or waiting in a cell with Bubba until your daddy's attorney shows up to bail you out."

"What did we do?!" one shrieks indignantly.

"For starters," I explain, "you didn't take your job seriously. You were working a rescue. You had a victim to tend to. That should have been your first and only concern and the only thing your eyes should have been fixed on. Secondly? Learn some respect. Those are my tits to stare at." I smirk before heading for the door. "Watch your back, boys."

God, I love being a cop. We're not going to track them, but they don't know that. They'll simply be more aware of the speedometer as well as their surroundings. My bet is they won't chance drinking and driving either. Makes our job easier. Check, check, and check.

My smile couldn't be any bigger when I see my girl standing in the middle of the rental shop lobby waiting for me. I step up behind her and wrap my arms around her shoulders. "You ready, hot shot?"

The rain has relented, down to a drizzle, but the run off is still going strong. However, I drive a rugged Jeep and am quite familiar with which routes to take to avoid the flooding. We're soaked to the skin – literally. I'm bare chested, due to having given away my T-shirt and Libby is in only a sports bra. I want to get the hell out of here. The chill of the air conditioning has had Libby's nipples hard since we walked in the building and it's driving me crazy.

She giggles as she tilts her head to look up. "Hardly a hot shot. We were both out there and just doing our jobs. Where did we leave your friends' helmets?"

"At the counter. I'll go get . . ."

"That's them! Can we get a statement?" The shout rings throughout the building from the lookout lounge above. A lot of tourists use it after a day of hiking or biking to savor a cocktail or take pictures and enjoy the views of the canyon range. Libby and I glance over to see a woman with two men carrying camera equipment rushing toward us down the stairs.

"Oh shit," I mumble as I quickly grasp her elbow and lead her toward the counter to collect the helmets. "Word got out." I quickly change direction and veer us toward the exit. "Screw it. I'll buy them new helmets. I think they're due for new inscriptions, don't you?"

"I don't know those people," she says as we start to run. "I don't want them to hate me for losing their gear."

"Not possible, Libby. They are going to love you." I slam the release bar on the door to get us out and we run hand-in-hand into the puddle-filled lot and drizzling rain toward the Jeep. We watch for the gulleys in the mud that have been caused by the water run-off and jump over those, splash through some puddles, run our asses off, then climb in as fast as we can to avoid the shouting media team behind us.

Locking the doors, I fire up the Jeep and take off – leaving three dejected looking reporters and some high flying water in my path as my tires hit the puddles. Yes, I could avoid this really big one in front of us, but as the three idiots from the locker room step outside under the awning to light up cigarettes or joints – hard to tell – I find my final revenge, dousing them in an approximate four-foot wave of muddy water.

"That wasn't very nice!" Liberty scolds.

"Smoking is hazardous to their health." Turning to look at her before pulling out of the parking lot, I add, "So is being too busy staring at you to do their job." She rolls her eyes. I grin slyly. "Now they know."

She really doesn't see herself the way I do; the way others do. She is stunning. Eyes that hypnotize, a voice that narrates your dreams. So smart, compassionate, witty, a body I want to explore every inch of and start all over again when I'm done.

The presence of an angel. A once in a lifetime chance. I'm a lucky bastard, though. I'm getting a second chance.

The trip takes longer than it normally would; the upper roads congested with seasoned drivers who knew well enough to stay away from flooded intersections. We wouldn't have been out in it at all had it not been for the rescue mission.

As soon as we arrive in the parking lot of my complex, the skies open up once again. It's like a deluge from hell, but no lightning or thunder, and the wind has died down.

"Ready to make a run for it?"

"Why bother?" She giggles. "Maybe this will wash the mud off our shoes."

"Wait there." I throw open my door. "I'll come around for you." Her seatbelt is off by the time I get to her side. She pushes the door open and my chivalrous intention of carrying her in is halted as she holds up her hands.

"No, wait! I've got something I need to do." Puzzled, I step back and watch as she hops out and rushes past me into the parking lot. She stands in an open spot and looks toward the sky; the pouring rain pelting her skin like a shower from heaven. She stretches her hands out and starts to slowly spin in a circle before she yells as if it's a revelation, "I'm not crying!" She does a little happy dance – much like a kid who's found the joy of puddles versus a boring bath – and spins again before she runs back to me and jumps into my arms, wrapping her legs around my waist, and shrieks, "I'm not crying!"

I stare at my wonder of wonders in total confusion yet grinning like a fool because I know Liberty, and her absence of tears is somehow of significance to her. "Okay."

"For years I've cried in the rain, Lucas," she explains through heavy breaths, "so no one could see my tears." The dam breaks as her eyes fill with a different kind of salty tears –

the happy kind – as her smile lights up with the most beautiful smile I've ever seen. "You fixed what was broken, just like always."

She squeezes me so tightly, there is suction between her skin and mine due to the moisture that makes a popping sound when I draw her head back and take her mouth in a searing kiss. I fixed what was broken? If only she knew how broken I'd been without her. I don't know as if I ever cried in the rain, but I always found the grey, wet, foggy weather fitting for my mood over the abundant sunny days in California. They were rare, but I wore them like armor. A good excuse for solitary confinement to *read a book*; instead using the time to reminisce, recall the girl in the window waving goodnight, conversations, bike rides . . . her promise.

"Let's go home," I murmur against her mouth before I carry her through the puddles toward the building. She's so light in my arms, weightless really, such a perfect fit against me. We weren't broken; we were each missing our piece of the puzzle to make us whole again.

We drop our shoes in the hallway; Libby shucking hers off behind me while still in my arms, giggling as they hit the floor. Our bodies have been locked together since the parking lot – the walk through the lobby, the ride on the elevator, the distance to my door. I can't put her down and it's still not enough. I rode that damn bike with blue balls this morning, but I'd already made the reservations and promised myself I wouldn't rush her. However, the memory of this morning's session of a dry hump on the sofa has me ready to explode. That look in her eyes, her stuttered breaths followed by the hum of satisfaction. She has no idea how good we can be.

I fumble with a concentrated determination to enter the code to my lock into my phone with one hand while holding her tight to me with my other arm and she turns the knob for us. Once inside, the door closed behind us, our worlds collide.

And what a collision it is.

Pinned against the wall in the entryway, her desperation is equal to mine as she writhes and moans against me. Our mouths clash in a frenzied mix of tongues, teeth and nips that will bruise, but never has pain felt so good. It's a battle for control, and as much as I'd like to give in to her at least a little, that's not my style. I'll follow her lead, but I take the reins when it comes to the ride. Admittedly, I may have some issues with control, but never at the price of a woman's pleasure.

I am not my old man.

I'd always pictured my first time with Liberty to be sweet, slow, gentle. On a bed with lush linens, taking my time appreciating every curve, every moan, every soft silky inch of her skin. But right now? The need to be inside her, connected in a way that wipes out the agony of so many years apart and confirm this is not some fucked up dream I will wake from tomorrow, is agonizing.

She arches her back against the wall, her full breasts thrust forward, demanding my touch as her thighs squeeze tightly around my waist. Her sports bra zips on the front, making for very easy access with one slide of the zipper, and it only takes a moment before I have two full, magnificent breasts in my hands – nipples hard and peaked – imploring me to take one in my mouth.

"Lucas." She gasps as she grips my hair in her fingers and pulls in the most delightful way. The sharp sting of pain sets every nerve ending on fire. *Desire.* "More," she whimpers.

"How much more, Liberty?" I murmur before tugging her nipple between my teeth and pinching the other between my thumb and finger.

She shifts her hips forward, seeking friction from the steel rod in my shorts begging for its own attention and moans loudly as she rubs against it. "All of it. Everything."

I should carry her to the bedroom, strip her down properly, taste her, tease her, but she's in the moment. And in this moment she wants spontaneity, passion, lust, confirmation – just like I do.

Who am I to deny her?

Chapter 28

Liberty

"Drop your legs, baby," Lucas whispers low against my ear, his hands inside the band of my shorts, squeezing my butt cheeks. Never so happy to get out of wet clothes yet reluctant to lose contact with the stimulation I'm receiving to my hardened nipples against his chest, as well as my extremely needy clit, I release the grip I hold on his waist and let my limbs drop.

He slides my wet shorts and panties over my hips; the weight of the rain soaked material causing them to fall to the floor without assistance, and I wriggle my feet to shake them off. Frantically, I reach for the waistband of his gym shorts, assuring I've captured both bands to include the jerseys underneath, and they drop in simultaneous splendor to reveal the most spectacular penis I've ever seen. And to be honest, as an NP, I've seen plenty. Not many at full salute, but even flaccid his would be a sight to behold.

Breathe, Liberty.

Tempted to either drop to my knees or take it in my hand, the decision is made for me as he lifts me once again, one arm wrapped around my back, the other coaxing the back of my thigh so I'll wrap my legs around his waist again. He aims our pelvises perfectly for pleasure, and slides slowly against my wet and welcoming heat, teasing me over and over.

"I don't think you're wet from the rain, Liberty," he taunts. "Is this for me?" I only whimper and nod shakily, desperate to feel him inside me. I've never been so needy; so wanton. Eighteen years. Approximately ten of them oblivious to realizing this was what I needed, until now. As he begins to enter me, he hesitates, eyes on mine as he acquiesces, "We should have been each other's first."

So much truth in so few words. We should have been. I believe we would have been. I match his words with my own. "We can be each other's last."

He wraps his hand in my hair, lowers his mouth to mine as he thrusts and pulls me down onto him in one swift move, taking my breath away, and groans, "Damn right we will."

He's in full control as he moves us in time – purposeful grinds with powerful and harsh thrusts that stimulate my clit, making me gasp and moan. I don't have to plead for *'harder'*, *'faster'*, *'more'*. He knows what he's doing; reading me like a well-worn book. With every thrust, every concentrated move geared toward my pleasure, he brings me closer and closer to the edge. The cliff I want to fall off, knowing he'll be there to catch me.

"Eyes open, Liberty," he breathes. "I want to watch you come undone for me."

His words, his eyes on mine, one last hard thrust, and I. Am. Toast. Not to mention hyperventilating as I nearly weep sobs of ecstasy with every involuntary pulse of my orgasm. My thighs quiver as I hold tight to him. My heart pounds in my ears.

"*Fuck, Libby,*" he groans so low I feel his chest vibrate as he buries his face in my shoulder, his teeth sinking softly into my skin, and releases so hard I feel every single jet of it. Either he has a low fever or our body temperatures must run a degree or two different from each other; his warmer than mine.

Sorry, it's the medical professional in me.

We stay this way, glued to each other, catching our heavy breaths, until Lucas softly kisses my temple and whispers, "Did I hurt you?"

My head bangs against the wall behind me as I jerk back in shock. Resisting the urge to say 'ow', instead I protest, "No! God, no. Why would you think . . ."

"I was a little rough," he confesses, though totally unnecessary.

My smile blooms slowly as my fingers dance through the locks of his still damp hair. "It was perfect." It really was. I've never been taken like this – so passionately. As if need didn't allow for steps to the bedroom, methodical undressing, mechanics of comfort.

He winces as he gently smooths his thumb over the sting at the crook of my shoulder and whispers regretfully, "I bit you."

"Uh oh." I worry my brow. "Did you leave two deep puncture wounds over the jugular?"

He stares at me, his eyes widening in puzzlement before he narrows them. I burst into a fit of giggles. He scowls.

"Smartass."

He lifts me away from the wall, smacks my bare butt and carries me through the bedroom, into the bathroom and sets me on the counter.

"Share a shower?" He shrugs and chuckles. "Wouldn't be our first today."

I close one eye as if calculating, my mouth twisted. "If memory serves, this would be our third."

He kisses my forehead before turning to start the shower faucet. "I promise to make this one more enjoyable."

"Less eventful would be good," I say wryly.

He turns back to me and slowly slides the straps of my sports bra off my shoulders and carefully removes the band holding my wet messy bun in place – my favorite dimple prominently displayed as he grins impishly and winks. "Don't spoil all my fun, Liberty Bell."

The warm water feels like heaven as it pelts my skin. Quite a change from being doused in cold buckets of the same thing from a different source. It's like the goosebumps I've been wearing since entering the building soaking wet, caused by the air conditioning, and the goosebumps caused by that life changing orgasm. Sex has never been that good. Nor has it ever stirred so many emotions.

Lucas snatches my shampoo that Mallory packed for me from the corner shelf of the shower and pours a dollop in his hand. "Coconut and vanilla, huh?" He breathes in a deep nose-full of the scent before he starts to wash my hair for me, massaging my scalp slowly. "It's just like you to bring a ray of sunshine to a rainy day, make all the clouds go away, leave a smile wherever you go." He tips my chin up with soapy fingers. "Make a boy fall in love with you so incredibly hard, he grows into a man who's incomplete without you. Not just a memory, but the sum of his whole. He gauges any possible relationships to what he had with you and none have measured up. He's alive, but he's not living."

"You're making me cry in the rain, Lucas," I whisper through tears below the drops bouncing off of him from the showerhead above. He's describing his life without me. It's a mirror of my own. We were young, but we were old souls.

He drops his forehead to mine, taking my cheeks in his palms. "It's a shower, Libby. And I don't ever want to make you cry. I want to make you mine. I never stopped loving you. I need to be whole again."

This is the slightly insecure Lucas I remember. The boy – now man – who would pour his heart out to me, but still need reassurance that heart was safe in my hands. The boy who would have moved heaven and earth for me yet never puffed his chest in victory when he succeeded. Never took credit when he *let* me win the bike race – which I knew he had done. Just smiled and told me *'Good job, Libby'*. Carried my books from school even when the other kids made fun of him; even when I told him he didn't have to. Gave me his sno-cone when I dropped mine at the carnival. Carried me piggyback when I could have walked. A gentleman in kids' clothing. And the list goes on and on . . .

"I never stopped loving you either." I move forward to kiss him and as I do, we both end up directly under the showerhead, much like the first half of our day has gone. The only difference being water temperature.

He steps back just enough to move us out of the downpour. When the kiss ends, he chuckles. "Didn't get enough of the direct hit today, huh? Tilt your head back, let me rinse your hair."

We take turns soaping each other up, lingering on body parts hyperreactive to slippery hands and tense grips until we've both released moans loud enough to penetrate the walls into the condo next door. Watching Lucas release onto the shower floor by way of my hands is a thing of beauty. I'm in no hurry to wipe my fingers clean this time. And when he licks his after my release and hums?

I wonder if this is how patients feel during palpitations.

He wraps a big, fluffy towel around me before I step out, grabs another for my hair, then reaches for one to wrap around his waist. I'm clean, I'm warm, and still reeling from not just the day I've had, but even more so from the last hour.

How is this my life?

Two months ago I caught my fiancé in a Vegas hotel doing the doggy with my archnemesis. I've suffered his pleading for forgiveness, excuses, tolerated his radiologist buddy pleading on his behalf – without punching either one of them, mind you. I've had to confer with them both over a little boy receiving proper care. I've endured the humiliation of all of those doctors in Vegas for the bachelor party knowing I was cheated on. Probably been the brunt of their jokes ever since. Unless, of course, Mallory was within hearing range. *Pretty sure they want kids someday.*

Three days ago I was pining for the love of my life from years ago, just as I had been *for the last eighteen years.* The boy of my childhood dreams. The best friend I thought I owed an apology. All those years never once considering the possibility of sex; just the kiss I never gave him. Now I'm stepping out of the shower with that boy of my dreams, after experiencing the best orgasms I've ever had.

As I step out, I smile to myself. Had it not been for Michael's cheating, I would have never transferred to the ER. I may never have found Lucas. Maybe I'll send Arseen some roses. Big fat black roses with really sharp thorns on long stems. I can be thankful . . . and spiteful at the same time. Can't I? She did me a huge favor, but it doesn't make her any more likable.

"What are you grinning about?" Lucas asks as he takes the

towel off my head and starts to squeeze the water from my hair.

"How lucky I am." I stand on my tiptoes and plant a kiss on his mouth. "I hate the circumstances that brought us together but . . ."

He places a fingertip over my lips. "Adam's circumstances would have been the same regardless. We can't change the world, Liberty. We can only try to make a difference in the tiny pocket we live in. Look at what you did today."

I snort and roll my eyes. "Yeah, right. Mister . . ." I lower my voice, mimicking the man's baritone vocals, "I'd have to take you to dinner before I let you hop on that playground, young lady."

His eyebrows rise as he squeezes the locks of my hair with the towel and tugs my head back, holding my gaze, the stunned look on his face almost humorous. "Excuse me?"

Furrowing my brow, I crinkle my nose in slight embarrassment. "I probably should have explained I needed to check his femoral pulse before I reached for his crotch."

Lucas stares at me for only a moment before he bursts into laughter; the sound of which lights my heart. It's sincere. Mouth open, straight white teeth, that dimple making its star studded appearance as his eyes gleam. He uses the towel he's been drying my hair with and stretches it across the back of my neck to bring my face to his, holding it tight in his hands. "You are incredible. It was probably the best distraction you could have given him. Not to mention making his heart jolt." He kisses me once, twice, then again. "I'll let you check my femoral pulse anytime you want, baby. You also have access to my playground without asking."

I feel the ever growing hard-on between us and glance down, then look back up and arch my brow. "Back again? He's an active creature, isn't he?"

He grips the towel in his hands firmer, bringing my face closer. "He's found his perfect fit. He'll always want you, Liberty."

Feeling that low swirl of temptation in my belly, I eye him skeptically while holding back a giggle, I question, "Do I get dinner first? Mr. Kiesner said . . ."

He swallows any words I might have had left with a harsh kiss then carries me to the bedroom. He laughs before tossing me on the bed. "Never mention that old man's name again when you're naked with me. Now, get dressed and I'll take you to dinner."

"I wanted to call the hospital and check on him." I shrug when Lucas spins at my words. "Curiosity gets the best of me sometimes. Can you find out which one they took him to?"

Lucas's chin drops to his chest as he pinches the bridge of his nose and his shoulders shake with silent laughter. "It's Liberty, Tanner," he whispers to himself, though I hear it. "Why are you even surprised?" He glances up, rolls his eyes and smiles, then shakes his head. "Let me make a call."

Chapter 29

Lucas

Leaving Liberty in the bedroom to get dressed, I snatch my phone from the kitchen counter to fulfill her wishes and make her happy. Getting the patient's updates will be on her, but getting his location will be easy for me. Roger and Reece should know. Just like Liberty to be concerned with the outcome. Her instincts were spot-on though. What would have happened to him if she hadn't insisted we stick around and ensure he made it back safely? Would it have even occurred to me?

Me: Any chance you know where they took the patient from the trail today?

Roger: Abrazo. Any chance you're going to tell me why you're asking?

Roger: *???*

Roger: *Tanner, I'm only asking as a concerned friend.*

I sigh as I stare at my phone. He's either truly concerned that something has happened or laughing his ass off as he waits for my response. These guys think with their dicks when they're not on the clock, and protocol is to move on to the next case, unless there are legal circumstances or ramifications involved. My hand itches before caving to the overwhelming urge to ignore him.

Me: *Liberty wants to check on him.*

Roger: *Not keeping her distracted enough riding the pony? Shame she's thinking about another man while in your company.*

I knew it! Asshole!

Me: *Fuck you, Roger.*

Roger: *Reece says you're making his teaching skills look bad. He's offering to be your proxy in the interim until you read the handbook on his counter. You know the code to get in.*

Me: *Be sure to tell him the scorpions will be somewhere between his sheets . . . or in his shoes . . . or his sofa cushions. Or maybe hidden in the . . .*

This ought to give him plenty to do when he gets home. Reece's one obsession is scorpions. They scare the shit out of him. He puts his shoes in the bathtub and uses a uniquely bent toilet brush that he crafted himself to scrub inside them before he puts them on . . . every single time. He also never leaves his shoes anywhere but on a rack. Want to freak Reece out? Just leave his shoes on the floor.

Roger: *He's apologizing as I text. Best put him at ease. He doesn't look so good.*

Reece: *Tanner! I was only kidding, man. I will swear celibacy for a month! I will buy the pizza AND the beer for the first five* *games this season. YOU KNOW THOSE LITTLE FUCKERS GIVE ME NIGHTMARES!!!! PLEASE!!!!*

Roger: *Gotta go*

Ah, they've been called out for an emergency. When will Reece learn? He lives on the third floor. Scorpions are rarely found above ground level; usually only if an idiot haphazardly brings one in. I should put his mind at ease, but it will wait. No distractions while they work. Snatching a note pad off the counter, I jot one down quickly to keep it handy:

Didn't think the crabs you keep catching would get along with the scorpions so I decided to let you off the hook . . . this time. Might want to get those critters treated.

Tanner

Yeah, I think I'll tape it to his door tonight so all of his neighbors will be sure to see it before he gets home in two days. Proxy, my ass. Not funny, Reece.

Libby enters the living room dressed in a tank top, pajama shorts, barefoot, her hair still mildly damp. Mind you, I've yet to shed the towel around my waist and advance to proper attire but it only takes me ten minutes to be ready to walk out the door. Miranda spent an hour just putting her face on, another to do her hair, and half an hour more to choose an outfit to wear. And Libby is beautiful without having done any of those things. There is no comparison.

Why did my mind go there?

"Didn't you want to go out to eat?"

"It's still raining." She sours her expression. "I have been wet for the better portion of the day. Besides, we had Chinese last night, I had Italian takeout the night before, and if I keep it up, I will have buns of bubbles before I know it."

I cross the room in seconds flat, taking her in my arms, her ass in my hands as I squeeze two perfectly rounded cheeks. Her ass is spectacular; firm, curvy, two tiny indents at the bottom of her back right above each cheek that would fit my thumbs as I grip her hips when I . . . "I could use a little more to fill out my palms."

She pushes at my chest, though I don't budge, stares up at me from the eight-inch height difference we share, and narrows her eyes. "I'm not growing a bigger ass for you. Now go put some clothes on, put the python away, and come help me find something to cook."

She noticed.

"Python, huh?" I say playfully.

The doorbell rings before we can finish our banter. Liberty frowns, looking to the door and back to me, glancing at the towel around my waist and points to the protrusion. "I'll get it. Go put that thing away."

Leaving the bedroom door partially open in order to listen as Libby answers the door, I throw on some jerseys in a hurry and slide on some sweats. Soft inaudible voices start before I hear Libby's surprised, if not slightly inappropriate, comment.

"Oh, you're the one who gives good head."

The familiar sound of John's chuckle follows. "I can attest to that."

Libby gasps loudly and quickly backtracks. "Oh God! I did not mean to say that. I-I just read the inscription in the helmet and-and it was the first thing that came to mind when-when you introduced yourself and I-I . . . oh God, oh God." Her embarrassed fumbling is followed by a desperate shriek. "Lucas!"

"It's alright, dear." Ava laughs, as does John, and I rush to grab a T-shirt. "I've been accused of much worse. I take it you're not a fan of blow jobs?"

"Ava!" I scold harshly as I return to the living room, my arms through the sleeves of the T-shirt, thumbs in the neckband ready to throw it over my head. "Toss her crumbs, not the whole damn loaf at once. She doesn't know you yet." I slide the T-shirt over my head.

Both she and John happily step past a dazed Libby – John with pizza boxes and a six-pack in his hands.

Fuck my life.

John sets the boxes and beer on the counter. "Thought you two might want an easy meal after, you know," he shrugs and snickers, "a hard, wet ride."

The gleam in his eyes indicates he's not just talking about sex, as is his usual, but they know we rode today as it was their helmets we borrowed. I study them both. "And you're being generous, why?"

"You're all over the news," Ava informs me. "The reporters might not know who you are, Tanner, as they're referring to you both as good Samaritans." She lifts a brow. "But we do. Now all you have to do is introduce us to this gorgeous young lady with the stunning eyes you're keeping company with." She places a hand on her hip and dips her chin. "Then you can tell us why you've kept her hidden."

Libby's still standing at the door which remains ajar, observing the three of us, unsure if she should thank them for the dinner or ask them to stay.

"It's a damn good thing you did for Marty," John commends her. "I've been to the hospital to see him already. He's out of surgery, groggy, but he's gonna be okay. The TV news reported it while I was there and I saw a soaked Tanner with his arm around you. Recognized Roger and Reece too."

I'm a little confused by his words as I didn't note any reporters other than the ones we dodged on our way out of the building.

"You know Martin Kiesner?" Libby's mouth is agape as she

stares at John.

John nods. "I do. He was my brother-in-law." Ava reaches out to place her hand on his arm as he finishes. "Still is, I guess. He was married to my sister. Childhood sweethearts. We lost her ten years ago. Never remarried. Don't think he ever will."

Libby and I exchange glances before she asks him, "How did you know about his accident?"

"I'm his emergency contact." John shrugs. "He's not much for people. Can't get the guy to smile if you pay him to. I can't remember the last time I heard him laugh."

"I can," I say without thinking, then wink at my girl. It was today in the pouring rain, injured, while Liberty was trying to treat him. Her cheeks flush with the slightest glow of pink. "Sometimes it just takes a magic touch."

Knowing John is going to be her best bet for the update she wanted on Martin's condition and the fact I really would like for some of my favorite people to get to know the love of my life, I ask them, "You guys want to join us for pizza?"

Libby's phone rings where it sits on the counter. Let me correct that. It belts out the tune from the *Wizard of Oz* "If I Only Had A Brain".

She releases the doorknob – finally – and rushes to the phone as she holds up a finger. "Excuse me." She snatches the phone up quickly as if slightly ashamed of the ringtone assigned to the caller. She answers, but errantly hits the speaker button for all to hear. "Hey, what's up?"

"Eighteen years," the voice says slowly before she taunts, "You know, Libs, there are much better exercises than bike riding to make you walk crooked. Fun ones even. Like, I don't know, maybe fucking his brains out! What were you thinking?!"

Ah, Mallory. I'd know that sharp tone and smartass attitude anywhere. Unaware her phone is on speaker until John and Ava chuckle, Libby pulls the phone away from her ear and turns the speaker off. She holds up another finger before heading toward the bedroom, face flushed with embarrassment. "I'll be right back." Before reaching the door and slamming it behind her, we all hear, "I am going to murder you!"

Ava snickers. "She is a firecracker."

I shake my head and chuckle. "She sure is."

"That's what Marty said too," John adds. "He was groggy as hell, but he had to tell us about the *little gal with crystal eyes named Liberty* on the trail. Who is she?"

Staring at the door she slammed moments ago, I smile. "My everything."

Chapter 30

Liberty

"Do you have to be so crude?" I whisper shout into the phone as soon as I slam the bedroom door behind me.

Mallory snort laughs so hard she chokes. "Me? Did you know your nipples were on proud display for all of Phoenix to see? Good thing I packed your blue one. Imagine if you had been wearing a white sports bra."

"My what?!" I shriek and nearly drop my phone as I pull it away from my ear and stare at the screen. She's joking, right? And here I stand, braless, having answered the door without hesitation, or two working brain cells.

No good deed goes unpunished.

"You can thank me later for packing more than just the lacy naughty things. I knew there was no way you'd go three days without exercise," she hesitates and laughs, "unless of course you were doing gymnastics in the bedroom."

"You open a conversation with hints of fucking his brains out," I sneer. "I was on speakerphone, you idiot. Do you know who's standing in Lucas' living room right now?"

"First of all, I didn't *hint* at anything, I was pretty straightforward. And, since I'm not there, I can't say as I do," Mallory informs me as if I didn't know. "Please enlighten me."

"Ava Mynx," I enunciate slowly and give her a moment for the information to sink in. Lucas had only identified her as Ava – no last name. She identified herself at the door. Her unique passion purple logo flashes through my mind. You know, the one on at least two dozen paperbacks in Mallory's room!

"Y-you're in, in the same place as *the* Ava Mynx?" Mal asks on a shocked whisper. "Holy shit."

"I'm about to go eat pizza with her."

"Just one question," she says, though by her tone I'm hesitant to indulge her.

I press my fingertips to my forehead. "Go ahead."

"Got enough pizza for one more?"

A smile blooms as I think of my best friend meeting her favorite erotica writer. I owe her. I didn't arrange it – it's totally coincidental – but if I have to, I'll tie Ava to a chair until Mal gets here.

"I can always order more. How soon can you be here?"

"Pin me the address. I'll be out the door in minutes."

I smirk, though she can't see it. "With a bag of books to be autographed, no doubt."

"Get off the phone and pin me the address, Libs!" she huffs as I picture her running to her room. "Never waste an opportunity."

Entering the living room once again – this time with a bra on and a smile on my face – I look to Lucas. "Mal would like to join us. I already told her that would be fine. You guys don't have to wait to eat. I can order another pizza."

My phone in hand makes it tempting to hold it up and take a quick pic, but I behave and simply bank the memory of the look on his face. "Your friend Mallory? The one from the hospital? She's coming here?" He points his finger at the floor as if marking his territory.

"Well," I propose slowly and point to the other side of the room, hiding a grin. "We could put her in the corner over there if it would make you more comfortable, but I promise her rabies shots are up-to-date. And she hasn't bitten anyone since. . ." I scrunch my nose and twist my mouth to the side, ". . . the last time."

Due to the way Lucas is rubbing his chin with one hand and staring at me, I can't tell if he's planning my punishment or pleasure. There's admiration in his eyes, tipped with a heated flare as he arches one brow. *Restraint.*

Ava giggles as she looks back and forth between the two of us. "I really like her."

Lucas sighs and shakes his head. "Text her and let her know the code to get in the main door is *89516#."

"I take it these ladies can be trusted with the door code?" John asks.

His eyes never leaving mine, Lucas answers his question, "Both Liberty and Mallory can be trusted with your lives. They save them every day." He crosses the room and takes me in his arms, burying his face in my neck, and whispers, "You've been saving mine for 25 years."

We put the pizzas in the oven on warm and pop open a couple beers for the guys while Ava and I enjoy a glass of wine. Within twenty minutes of simple conversation, we're chatting as if we've known each other forever.

"What the hell do you think you're doing?!" The familiar growl of Mallory Tompkins comes through loud and clear from just outside the door. "Do you not make enough trouble in our building? For God's sake, take those filthy underwear off the door!!"

"What are you doing here!?" another female voice demands. "Oh, let me guess. You're probably fucking one of the firemen. Or is it both? Wrong floor though. They're one flight down."

"Bitch, I warned you about that mouth," Mallory threatens. "There's a stairwell right there. I can show you four flights down with one push."

Lucas is white as a sheet as he jumps up from his position on the sofa, joined quickly by the three of us. He throws the door open to find a fuming Mallory and Miranda Nelson arguing in the hallway as well as a thong taped to his door and a pair of panties hanging from the doorknob.

"Tanner," Miranda sobs as she tries to throw herself at him. "She threatened me with bodily harm. You must have heard her."

Lucas is quick to take her by the shoulders and hold her away from him. His voice is harsh and his jaw is set firm. "What are you doing in this building? You have a restraining order."

"You didn't mean it," she cries. "I know you didn't. You were just mad about the box. Roger and Reece were so mean to me and . . ."

"Get out before I call the police," Lucas warns through a

clenched jaw.

"B-but you are the police," she sobs and tries to move closer to him once again, but Ava steps between them, preventing her advances.

"Miranda!" a woman shouts from down the hall as she makes her way toward us. "What are you doing in the building? You know you're not supposed . . ."

"Aunt Shelley!" Miranda screams as if she's been wounded. "These people are being mean to me!"

The woman approaches Miranda with care and places her arm around her shoulder. "Come on," she says with a shake of her head. "Let's go."

"Shelley," Lucas warns, his voice low and resigned. "Out, or I'm calling it in."

A remorseful Shelley nods. "I understand, Tanner."

"Who gave her the new code?" Lucas demands.

As if the last few minutes haven't happened, and a whole new personality has taken over the woman caught hanging panties on a door that doesn't belong to her – a little like Sybil – Miranda Nelson smiles evilly. "I have my ways, Tanner."

He lifts a brow, his voice flat. "And I'm sure the Dennison firm would love to know what they are, as well as the orders you've violated."

Her evil smile drops immediately as her eyes flare with shock . . . and fear. "You wouldn't dare!"

He nods before he turns his back to her and calmly says, "Monday morning, count on it." He corrals us back inside, closes the door and locks it behind him.

"Well," Mallory says lightly as she sets her carefully packed rucksack of paperbacks by the sofa. "I see she's spreading joy wherever she goes." She crinkles her nose in disgust and looks to me. "I wonder if she's been delivering panties to the dude on the ninth floor. He has been checking the hall before he gets off the elevator a lot lately." She snaps her fingers at Lucas. "Grab me a trash bag and some disinfectant. Got any rubber gloves?"

Lucas eyes her warily. "No."

Mal shrugs. "Then get me a fork. That'll do."

"A fork?"

"Yes." She scowls as if second guessing her order is a sin. "You don't expect me to touch those filthy things, do you? You can't be so daft as to think she left you clean panties. That out there is sniffing material."

Ava's burst of laughter fills the room. "Where have you been hiding these women, Tanner?" She smiles at Mallory. "Tell me dear, do you happen to read?"

Mal doesn't miss a beat as her face lights up. "I don't think I've missed a page you've ever written, *Ava Mynx*." She turns back to Lucas. "Now, hurry up with those supplies. I have a hand for Ava to wear out."

Lucas stands frozen; the only thing moving is his eyebrows as they reach higher and higher on his forehead. "You have a what to wear out?"

Mallory rolls her eyes and shakes her head. "Typical male. Women don't wear their hands out the way you men do. We have toys to do the work. Liberty had to get a new one after some idiot got one stuck up his . . ."

"Mallory!" I shriek so loud I can hear my own echo.

Lucas turns slowly, an impish grin lighting his handsome face as he mouths, "Dildo?" I simply close my eyes in lieu of answering before I feel his breath at my ear as he whispers, "Don't ever use it alone again. Facetime with me if you get lonely, and you have to name it Lucas. Got it?"

I glance at his hand then back up at his face. "Are you naming your hand?"

"No need," he says confidently. "It's got the same one it's had since the first day I used it." He traces a soft line with his finger from my forehead to my chin and whispers, "I guess in a way, you were my first after all."

Throat clearing bursts our bubble before Mallory demands, "Trash bag, fork, and disinfectant. Hurry up before your neighbors think you're a pervert."

"She does have a point, Tanner," John agrees. "Wouldn't want to take away from the firefighters' reputations."

"Or ours," Ava adds with a lifted finger.

Four of us chuckle while Mal's gaze drops to the countertop and I see a flash of disappointment as she waits for the supplies to remove the unmentionables attached to the door. Recalling our conversation from so long ago in Vegas when she described what she wants makes me wonder.

"I would rather have a fun guy who is willing to work for it than one who thinks he's got it in the bag just because he makes a shit ton of money and he's hot."

Lucas must notice it as well because he immediately rushes to defend his friend. "Reece is more talk than walk. You guys know that. He seems pretty hung up on some woman he won't identify."

"Ah yes," Ava drawls. "The one he calls 'kitten'. And he still won't tell you who she is?"

"You know Reece," Lucas says easily while he pulls the disinfectant and trash bag from under the sink. "Must be the Texan in him. They're like bulls on the outside, but all mushy and sweet on the inside. He's a talker, but discreet."

The corners of Mallory's mouth tip in a smile she tries to hide as she dips her chin. Seems she and I have a conversation that needs to take place later. I've been a little busy reacquainting myself with the love of my life to get the deets on what happened when Reece chased after her last night. I so want to see her happy.

"I'll get the mess cleaned up," Lucas tells her as he tries to get past her around the counter.

"No you won't. Hand it over, Lucas. I may bag it and drop it at her door later tonight anyway." She snatches the items out of his hands.

"You know where she lives?" A shocked and somewhat nervous Ava asks.

Mal scowls and gestures with her middle finger held up high. "Unfortunately, one floor up from us. She's the bane of our existence and the pain in all of our asses."

Ava nods exaggeratedly. "That explains the confrontation in the hallway."

"Not at all." Mallory shakes her head. "A true confrontation would have been me scratching her eyes out. Why the hell was she here and why was she taping unmentionables to your door, Lucas?"

"Whoa, whoa." John holds up a hand. "That's the second time I've heard that name. Who's Lucas?"

Lucas rubs the back of his neck nervously before Mallory whirls on him feigning surprise. "Wait! They don't know?" She turns back to Ava and John. "Lucas is his stripper name. It's what we all call him down at *The Tempest*. You should see the way he strips off those cop uniform pants in one swift pull. Velcro is the best. The ladies love it. He even has some avid male fans."

"Mallory!" I grind through teeth that are close to cracking.

Lucas glares at her as he draws deep breaths next to me and growls slowly, "I haven't had *my* rabies shots, Liberty. Rein her in or I will be locking her in a kennel." He turns slowly; the flare in his eyes severe. "Commonly known as a jail cell."

I step forward and yank on her arm, moving her toward the

door. "Let's go remove some undies, shall we?" I lean in close and whisper, "Before I use that fork to poke you in the ass."

Outside in the hall stands a man, a very confused man, though seemingly familiar. I'm sure I met him last night outside the hospital. His hand is raised as if readying to knock on the door, though unsure if he should.

"Wiley, right?" I greet him.

"Uh, yeah," he stammers, looking at the lingerie hanging on the door, then back to the two of us, and his face scrunches. "Is Tanner here? I saw the news and just wanted to check on you . . . two." He glances at Mallory. "Now three?"

"Hey, Wiley," Lucas says from behind me. "What's up?"

"Uh," Wiley stammers once more as his eyes flit from Lucas to me to Mallory, then the door. "You went to college, didn't you, Tanner?"

Lucas snorts. "Yeah."

Wiley scratches his head as if confused. "We used to hang socks on the doorknobs. What year did it change?"

Lucas pinches the bridge of his nose before he runs his hand down his face and takes a deep breath. "You want pizza, Wiley? John and Ava are here."

Wiley ponders for a moment and glances at Mallory before looking back to Lucas, his brows furrowed. "Does this mean I would have to be her date?"

Mallory holds up the fork in her hand, her scowl fixed on Wiley. "I have a fork and I'm not afraid to use it."

"S-so, that would be a no?" Wiley asks.

Mal narrows her eyes. "A definite no, you moron."

Wiley rushes past us in the door. "I'd love some then." He whispers to Lucas on his way past. "She's way too young and meaner than any of my ex-wives."

Chapter 31

Lucas

"So why the hell do you have underwear hanging on your door?" Wiley asks as soon as his ass hits the couch, beer in hand.

Liberty and Mallory are removing and disposing of it as we speak. I could have done it myself, but Mallory was insistent she do it. As it is, I'm so livid I'm ready to combust. I've put up with Miranda's stalking tendencies for the last two months. Tendencies, hell. She's nuts. No two ways about it. And I'm done. The Dennison Law Firm will be notified on Monday of her violating a no-contact order. As an officer of the court, this will pretty much ruin her career. But she's been given so many chances and now that Liberty is in the picture, I'm not willing to give any more. Miranda can go back to Wyoming. She can go wherever she lands as long as it's not here. Quite frankly, she can go to hell.

I shoot him a wry look and grumble, "Miranda."

He groans as he swipes his hand over his five o'clock shadow. "You missed with the holy water, didn't ya? Damnit, Tanner, I told you we shoulda bought the power jet sprayer." He throws back another chug of his beer. "Women," he grunts. "Can't live with 'em, can't pay 'em enough to shop 'til they drop . . . dead."

That renders a laugh from the other three of us in the room. Libby and Mallory join us once again, only the disinfectant in Mallory's hand and she sets it on the counter. They both wash their hands at the sink.

"Where's my fork?" I ask Mallory.

"It's Oneida, isn't it?"

My face squirrels in confusion. Silverware is silverware, isn't it? It looked sturdy, felt weighty in my hand, sold by the set, service for eight. Enough to serve the gang if, on the rare occasion it isn't finger-food. Unless of course it's Wiley. He'll hold the plate to his tongue and lick the remaining crumbs off.

Married three times, folks.

I shrug. "I don't know."

"Google it," she says cockily with a tip of her chin. "It's the Pilot pattern. You can order them individually. I wouldn't take the chance of running that thing through the steamer at the hospital. Probably give the patients oral chlamydia."

"I am in love," Ava says adoringly from her place on my couch as she stares at the newcomer.

Mallory's face lights up so bright, it nearly makes her unrecognizable. I mean, really, it almost convinces me there's a nice person somewhere deep, deep, deep inside there. "Enough to sign my collection of books for me?"

"I'll even sign your boob for you, sweetheart," Ava tells her with a playful smile.

"Really?"

"No, dear," Ava deadpans. "But I would be happy to sign every book you brought with you. I even have an author's copy of my latest that doesn't release until next month that I can let you have early if you'd like."

"Oh my God!" Mallory virtually throws herself at Ava and wraps her in a hug. "I swear I won't tell anyone what's in it. Well, maybe Liberty, but she's trustworthy."

Libby holds up her hands. "I'm good, Mal. You can keep it under wraps until release day."

"So, what is it you ladies do at the hospital?" John inquires.

"Libs is a nurse practitioner in the ER," Mallory answers as she digs through the rucksack and pulls out a pile of paperbacks, "and I put people to sleep."

As is the usual Wiley – aka open mouth and insert foot before engaging his brain – he asks, "Permanently?"

Mallory smiles sweetly, then winks. "Only the ones that piss me off."

A wary Wiley gulps hard. "What hospital do you work at?"

"Why?" Mallory teases with a wink. "Got an upcoming surgery planned?"

Glancing at Libby, I smirk. "What corner were you going to put her in?"

Two agonizing hours and one harsh realization later, the guests are leaving. Somewhere in the midst of pizza, beer, constant chatter, and the music of laughter, I lost myself in the memory of being with Libby for the first time this afternoon. The feel of her wet naked body against mine, the passion and desperate need I'd never felt before, the sound of her moans as we were skin-to-skin and . . . oh shit!

Not once from the moment we got inside that door until the rampant thoughts of doing it again had it occurred to me we hadn't used a condom. I hadn't even inquired about birth control. My golden rules of birth control combined with condoms weren't on my radar, which now explains the burning that is reaching from my chest to the deepest, darkest pit of my belly. This is how mini Monterreys are made. This is how the bloodline of the devil is extended.

"Got a little heartburn there, Tanner?" John asks with a chuckle as he pats my shoulder. "That pizza was a bit spicy."

Releasing the fist I hadn't realized I had held to my sternum, I fake a light cough. "Next time, leave the jalapenos off."

"We'll walk Mallory to her car," he offers, then bends to pick up the rucksack full of signed paperbacks. "You two enjoy the rest of your evening. Liberty, it's been a pleasure meeting you."

Libby's smile is genuine as she extends her hand to shake his. "You two as well."

Ava takes Libby in her arms and squeezes her tightly. "Don't worry about the helmets, dear. John and I will pick them up later. Someday the four of us can ride together." She laughs and tilts her head. "Preferably after monsoon season is over."

"Give Martin my best," Libby tells her.

Ava takes her hands in hers. "Sweetheart, I think you already did. Thank you."

Wiley clears his throat before muttering softly next to me, "Think I can stick around until John gets the *kitten* to her car? I swear that woman has claws."

The devilish grin on Ava's face indicates she heard as she

mouths at me, "That's Reece's kitten?"

I place a hand on her shoulder, leading her to the door. "Pleadin' the Fifth, Ava."

"Oh shoot," she whispers. "I should have highlighted a few paragraphs for her. She could have that man on his knees before he could say . . ."

Leaning in close, I keep my voice low. "Think he's looking to be on his back while she's sitting on his face."

Her eyes twinkle with delight as she whirls her head up. "Oh my. I have full pages to cover the subject of . . ."

"Good night, Ava."

The door closes behind them and I rest my back against it before I pinch the bridge of my nose.

"I like your friends. They're interesting." Liberty's puckish grin only makes her more beautiful.

"They're nuts," I grumble before moving away from the door and taking a place next to her on the couch. "But I wouldn't trade them."

"Want to tell me about Miranda?" she asks, avoiding my gaze as she lifts her wine glass to her mouth.

I wait for her to face me. We all make mistakes. Some big, some small, some disastrous. Miranda was my Chernobyl. A disaster waiting to happen. No, she didn't cheat on me, but we weren't a couple – certainly never engaged.

"Have I asked you about the good doctor, Libby?"

She sinks her teeth into her bottom lip; her cheeks flushing the slightest shade of pink. "No."

What is wrong with me? Liberty and I have always shared everything. No secrets, no lies. No, I haven't asked her about her about the former fiancé. But I haven't suffered having him thrown in my face either. I wouldn't know the guy from Adam, but I hate him already without the formalities. He hurt her. I don't need more than that.

Tugging that bottom lip from between her teeth, I lift her chin. "Miranda was everything you weren't, just like every woman I've ever been with. Brunette, redhead, brown eyes, red lips. Anything but pink." I drop a soft kiss on her mouth. "Because I knew it had a flavor. I was willing to die never knowing what it tasted like before taking the chance of having it tainted. Call it obsession, call it crazy." I plant another kiss on her mouth before finishing. "I called it hope."

"You never had a blue or green-eyed, blonde girlfriend?" she asks, surprised.

"I've never had a girlfriend, Liberty." I shake my head slowly. Maybe this will be the best segue to the truth. "Couples generally lead to dreams of white picket fences around yards filled with kids and toys." My gaze finds its way to a landscape picture on the wall – I have no family portraits to hang – and I can't look her in the eyes. "It's never going to happen for me, so I never considered starting something I wouldn't finish."

"Y-you can't have kids?" Her voice is but a whisper, but as I turn to see the crease of her brow and unwarranted pity in her eyes, it almost makes me reconsider.

Almost.

Closing my eyes and holding steadfast to a decision I made so many years ago, I steel my tone and tell her, "No, Libby. I *won't* have kids." I open my eyes to see a rather dazed expression as she stares at me. "Speaking of which, do I need to run out and pick up a Plan B for you?"

That dazed expression? Yeah, have I mentioned her eyes have a tendency to brighten or darken with sudden flashes of emotions? Tears, happiness . . . anger?

"A what?!"

Irises surrounded by solid white, the green two shades

brighter, the blue one shade darker in three seconds flat. Yup, that would be anger.

"I didn't wear a condom and I didn't ask about birth control." My hand rises in an effort to placate her. "I take full responsibility. I was so caught up in us, so desperate to . . ."

"Just stop, Lucas!" she growls in frustration as she buries her face in her hands.

"Libby," I utter a plea. "I thought of all people you would understand."

She lifts her teary eyes to meet mine. "Understand what?"

"I will not poison this world with one more Monterrey." I feel the tears brim my own eyes and the burn in my chest as I recall the pain and misery from years ago. The mother I barely recall, my best friend and all the years I lost with her. The day-in and day-out cruelty I suffered under his reign. The childhood that was taken away. "I don't have to carry his name but his bloodline ends with me too. He took everything from me. I refuse to let him take anymore."

"He's dead, Lucas," she says softly, reaching for my face and brushing a wayward tear from my cheek. "He can only take what you give him now. Though it sounds like you're giving him exactly what he would have wanted if he were alive."

I shake my head and close my eyes, my chest squeezing in anguish over a decision I made years ago, though I never felt it was a choice. It was necessity. "It ends with me, Libby. I'm sorry."

She rises from the sofa and my eyes follow her movements. She stands before me, studying my face for the longest time. Her shoulders rise and fall with a deep sigh before a sad smile ever so slightly stretches the beautiful outline of pink as she acquiesces, "I guess you have forgotten some things." She heads for the door, slipping her shoes on before she reaches for the knob.

"Where are you going?"

"I need to take a walk."

"It's still raining, Libby!"

She turns to me before twisting the knob and nods slowly. "Exactly."

So no one can see her tears.

The ones that I just caused.

Chapter 32

Liberty

"Okay, we'll wait 'til we're 32."

The words of our youth ring in my ears as the cold rain pelts my skin. It's an ugly drizzle; a mix of scattered fat drops and mist. Just enough to wash with my tears and leave a slight salty taste as the moisture rims my lips. They were happy tears this afternoon when Lucas held me in his arms. Now? They're drops of misery.

Soaked to the skin, I sit on the curb in the parking lot close to the building. I know better than to walk around in the dark, especially in a strange part of the city – I'm not stupid. But I had to step out and take a breath. Besides, I'm well aware of Lucas' presence right inside the door of the complex as he watches and waits for me to come back. Always protective, always the gentleman.

I want to understand his dilemma. Is it the trauma, or is his hatred for his father so strong that he will never get past it? It's not the name – even he doesn't carry it. Is it fear? After seeing him with Adam, I have no doubt he would have indubitable paternal instincts. Children have always been in my plans – eventually. But for some reason, I never pictured myself having them with Michael. And now I know why.

The magic number 32. Someone else's dream. It was never meant to be Michael's and mine.

This is crazy. I'm crazy. How could I have possibly expected his dreams would have remained the same as mine? We were kids! Bike riding, bubblegum chewing kids. I could be married with kids and a house in the suburbs with anyone else, but if ever asked who my soulmate was, the answer would remain the same: Lucas. Always Lucas. Some people say there's no such thing as soul mates. Others say you can have many. Some say you never find one. I guess it's a good thing I don't listen to unsolicited opinions. I've always known. Question is, what sacrifices do you make for the sake of harmony?

A car door slams from somewhere in the parking lot. "Liberty?" The now familiar voice belonging to Wiley sounds from close by and I look up to see him approaching with an open umbrella in one hand and a six-pack in the other. "What are you doing out here?"

"Just thinking, Wiley."

"In the rain?"

Swiping the back of my hand across my cheek, I sniffle. "It's easier this way."

He glances at the entry door to see Lucas, then back to me. "Ah, lovers' quarrel?"

I chuckle to myself more than him. "No, just wishing I could go back in time and change history, ya know?"

He plops down next to me on the curb and hands me the umbrella. "I'm a good listener, but it usually takes a beer or two." He twists the tops on two beers and hands one to me, takes the umbrella back, doing his best to shelter the both of us, though I'm soaked to the skin. "Yeah, yeah, I know, you don't need it but it would look pretty bad if I didn't share. Humor me. Now tell me what's on your mind, kiddo."

"How long have you known Lucas?" I ask before raising the bottle to my lips and taking a swallow.

"Lucas?" He squints one eye and his mouth twists as he considers. "Only since I heard you call him that. Tanner? About three years. Was I shocked when I heard what had happened to him? Yeah, I was. But I always knew there was something. He's different from the rest of us; guarded, reserved." He nudges my arm. "But I've always felt a connection with Tanner that I don't feel with the rest. If there were one of them I could go to for something or could hold a secret, it would be him. We all have secrets, Liberty. And we all have histories, regrets, bad decisions we made or things we've done in our past that we'd like to change. Take it from someone who knows. If you let your history dictate your future, you may as well never grow old . . ." he lifts a brow and dips his chin, ". . . because you will always be stuck in your past."

"But you can have good memories that help you overcome the bad from your past, can't you?" It's as much a plea for confirmation as it is a question.

Wiley flashes what he thinks is a knowing smile and winks. "I believe that's what you've done, Liberty. I've never seen Tanner so happy. You've literally given him a future he never thought possible."

"I think he forgot an important part of it," I whisper into the dark, unsure if I should be sharing such a private part of our lives.

"What do you mean?"

"He doesn't want kids, Wiley." Knowing I'm probably sharing too much, I still can't help myself because I know Wiley has heard the story. "He's afraid he'll taint the world with his father's genes."

He nods slowly, staring out at the dark parking lot. "Has he fixed it so he *can't* have kids?"

I ponder his question for a moment. Lucas wouldn't have been worried about condoms or birth control if he were shooting blanks. "You mean like a vasectomy?"

"Yeah," he nearly grunts. "Like that."

"No." I shake my head. "He just doesn't want them."

He sounds resolved as he shoots me a wry look. "He's not a complete imbecile and it's not too late then. Once he pulls his head out of his ass, he'll figure out just how damn lucky he is."

"Is that what you meant by bad decisions?" I ask him, studying the face of a man I would have guessed to be about fifty suddenly look ten years older as sadness and remorse envelop his amber eyes.

He grins ruefully. "Sometimes we make snap decisions due to choices that were taken away from us. Some are reversible, some aren't. Give Tanner time."

Lucas' shaky voice sounds from my right. "Libby, would you please come back inside?"

Wiley hands the umbrella over and rises from his place next to me; his jeans now soaked from the rain. He pats Lucas on the shoulder. "I'll leave you to it. Don't be a dumbass. There ain't enough room in this building for two of us."

"Wiley," I call after him. "You can take your umbrella. I don't really need it."

"Keep it, Liberty," he says as he looks toward the sky. "I don't want anybody to see mine either."

My heart breaks a little for him as I watch him walk away. Wiley portrays himself as the jokester of the group, but I think he hurts. Decisions, regrets, secrets, history.

Lucas extends his hand for me to take. "Please come back inside with me, Libby. I need this to be real, to touch you, to know this isn't some fucked up dream. We'll work it out. I promise."

I don't reach for his hand and instead meet his gaze. "Does the number 32 mean anything to you, Lucas?"

He slides his fingers into damp pockets and rocks on his heels, eyes never leaving mine. "Of course it does. It was the original plan. We weren't supposed to date until we were thirty either."

Fresh raw tears slide down my cheeks as he takes a seat next to me on the curb. He does remember. He places an arm over my shoulder and pulls me close. "Your dad must be watching over us pretty closely. Definitely making us stick to his rules." He kisses my temple, holding his lips to my skin as he chuckles. "Doubt he'd appreciate me fucking you up against the wall this afternoon but we can hope he was busy playing canasta at the time."

I giggle against his shoulder, burying my nose in his scent. We will work it out. We always did, one way or another. I hate his father too. He took so much from Lucas. But people can only take what you're willing to give. Lucas was half of his mother, too. That has to count for something, doesn't it?

"Come on," he says softly as he pulls me to my feet. "Hot bath and a dry bed sound good?"

"With you in it?"

He swipes the wet hair away from my forehead before he kisses it. "Try and keep me away, Liberty Bell."

"I am on birth control, Lucas," I assure him. "Not that I've needed it, but it's an implant and it would be a pain to have it removed and replaced so I just kept it."

"Thank God," he breathes in relief, sliding an arm over my shoulder and leading me toward the door. "I don't think I could take anything between us. You were my first for that. I plan on you being my last . . . ever."

"This is moving so fast, Lucas."

"For anybody else, I suppose it would be." He enters the code and pulls the door open so we can slip inside. "Just think of where we'd be if we hadn't been screwed out of so many years together. We'll slow down if you want, I'll even take a step back." He blows out a deep breath and stops to turn me in his arms. "But I will not step away. A lot changed for me over the years, Liberty. The only thing I had to hold onto were the memories of you, and even those felt like wishful thinking after a while, but they never dimmed. I've got a lot going through my head right now, but my heart is so fucking full, I don't want to deal with both at the same time. I just want to be happy for the first time since I lost you. Are you happy, Libby?"

Without hesitation I throw my arms around his neck and pull him down to me until his mouth meets mine. I don't want to slow down and I surely don't want him to step back – definitely not away. His response is instantaneous; the unsurety in his question replaced by a confident grip to the back of my neck and a hold around my waist as he takes full control of the kiss, coaxing my lips open with his tongue.

"So happy, Lucas," I whisper against his mouth as the kiss ends.

"Go crazy with me, Liberty." He leans his forehead on mine. "I waited years for one tomorrow. I want you to be all of my tomorrows. I want you." He does it again. A kiss that makes the rest of the world go away. A kiss so deep it begs and pleads while at the same time steals and claims. Only Lucas could ask and demand at the same time. Incomparable kisses that I feel are mine and mine alone.

He lifts me off my feet and I wrap my legs around his waist. "We are not repeating this afternoon, Libby," he mutters against my mouth as he carries me toward the elevators, his voice deep and severe. "We are making it to the bedroom this time. I plan to savor every last inch of you . . . over and over."

"Do I get a shower first?"

"Eventually." He chuckles. "I'll keep you warm."

Totally sated and a lot tired, I lay my head on his chest and trace my finger over the Liberty Bell tattoo. The others on his upper arms vary; one of the PPD insignia and a script that reads: *The Promise of Tomorrow.* Singular. Not promises. Just one. Mine. Decisions, choices taken away.

"Would you check on Wiley in the morning?" The question leaves my mouth as the prior thought takes hold.

He tips my chin with two fingers and quirks a brow. "That's twice now that you've thought of another man while naked with me, Liberty. Is there something you're not telling me?"

"No," I huff and sit up in bed. "He seemed off tonight. Kind of . . . depressed. I'm a little worried about him. Our conversation seemed to drum up some memories for him that maybe weren't so pleasant."

"What did you talk about?"

My mouth twists to the side, uncomfortable with the confession that I may have spoken out of turn about our own issue. "Us," I say sheepishly.

He furrows his brow as he considers. "How much of *us* did you discuss?"

I shrug one shoulder. "Not much. He was more advising than curious. I thought he knew the whole story."

"Nope." He shakes his head. "He only knows what happened, because I'd already recited it to Roger and Reece. He was a little late to the party that night. He said if I ever wanted to give the details or talk about it again, he'd be my ears."

"He thinks the world of you, Lucas. But he seems regretful of some of his own life decisions. Sad, ya know?"

Lucas snorts. "He has been married three times."

"Three times?!" My eyes nearly bug out of my head.

He nods. "Doesn't exactly reminisce fondly about them." He closes one eye and looks up toward the ceiling. "In fact," he drawls, "he's never really reminisced about them at all, other than to mark them off as the alimony payments conclude."

"No sentimental or emotional value in his discussions about them?"

"Not a lick." He shakes his head. "No discussions at all, really. He's not much of a talker. We don't even know their names other than wife numbers one, two, and three."

"You don't find that odd?"

He shrugs his shoulders against the mattress. "Hadn't really thought about it."

I snatch my pillow from behind me and throw it at him. "You are such a man. What is wrong with you guys!?"

He tosses my pillow back to my side of the bed and yanks my naked body down to his. "I am all man. You should know that by now, baby." He flips me onto my back and rolls over on top of me, rubbing an ever growing hardness against my thigh. *Dang! The man is virile.* His eyes pierce mine as he narrows them and growls, "Now, you want to tell me what's *wrong* with me?"

"N-nothing," I stammer in protest. "I didn't mean that part." I tap his temple with my index finger. "I meant this part. You need to use your head sometimes."

He grins impishly as he places the tip at my entrance. "I am using my head right now, Liberty." He inches in slowly at first, lifting my leg at the knee to gain better access. "And if you ever speak another man's name while naked with me," he slides in a little more, teasing, "in bed," *a little more* "I'm going to put a gag on you." He thrusts hard, and I'm the fullest I've ever been.

"Lucas!"

"Mmmm," he hums as he pulls back and thrusts again. "Good girl. Mine is the only name I want to hear in our bed." *Our bed.*

The man is a demon in the sheets. Relentless. However, never taking without giving first . . . a few times.

It's two o'clock in the morning by the time I'm freshening up in the bathroom from our last round and sliding one of his T-shirts over my head. I could sleep in nothing, but he's the one who made the rules, and our discussion is not over.

Lucas is sitting back against the headboard waiting for me as I step out of the bathroom and stand at the foot of the bed. He looks puzzled as he takes in my attire. "You look good in my shirt but I prefer you naked." He pulls back the sheets, inviting me in. "Come on."

I hold up a hand. "Not yet. They were your stipulations and I don't want a gag. Are you going to check on Wiley in the morning?"

"What?"

I fold my arms over my chest and arch a brow. "I'm not in the bed and I'm not naked. I can say his name. Are you going to check on Wiley in the morning?"

"You were serious?"

"He's your friend, Lucas. By extension, kind of mine too. I like him and I'm concerned. He was carrying a six-pack after having had drinks with us. Does he always drink like that?"

The blank look on his face is met with my own expectant glare. He scrubs his hand down his face, ending with a scratch of his delectable soft, trimmed facial hair before he rolls his eyes. "I'll go check on him in the morning."

"Oh good." I bounce on my heels and giggle. "Can I get naked now and hop back into bed?"

He laughs, knowing I've won the battle but he gets his prize; a naked me.

He curls his arm around me and pulls my back to his front as I get comfortable. "I always knew it was your heart that made you who you are. Beautiful inside and out. I love you. You know that, don't you?"

"I love you, too. Always have."

He kisses the tip of my shoulder and buries his face in my hair. "My first, my last, my Liberty."

Chapter 33

Lucas

Wiley squints and rubs the heel of his palm over his left eye before raking the same hand through his hair, leaving half the strands standing straight up. He looks like hell, could use a shower, probably a Sunday service, and a few cups of coffee.

"Tanner? What the hell brings you around at the ass crack of dawn?"

"The ass crack of dawn is five o'clock, Wiley. It's ten in the morning."

"No shit?" he fires back, scratching the back of his head. "Huh, good thing it's Saturday."

"It's Sunday, Wiley," I correct him, now more than concerned with his present state and seeming confusion. Maybe Libby was correct. "You gonna let me in?"

"Sure," he says casually, opening the door. "Come on in. What's up, Tanner?" He holds up a finger. "Wait a minute. Where's Liberty?"

"She's upstairs," I reassure him as I step inside. "Wanted me to check on you and to be honest, I can see why. You look like hell and unless you had a party I wasn't invited to," I wave my hand around the living room, "you drank enough for six people."

"I kinda went overboard last night." He winces with his confession.

"No shit," I deadpan.

Moving to the kitchen, I collect a mug from the cupboard and start a cup of coffee in his Keurig. "Sit down. We'll start the detox and I'll help you clean up."

"You don't need to clean up my messes, Tanner. I gave up long ago."

"Start at the beginning, Wiley," I order as I snatch a trash bag from under the sink. *Bread bags, my ass. He buys them. Green ties.* Setting the cup in front of him on the breakfast bar, I move my way toward the living room to collect the many bottles on the coffee table. He's not a slob per se; just messy. "Let's hear it. What set you off?"

"It doesn't matter, Tanner." He takes a sip of his coffee and breathes a long sigh. "This will pass, just like it has a thousand and one times before."

"Was it one of your exes?" I throw another bottle into the bag. "Coming back for more money?"

He grunts, then lets out a pitiful sound I can't even describe before a nearly inaudible whisper, "Not money. What this one took was priceless."

"Which number was this?" I inquire. "Gotta tell you, Wiley, your track record isn't exactly stellar. Maybe you ought to skip the vows and just get laid once in a while. Take a page from Reece and Roger's handbook." I add the last bottle to the bag and carry it to the recycling bin, opening it to see it's half full of various liquor bottles. "What the hell, Wiley? Your liver needs its own detox regimen from the looks of this. When's the last time you emptied this thing? And don't bullshit me."

"Last week," he grumbles, then raises both hands in the air as if defending his imbibing. "I binged, okay? Sometimes I get triggered. It's the only way I can sleep."

His coffee cup is now empty so I start another for him. Intrigued by his half-assed admission, I prod further. "Triggered by what?"

He stares at his folded hands in front of him, though he looks to be a million miles away. His voice is wistful as he speaks, maybe for the first time out loud to someone other than himself. "Don't get me wrong, Tanner. I am so damned happy for you. I gave up looking for my own Liberty. Amy and I were so fucking young and not ready. We had a plan, an agreement. We'd give him up for open adoption, in the hopeful event that someday he'd want to meet us. I held him once right after he was born. There is no feeling in the world like it, to see something you know is a part of you, that you created, so tiny, so vulnerable. You want to give them everything, but you know you're not capable, so you hand them over to people who can, and hope they take good care of them."

My eyebrows must meet my hairline in shock. Wiley has always said ex-wives were expensive enough, kids would break the bankroll. "You've got a kid?"

"Somewhere out there. Not a clue where."

"If it was an open adoption, you should have access to the

records, Wiley."

His folded hands separate and clench into fists. His face reddens and his jaw tics. "Ten hours," he grinds through a clenched jaw. "Ten hours is all it took for me to realize I was making a mistake. We could have made it work. It would have been hard at first, but not impossible. People do it all the time.

"I showed up at NMC in Sahuarita, middle of the night, to try and change her mind. Found out she'd already done that on her own. She'd packed up and took my kid with her. The night nurse told me she and *daddy* went home earlier that evening."

My eye twitches as I stare at him in disbelief, my stomach curdling with this morning's breakfast. Removing the full cup from the Keurig, I set it in front of him, because, well – I need to sober him up for the rest of the story. "She stole your kid?"

His eyes flash with a heated glare, tears rimming the edges. "She stole my kid. I went to jail that night for destruction of public and private property, reckless behavior, and assault." He rolls his eyes. "Not the nurse. I would never punch a woman. It was a security guard."

He pauses to take a sip of his coffee. "I got out three days later because my old man thought I should sit and stew for a while. It was enough time for Amy and whoever my replacement was to get out of town and disappear. Got a letter a week later telling me how sorry she was, but it was," he uses air quotes and snarls, "*for the best.* Her first love had shown up and she wanted a life with him. Promised that my son would be well cared for. Told me to not look for her because her name was already changed and I'd never find her. No return address. The hospital wouldn't tell me shit because I'd already signed adoption papers." He shoots me a wry look. "I wasn't in real good standing after having torn up the place, either.

"I gave up after a few months and went back to college, angry and broken. Eventually ended up finding a doctor down in Yuma willing to do a vasectomy on a 21-year-old kid. I swore I'd never go through that again. I wanted the kid I was supposed to have." He lets out a bitter laugh. "The doc botched the vasectomy; irreversible. Two of my exes eventually decided motherhood was more important than me. Still wanted the alimony though, so they didn't remarry. The last one," he snorts a self-deprecating chuckle, "just plain didn't like me."

Ah, his trigger is making sense now. His conversation with Libby. That's why my eye twitched.

"That's a helluva story, Wiley." I dip my chin and look him in the eyes. "Liberty told you I don't want kids, didn't she?"

"Yeah, she did." He nods slowly and his forehead creases. "She took it pretty hard. Don't be a dumbass. You are not your old man, Tanner. I was an idiot for what I did. I take responsibility for my decisions, but I let my pain dictate those. I try to find solace in the thought there is a productive member of society out there with my DNA, whether I got to raise him or not." Tongue in cheek, he adds, "A little like those college sperm donors. I think my ex-wives were always afraid he'd show up at the door someday."

"Is that what you're hoping for?"

He shrugs. "I am. As well as his mother." He closes his eyes and shakes his head as he acquiesces, "Amethyst Tanner was not a woman you ever get over."

Yeah, that breakfast that was curdling in my stomach? It's now in my esophagus about to make a reappearance in a very unpleasant way. I gulp hard and feel the burn as my stomach edges on revolting. *They were both named after gemstones.* My voice is shaky as I stare at him. "What the fuck did you just say?"

"That I never got over . . ."

"No," I choke through a scattered breath, indicating I'm on the verge of losing that breakfast. "Her name."

"Amethyst Tanner?"

Knowing I won't be able to grab the trash can from under his sink fast enough, I lean over the sink – garbage disposal side – and gag as the pancakes Liberty fixed us make their second appearance.

"Jesus, Tanner! Don't take it personally. It's not like I held it against you, it's just a name!" Wiley holds a backwards hand to his mouth, ready to join me in a retching contest. "You okay?"

I flip the switch on the disposal, snatch the sprayer from its holder and rinse the sink. He can bleach it later. As I scoop water into my hand from under the faucet to rinse my mouth out, visions flash through my mind; all those asshole's dominant features, yet none of them passed on to me. Black hair, dark eyes, the smarmy mustache. I have no recollection of height, but when you're only twelve and a late bloomer, a monster is huge no matter their size. Records! They'll have records from his imprisonment.

I've never had reason to question it. His name is on my fucking birth certificate! Lorenzo Monterrey. It's on the copy we collected from the county courthouse in *Sahuarita* after the original was collected by the authorities and never returned – just like everything else.

Leaning on the edge of the sink, breaths flowing through my mouth so I don't smell what I've just left in it and spark another round of heaving, I stare at Wiley, intensely studying his features for the first time. Hair the color of mine with some gray scattered throughout, light brown eyes, sharp jaw, tall. "When was your kid born?"

"August 10th, 1994," he says softly. "The best and worst day of my life. I spend it alone every year. Just me, a single cupcake, and the Polaroid I have of me holding him. His birthday is coming up soon. He'll be 30 this year."

"Yeah, he will," I murmur before pushing off from the stability of the counter, desperate to find some fresh air, the ability to take a deep breath. "I gotta go."

Running for the door, ignoring Wiley calling after me, my only thoughts at the current time being, *now I hate my mother too* and holy shit! I think Wiley Bergman, of all people, is my father. I want to scream, cry, and fist the air in victory all at once. She lied to me, I didn't have to grow up in that hell hole, and that fucker's blood isn't running through my veins.

I make my way down three flights of stairs, two at a time, and rush out the front door in a dead run across the parking lot. No phone, no water bottle, and no car keys. Stupid, I know. It's already 95 degrees, forecast of 118 today.

The firehouse. It's only three miles away. Reece and Roger won't ask questions – maybe. I know their captain. I'm a public servant, officially allowed on the grounds. They'll let me hide . . . for a little while. Hopefully long enough to strangle this urge to murder people who are already dead, deal with the demons that have resurfaced, and exorcise the new ones that have weaved their way into my life.

Did Aunt Ruby know? She told me she and my mom were estranged for years; ever since college. It made sense as I had no recollection of her other than stories mom told me when the asshole wasn't around and seen pictures she had shown me; the same ones Ruby had. *The Tanner gem girls*. Amethyst and Ruby.

Halfway to the firehouse I stop in my tracks. What the hell am I doing? My whole world is sitting in my condo waiting for me to come home and I'm running away? Old habits die hard. I've been running for eighteen years because I had nowhere to land. I do now though. I'm going home. To Liberty.

Once back inside my building, I head for the stairwell and take a seat on the bottom concrete step. I'm soaked with sweat, breathing hard, and need a minute. I need a gallon of water too, but it can wait. I drop my elbows onto my thighs and let my head bow low. Wiley Bergman. Crude but funny, always willing to lend a hand – he stood in a dumpster searching for a childhood memory for me, for crying out loud – helluva portfolio manager, lousy rhythm keeper unless of course he's farting the alphabet, but a good friend. And now? Quite possibly my dad.

Admittedly, I would take Wiley Bergman any given day over that asshole who raised me. Is that why he seemed to hate me so much? How he could be cruel without guilt? Because I wasn't his?

How is Wiley going to take it when he finds out not only am I his son, but the woman he never got over has been dead for nearly two decades? Murdered by the man who played *daddy* the night Wiley went back to talk my mother into keeping me.

The way he talked, the look on his face, the pain in his eyes. The birthday he spends alone every year, with a cupcake and a picture of the one and only time he ever got to hold his son – the one he never got to know – is me.

I'm thrilled. I'm not a product of my old man! I'm the result of the love of Liberty Collins. But how do I tell Wiley?

Chapter 34

Liberty

"Hey, Wiley," I greet the wet-haired, freshly showered, somber looking man as he opens the door. "Is Lucas still here? He didn't take his phone and I can't reach him. He's been gone for quite a while and I wanted to make sure everything was okay."

He scratches the back of his head and scrunches his nose. "He didn't go home?"

"No, how long ago did he leave?"

He glances at the clock on the wall. "About an hour ago. He, uh," he scrunches his nose again, "got sick to his stomach and ran outta here like his ass. . . " he winces, "sorry, *butt* was on fire."

"He got sick? From what?"

He lifts one shoulder in a haphazard shrug but looks unsure. "I thought maybe he ate something for breakfast that didn't settle well."

"I ate the same thing he did!" I snap harshly as if personally insulted, though unwarranted as he doesn't know I cooked it. "It didn't occur to you to make sure he got home okay?"

He stares at me for a moment, then grimaces as the air deflates from his lungs and his shoulders sag. "I'm a shit friend, ain't I?"

"I wouldn't hand you a trophy, Wiley." I narrow my eyes. "You're lucky I'm not Mallory. She'd have you singing soprano by now. I need to find Lucas."

"Hang on," he says, turning away from his door. "Let me grab my keys and phone. We'll go together." He locks the door behind him and points toward the stairwell. "Let's take the stairs just to be sure. We know he ain't on the elevator."

Before opening the door to the stairwell, he stops short with his hand on the handle. "Liberty, why do you call him Lucas?"

"That was his name. He'll always be Lucas to me. They changed it after . . ." I hesitate at the horrific memory, ". . . that night. I thought you knew the story."

"I got the short version, not the details. Who raised him after that?"

"His aunt and uncle in California. Why do you ask?"

"When is his birthday?"

"August 10th. It's his 30th this year. Don't say anything but I'd like to throw him a surprise party. I hope you'll join us."

Wiley's face turns white as a sheet as he leans on the door for support. A sickly groan leaves his throat as he places a hand over his mouth and gulps hard. "His dad killed his mom," he whispers. I only nod. "What was her name, Liberty?"

I think on it for a moment, my brows lifting and lowering. "I always called her Mrs. M. Let me think . . ."

"Amy?" he sputters weakly before I can respond.

"Yeah," I reply, surprised he would know this, or be a good guesser. "That's what my mom called her. But we were taught to address the adults by their . . ."

"Oh God," he groans as if he's been punched in the solar plexus and drops to his knees. "No," he cries into his hands, body crumpling forward, shoulders trembling as he rocks his body back and forth. "No, no. God no."

I'm unsure how to help him. His cries sound as if they're coming from a wounded animal. As professionals we're taught to approach with caution; no sudden movements, don't touch unless it seems welcome. Do not leave yourself vulnerable to harm in an unstable situation. I don't know him well, and he's not a small person.

A sudden burst of anger and frustration leaves him as he looks up at the ceiling, his fists clenched in rage, and wails, "Why?! Damnit, Amy! We could have made it work!"

The door to the stairwell flies open and Lucas stands on the other side, out of breath and sweaty, as if having run from the bottom floor. "What the hell?"

Wiley looks at up at him with pleading, red-rimmed eyes from his crouched position before falling to his backside against the frame of the door. "I tried, Tanner. I swear to God, I tried."

Lucas drops to his knees next to Wiley and places an arm around his shoulder. "I know, Wiley. She made her choices."

"I would have come and gotten you if I'd known where you were," Wiley sobs next to him. "I would have moved mountains."

"I know you would have," Lucas says softly as he pulls a broken, sobbing Wiley against his chest. "I know you would have. He was a sneaky asshole."

"He killed her, Tanner," Wiley sobs against his chest. "He killed my Amy. I would have never hurt either one of you. I loved you both so damn much. From the minute I held you, I was never the same, and I've never felt that way again."

I am totally befuddled by the scene before me. Wiley's Amy? He held Lucas?

Lucas' tear-filled eyes lift to meet mine. So much pain behind the amber flecked with green. "What can I do?" I whisper so low, it's nearly inaudible.

He extends his free arm to invite me in, so I drop to my knees on the cold concrete floor next to him, relishing the tight hold he pulls me into and the kiss to my forehead. "Go crazy with me, Liberty."

Half an hour later, we're all in Lucas' condo, seated on the sofa with coffees in front of us, though barely touched. I had offered to go home, leave them to some private conversation, but both refused and Lucas hasn't let me get far enough away to do more than pee. And even then, I'm not sure he didn't stand outside the door. The most I've gathered so far is it would seem Wiley is Lucas' father. It's not my place to make a judgment call, but if memory serves me right, I'd call it a personal win. At least these two like each other.

"We'll get a DNA test to confirm, Tanner," Wiley chuckles ruefully, his elbows on his knees as he drops his head and shakes it. "I've got no doubts, but I don't ever want you to question it."

"I think it would give us both solid peace of mind," Lucas

agrees, "but I'm counting on 100% match."

"Out of curiosity," Wiley squints as he presents his question, "do you have a strawberry colored birthmark in the shape of a heart on your right hip?"

Lucas smiles knowingly and nods. "100% match, Wiley."

My phone pings with a text from Mallory.

"*Heads up, roomie. You've got company. Mommy and Tom are here. Pretty sure she's figured out you're banging your best friend. Your bed was made and three Amazon deliveries were sitting on it. She's too busy grilling me after you didn't take her call. Rescue 911 or I'm giving them his address and letting her catch you naked.*"

Me: *What the hell are they doing in town?*

Mal: *Shall I ask? Quoting you, of course.*

Me: *I'm kind of in the middle of something.*

Mal: *Just swallow and call your mother. Small wonder you weren't picking up.*

Me: *I wouldn't be texting in the middle of oral sex either, you idiot!*

Mal: *So vanilla. Hurry up, I want to get back to Ava's book.*

Me: *I hate you sometimes.*

Mal: *Porn video will be set up and ready to play when you get back. This one teaches multitasking. 'How to talk with your mouth full'.*

Me: *I'll be sure to tell Reece you've honed your skills. Tell mom I'll call in a bit.*

There! That ought to shut her up for a while. What is my mother doing here? We just talked yesterday. She said soon, not tomorrow! Admittedly, she was excited to see Lucas, but they've never popped in unannounced.

"You okay?" I turn away from the screen to see Lucas watching me, his brows pinched.

My bottom lip finds its way between my teeth as I nod. "Mom and Tom are in town. She said they were going to wait, didn't she?"

He shrugs. "Maybe she's anxious to see me. It's been a long time."

"Do your folks live close, Liberty?" Wiley inquires. There's a hint of hopefulness in his eyes, maybe in his voice, that he can glean a little insight into Amy's life after they parted. "Do you get to see them often?"

"My dad passed sixteen years ago," I explain. "Mom remarried. They live in North Carolina. He's a really nice guy. She's happy."

His voice is sympathetic and sincere as he dips his chin. "I'm sorry you lost your dad."

Lucas takes my hand in his and squeezes gently, his smile lights his eyes with the memories. "Libby's dad was great. Used to fix my bike when it broke, pulled my first tooth, bought us our bubblegum . . ." He stops when he realizes what he's said may seem insensitive. He reaches over me on the sofa and squeezes Wiley's shoulder. "It's okay, Wiley. Not everything sucked. Libby's dad made things as good as he could."

"I'm sorry I missed it, Tanner." He sniffs and reaches for his coffee, changing his mind before he picks it up. "I'd give anything to get those years back."

"Eh," Lucas' voice lightens as he shrugs one shoulder. "If you're patient, you can get a second chance with a third generation. I'd be willing to share teaching the art of throwing a baseball or playing with Barbies." He turns to me and lifts my chin with two fingers. "I believe we've got two years yet, don't we? I'd kinda like a little time with you to myself."

My nose tingles and my eyes begin to burn, preparing for the tears I don't need to shed in the rain. "You mean it?"

His dimpled smile melts my heart. It's every dream, every

wish, every fantasy I've never let go of, yet never thought would come true being gifted me in one statement. "Only with you. Only ever with you, Libby. The way it was supposed to be." He slides his fingers into my hair, brushing his nose against mine, leaving a chaste kiss on my lips – apparently more respectfully conscientious of Wiley's presence than I am – before moving his mouth close to my ear and whispering, "The extra year will let us *multitask* in the meantime."

I jerk back so fast, I nearly fall into Wiley. "You weren't supposed to see that!"

He chuckles and winks. "Tell Mallory to send the link. We can watch together."

Wiley clears his throat behind me, the unsurety in his eyes as he turns to Lucas. "You'd actually let me be a part of my grandkids' lives?"

"Wouldn't have it any other way, Wiley." He holds up a finger and shoots him a warning glare. "Unless I catch you teaching them how to fart the alphabet. Think about it, long and hard."

My eyes flit back and forth between the two of them. "How to what?!"

Wiley rolls his eyes, his mouth curved upward on one side, much like Lucas' does. "It was a one-time thing, Tanner. No more gas station burritos. I promise."

Chapter 35

Lucas

Mrs. C – damnit! – Mrs. M arrives an hour after one rather inquisitive and insistent, yet loving phone call between her and Liberty. I receive a hug reminiscent of ones I've missed for years – AKA squeeze the stuffing out of me – this one joined by tears in her eyes and an unexpected sob as she clings. Introductions are eventually made, sans the intricate details, starting with Tom Mason and me, ending with Wiley and . . .

"Wiley Bergman?" Mrs. M gasps, stopping short of taking Wiley's hand in hers to shake upon their introduction. She studies the face of the man before her, slides her gaze to me then back to him. "Impossible," she whispers, shaking her head slowly. "From Sahuarita?"

Wiley nods. "Originally, yes."

Her voice is shaky as she inquires, "How do you two know each other?"

As Wiley says, "We both live in the building," I drawl, "Well . . ."

"Mom," Libby says slowly. "What's going on?"

Mrs. Mason rushes to her purse on the table by the door and retrieves a small manilla envelope from inside. She holds it to her chest with trembling hands. "Lucas, can I see you for a minute, privately?"

I want to indulge her. She had never been anything but kind and loving to me, but the words leave my mouth before I can stop them. "Is what's in that envelope going to tell me Wiley is my real father?"

"You know?!" she pitches high as Tom holds her steady on her feet.

"Just figured it out a couple hours ago, Mrs. M."

"Mom!" Liberty scolds as she slips her arm in mine. "How could you have withheld this from him? You knew what his home life was like!"

"Libby," I mutter softly. "Let her explain."

"Liberty," she starts and holds out the envelope for me to take. "This is why we're here today. I received this a month after that night. Amy hired an attorney to deliver it to us if anything happened to her. I had no way to get this to Lucas. He was a child. No one would tell me where they had taken him. Your dad and I pleaded with the authorities, but they were unmovable. They told us it would put Lucas in danger because of Lorenzo's criminal activity and connections. They reassured us he had been moved out of the state and would be well taken care of and safe but they would tell us nothing . . ."

"Wait a minute," Wiley interrupts, holds up a hand, his fingers curling into a white-knuckled fist. "Lorenzo? Lorenzo Monterrey?" He stares at me, his jaw so tight it tics as his face fills with mortification. "That's who raised you?"

I nod reluctantly as Liberty squeezes my bicep gently. Wiley pulls me away from her and wraps me in a hug so tight it nearly drains the air from my lungs. "There aren't enough apologies in the world, Tanner." His breath is shuddered as his voice cracks. "How in the hell did you turn out the way you did?"

I relish the first hug from my real father and whisper the truth, "It's not his blood running through my veins, Wiley."

"There are letters in there for both of you," Mrs. M states, then turns to her husband and shrugs. "I guess we don't have to hunt Mr. Bergman down after all."

He slides his arm around her shoulder and kisses her forehead. "What have I always told you, sweetheart?"

"If it's meant to be, it'll be," she starts, and they finish together in unison, "but persistence and stubbornness will win you the prize every time."

She giggles as he tips her chin up, places a kiss on her mouth, and says, "It worked for me."

Mrs. M looks happy. That alone earns a lot of respect for Tom Mason. Mr. C was an icon to me, my very own hero. It would take a helluva guy to fill his shoes. And if he can make Libby's mom smile like that, he must be one of the good ones.

"Who was Lorenzo to you, Wiley?" I ask him, pulling two sealed, letter size envelopes from the manila one Mrs. M handed me. Lorenzo hasn't meant shit to me for years, but Wiley's reaction and the shock and hatred in his eyes has my curiosity piqued.

He nearly spits in disgust as he answers, "My stepbrother."

"Mr. Bergman," Mrs. M approaches with caution, and compassion. "You might want to read Amy's letter. I don't know what's in it. It wasn't my place to open it. She left me one of my own. Maybe if we'd known the truth, we could have helped, but she never once made us question Lucas' parentage. We also never saw evidence of physical abuse on Lucas or Amy."

I nod in agreement. "He was an asshole, but his abuse was in the form of emotional and mental abuse."

Mrs. M shoots me a look of sympathy and regret before turning back to Wiley. "My instructions were to place Lucas with you if anything happened to her. But we had no access to Lucas, no way to find him, and they told us we'd put him in danger if we tried. They said Lorenzo had ties with a cartel and we'd be making Lucas a target. His safety was our priority. He was like a son to us, and we had to believe what they said and let him go."

"Mom," Libby cries. "Why didn't you tell me?"

"Liberty, you were a child. It broke your dad's heart to watch you cry night after night. He couldn't get you back on a bicycle, couldn't even get you to chew gum. You refused to make new friends. You wouldn't swim. He tried everything in his power to get you over it. The first time he made you laugh after that night, he cried. He belly flopped in the pool? Remember?"

Libby's sniffles break with a small sob. "His skin was so red."

Mrs. M nods somberly. "And his tears were hidden by the pool water."

"Oh God," Libby sobs as I take her in my arms. "Now I know where I get it."

"Pretty cool trait to inherit," I whisper against her hair then tip her chin up. "He would be so damn proud of you, Libby."

"He would be proud of both of you," Mrs. M adds softly. "I know I sure am."

The Letters

My dear Lucas,

I only wish I could have given you the life you deserved. We had so many hopes and dreams for you. By we, I mean your father and I. What I don't mean is Lorenzo Monterrey. Your real father is a man named Wiley Bergman. He lives in Sahuarita. He is a good man, Lucas. We loved each other very much. He can explain everything when you find him.

The only reason you would be receiving this letter is if something happened to me. Liberty's mom and dad will know what to do. You trust them. Do what they tell you. They'll help you find Wiley.

I would have run away with you years ago if I could have, but Lorenzo would have found us and things would have been so much worse.

Sometimes, the things we do for love hurt the most, but are for the best. Know that I love you to the moon and back and will forever be watching over you from the stars above.

Mom

****

My darling Wiley,

I don't have to wonder if you hate me. Please know everything I did, I did for you. Lorenzo came to the hospital with a copy of your transcripts from school to prove he had access, and promised to ruin you if I crossed him. He also brought along your stepsister who threatened to cry rape if I didn't do as told. They had access to your DNA at the house, Wiley, and I knew your dad would believe them. That's years in prison!!! A fate worse than death. I hated Lorenzo but I knew he would never physically harm our son. He simply wanted what was yours. He always did.

The only reason you would be receiving this letter is because I am dead. Our son's name is Lucas Monterrey. If he's still underage, people will be bringing him to you. If he's grown, please find him, Wiley. Let him know his real father is a good man, and not the devil I was forced to marry.

I never stopped loving you. I never found a moment's pleasure with Lorenzo. Never. And I can promise you, my dying thought was Wiley E. Bergman; the only man I ever truly loved.

Begging your forgiveness,

Amy

Wiley studies the letter in his trembling hand, swiping his face with his free one. I'm a little surprised he opened it here; thinking he might want to take it home with him and peruse the words one by one in private.

Apparently mine was intended for me years ago, close to the time she died. I fold the page and place it back in the envelope, unsure how I feel about the words she'd written. Nowhere amongst them did I read 'I'm sorry' nor 'forgive me'. The whole thing sounded like instructions and excuses. Rather cold, actually.

Aunt Ruby's words invade my thoughts out of the blue:

"No shame in apologizing, unless of course you feel it's beneath you." She would pair them with an arched brow and a dipped chin to stress her point; one which you'd have to be a blithering idiot to miss. Yeah, I'll call her sometime this week.

Wiley folds his letter as well and tucks it into the envelope. "I think I'll head back downstairs and leave you folks to visit." He nods at Liberty's parents. "Lauren, Tom, it was nice to meet you. Thank you for this." He takes a long, slow breath in and rolls his neck. "Now, tell me where I can find Lorenzo."

"They got to him in prison before he could testify." My voice is as flat as the emotions I feel. "He's dead."

"He's lucky," Wiley growls as he opens the door. "And so is

my old man."

"Wiley!" I rush out the door after him to see him entering the stairwell. "Wait!" He stops and turns, a puzzled look on his face. I grasp his shoulder and squeeze, convinced he's headed down the same rabbit hole I pulled him out of this morning. "Alcohol is not the solution. You binged last night. I am not going to let you spend the day alone at the bottom of a bottle."

His face sours as if I've told him he can't place any bets all football season. "Alcohol?! What are you talking about? I've got twenty nine birthday presents to buy over the next two weeks and thirty candles to put on a whole cake that I don't have to eat by myself. What's your favorite flavor, son?" A smile lights his eyes that brim with tears. "Best fucking year of my life."

He pulls me into a hug and squeezes before patting me on the back a few times; like a dad would, I suppose.

Son. I have never been called son. Who knew one word could carry such impact? It feels good. It feels really, really good.

"Mine too," I tell him, matching his grin. "Dad's choice. I'll eat whatever you pick out. Plan on joining us for dinner tonight. I'll text you the time. Pretty sure Libby will invite Mallory to join us."

He stares for a moment before he scrunches his nose. "She's mean!"

Pinching the bridge of my nose, I sigh. "She's Libby's best friend."

"So she really isn't mean?"

"She's Libby's best friend," I repeat slowly.

He chuckles softly. "You're going to make a damn good husband. If you can tolerate her, so can I." He winces and rubs his chin as if reconsidering that statement. "Might want to keep the forks away from her, and seat me at the other end of the table though." He turns to head downstairs. "Tanner?"

"Yeah?"

He keeps his back to me as he releases a wistful sigh and shakes his head. "We've got a lot of catching up to do."

"We do," I confirm, though a part of me fears he wants history on a woman I can't give him. I barely remember her. "But we've got a lot of living to do as well, Wiley. Football season starts soon. Can't break our routine."

He glances back over his shoulder and grins cockily. "No more betting for me. I've got grandkids to get ready for. Gonna spoil the shit out of them. See you at dinner."

Chapter 36

Liberty

"You can still stay at our place with me, Mrs. M," Mallory offers from her seat at the restaurant across from my mom. "This way I can enjoy your famous waffles in the morning and Libs can. . ." she smirks and winks at me, ". . .enjoy whatever Lucas serves her. She raves about his breakfast *sausage*."

I plan her demise in my head. I have access to scalpels. Gurneys that I can wheel down to the morgue. I can switch out toe tags and no one will be the wiser.

She must read my mind, as she bats her long lashes my way and singsongs, "Just *honing my skills* for helping out a friend." Aha! Payback for my text about Reece.

Mom flashes a stern look my way – the obligatory parental show of disapproval – but then Tom places a loving hand over her shoulder and plants a soft kiss on her temple, and whispers something in her ear. She softens, a playful smile blooming that she cannot hide, then cuts off another bite of her steak. "I think a hotel room sounds wonderful."

"What about my waffles!?" Mallory shrieks so loud she turns heads in the restaurant. "It's my favorite part of your visits!"

I've never seen my mother smirk, until today. Damn! She's good at it too. She looks to my bestie, a gleam of satisfaction in her eyes. "I'm sorry, Mallory. I've developed a sudden appetite for *sausage* myself. Maybe next time."

'*A cold day in hell*' would have been my answer had anyone asked if or when I thought my bestie could be stunned silent. Yet here we are. Satan is wearing a coat and his minions are shivering. Mallory's jaw hangs agape as she stares at my mother, lost for words. Can't say I'm not a bit shellshocked myself. My mom is naughty!

Wiley and Lucas snort-laugh in unison before Wiley drops his forehead onto the heel of his palm and murmurs, "I'll bet Thanksgiving dinners are a blast."

We arrive back to Lucas' condo after making arrangements for tomorrow with mom and Tom, who are staying at a hotel, and bidding farewell to a disgruntled Mal and a rather calm and happy Wiley. Quite the contrast from this afternoon.

I cannot imagine the thoughts flowing through Lucas' mind. The emotions stirred by the plethora of information shoved at him today. *Lorenzo wasn't, Wiley is, the secrets his mother withheld.* He'd been quiet on the drive home, tension obvious in the way he gripped the steering wheel, the tic in his jaw, the arterial protrusion in the side of his neck. I left him to process his thoughts. He hid the turmoil well at dinner, while we all sat together, or maybe distracted him enough. I knew better though. I could feel the undercurrent of stress in the way he squeezed my hand under the table, the way his thigh bounced under my touch. He was ready to crawl out of his skin. He either needs a ten mile run or . . .

He throws the deadbolt on the door, takes the clutch from my hand and tosses it on the table in the foyer, and leads me to the bedroom without a word. Once inside, he walks me backward toward the bed, eyes never leaving mine as he slowly lowers the zipper and peels the straps of my sundress off my shoulders. I'm braless; the ruched material having been enough to hide the now stiff nipples begging to be teased. His eyes don't follow the material as it falls, but his hands do, caressing the bare skin as it's slowly revealed to the cool air.

"You're the only one who could ever make it go away, Liberty." He moves a hand to my hair, tugging my head back to give him access to my throat. His other hand splays across my lower back, drawing me closer to feel his need, and he murmurs against my skin as he peels my thong away, "My two favorite colors, your calming voice, the goodnight waves from your bedroom window, your promise of pink. With me or not, you have always been my light in the dark, my port in the storm."

His patience snaps as he releases me long enough to yank his shirt over his head and throw it behind him. As he does, my fingers fumble with his belt to release the tab from its confines, pop the button on his jeans, and slide the zipper down. He wastes no time in sliding them off his hips, letting them fall to the floor and stepping out of them and his shoes simultaneously. I don't think I've ever seen him this tight, this hard, this . . . ready.

His tug on my hair is harsh this time, as is his kiss. The bruising pressure and drag on my bottom lip between his teeth stings, but he's quick to soothe it with his tongue. He's struggling for composure – the usual calm and collected man ready to explode – and I don't hesitate to relinquish all control to him. Lucas would never hurt me. This is his battle tonight; a need to purge the pain and anger he's held back for so long, and the new one he's been forced to deal with. The gentility in his touch and soft caresses disappear as he lifts me off my feet and virtually tosses me on the bed, following on his hands and knees.

The agony etched in his eyes and the crease in his brow breaks my heart as he nearly pleads, "Make it go away, Libby."

My hands wrap around the nape of his neck, my legs around his hips, and I voice exactly what he needs to hear, "Take whatever you need."

His hands slide under my butt cheeks, lifting me for the perfect angle and the perfect view. He thrusts hard, eyes fixed on our joined bodies, as if hypnotized. He's slow on the retreats, fast and hard on the thrusts, groaning each time he buries himself so deep I nearly scream. I watch him watching us; so concentrated on the connection. Soon his movements become erratic and his breathing so hard, I know he's close. He throws his head back, his eyes squeeze closed, his jaw locked with the last few thrusts, then holds himself deep inside as he meets his release.

"*Fuck*," he growls so low it sends vibrations to a very stimulated and sensitive part of me that, unfortunately, came close but didn't actually come. There's a fine line between pain and pleasure. I was here for his pain, not my pleasure.

He drops down on top of me, panting, burdening his weight on his elbows, and buries his face in the crook of my neck. "Libby," he breathes on a pained whisper. "I'm sorry."

"For what?"

He lifts his head and brushes a wayward strand of hair away from my face. "You didn't get to come."

Planting a soft kiss on his mouth and running a finger through his beard, I whisper, "No, I got to go."

"What?"

"Crazy." I smile softly. "With you. Did it work?"

His mouth lands on mine before I have time to see it coming . . . or lick my lips. "Pink," he whispers as it ends. "I always knew it had a flavor. And somewhere deep down inside, I knew you wouldn't break that promise. I love you so damn much."

The next morning, my mom and Tom join us for breakfast at a diner Lucas recommended. It's Monday morning; the business world back in full swing with bumper-to-bumper traffic. Bike couriers, briefcases, coffees to go, and constant time-checks via phone or watches as people hurriedly make their way down the sidewalk. The tenderness between my legs is preventing me from rushing anywhere. Ever the gentleman, Lucas was determined to make up for my lost orgasm by providing three in its place.

Mom and Tom are seated by the time we arrive, coffees in front of them, and what looks to be a shoebox on the table.

"You've been shopping already?" I tease my mom as we take a seat in the booth across from them.

The server appears and turns our coffee cups upright and starts to pour. "You want some time to look at the menus?" Her eyes dance with delight when she notices my breakfast companion. "Tanner!" She places her free hand on his shoulder and squeezes. She's pretty, blonde, young, probably mid-twenties. Her voice is teasing as she flirts openly, "You ready to get sweaty with me again?"

We all turn to Lucas as our eyebrows rise to the height of our hairlines. He narrows his eyes at our server and nearly growls, "Rephrase that, Ruthie, or you have just lost your bag stabilizer." He aims his gaze at me. "Roger's little sister. I help her with kickboxing at the gym." He looks back to the server. "Ruthie, meet the love of my life, Liberty Collins, and her parents, Lauren and Tom Mason. You may apologize in 5-4-3-2 . . ."

The *oh shit* expression she portrays with the puckered O shape of her mouth, the deep flush of her cheeks, and the wide eyes is comical. "It was just a joke!"

"One," Lucas deadpans.

"I'm sorry!" she shrieks, then tucks her chin to her chest. "I-I'll be back when you're ready to order." If the poor girl had a tail, it would be tucked in tightly as she scoots away from the table, coffee pot in hand, toward the kitchen.

Mom chuckles. "Never a dull moment with you two." She reaches for the box on the table. "No, I didn't go shopping. I brought these from North Carolina. I've had them in storage for a very long time. I thought Lucas might want them. You too, Liberty. There are a lot of the two of you together, and a few of Amy that I thought Lucas might want to have." She shrugs and adds, "Maybe even Wiley now that . . ."

"What are they?" Lucas bristles as his eyes move from the box to my mother. He knows what is in that box. History. I place my hand on his thigh under the table, but before I can squeeze, he intertwines our fingers and we squeeze together.

"Pictures from over the years that we lived next door to each other." Mom inches the box our way slowly. "There's a lot of you and Liberty, some of you and your mom."

"Any of Lorenzo?" Lucas snaps harshly, then sighs. "Sorry."

"No," Mom answers confidently. "I've double and triple checked. He was never one much for joining us. I would have burned them if there were."

Lucas stares at the box before moving it closer to me. "I only want the ones of Libby and me." He doesn't look up but adds, "I can check with Wiley and see if he wants any of her." He squeezes my hand tighter under the table then flashes me a smile. "The most important one I already had anyway. Been holding on to it for fourteen years."

Two fat tears fall from my eyes and Lucas reaches out with his free hand, palming my cheek to swipe one away with his thumb while he leans in to kiss the other. He whispers against my skin, "That, and a charm bracelet, a letter, and two pieces of bubblegum."

"Old souls with young hearts," Mom whispers wistfully as if reminiscing. "It's what your dad used to call the two of you."

Tom slides an arm over the back of the booth and gently drops it to her shoulder, offering comfort with the memory. This is why I love this man for her. They had both suffered loss of the worst kind, but there is no jealousy of ghosts. I've heard them speak fondly of their former spouses, followed by a hug for their current one, knowing how blessed they are to have each other. They really are the perfect pair.

When breakfast is over, Mom informs me they need to head for the airport to catch a plane back to North Carolina. My neck snaps as my head whirls toward her. "You're leaving so soon? You just got here!"

"Today is your last day off," she says, reminding me she is always aware of my schedule. "We needed to get the information to Lucas as soon as possible so he could find his father, but now that it's taken care of, we can head back and you can have your day to yourselves. We don't want to intrude. We'll be back soon, Liberty. How about October?" She raises a finger in the air and her eyes twinkle as she suggests, "Or, bring Lucas to the ocean."

I neglect to voice it's not my last day off. I put in for three more two days ago, bartering trade-offs with one physician and another NP – as soon as I found out Lucas was off until the end of this week. I have tons of banked vacation time as well – the honeymoon with an asshole that was never going to happen – and now I have better reasons to use it.

Lucas is quick to accept the invitation. "Sounds like a plan."

Chapter 37

Lucas

After saying goodbye to the Masons, Libby and I climb back into the Jeep and head north. It's a surprise for both her and the one other person who played a huge role in not only that night, but three years later when he handed me a little white box that he had kept safe, on the off chance he would ever see me again.

"Hey Tanner," Sylvie looks up and greets me with a smile when she notes my presence at the desk. She looks to Liberty and gasps. "Jeepers, creepers," she whispers in awe, "where did you get those eyes?"

"Sylvie!" I chastise with a scowl. The woman doesn't need a filter; she needs a muzzle. The art of diplomacy has escaped her once again. She still lets me know her daughter is available, just like the day I applied.

Libby giggles, then tugs on my arm to pull me down as she lifts up on her toes. "It's a song," she whispers in my ear. "Dad used to sing it to me. It's probably older than the two of us combined."

Ignoring Sylvie's inquiry, I make my own. "Is the Cap in?"

She continues to study Libby, as if fascinated and mutters, "In his office."

I tap lightly on the open door and wait for Sully to look up. He tips his chin when he sees it's me. "Tanner, what can I do for you?"

"Got somebody I want you to see." His eyebrows draw inward as I step inside the room and pull Liberty in behind me. He squints as he tilts his head.

Liberty lifts her hand in a timid wave. "Hi, Captain Sullivan."

His face splits in a grin the moment he recognizes her and a hearty laugh fills the room. He stands from his chair in a rush and rounds his desk, holding his arms out for a hug. "Liberty Collins. Who could forget those eyes." He embraces her in a fatherly hug, then takes her by the shoulders. He looks to me then back to her. "If I didn't believe in miracles before, I sure do now."

We spend an hour with the Cap, visiting and explaining how our reunion came to be. The discovery of my actual father leaves him speechless and dumbfounded, but happy as hell for me. Liberty thanks him profusely for delivering the box she left with him years ago. He doesn't ask, I don't elaborate. Somehow, I think he just knows it was a lifeline.

At six o'clock in the evening the all too familiar, obnoxious pounding on the door starts. No idea what delightful rhythm they're trying to follow, but as is the usual, they're failing miserably. Which can only mean one thing: Wiley is with them. This is either a visit for congratulations, feigned sympathy to piss Wiley off, or a *"Tanner has had enough sex and doesn't need anymore"* ploy to piss me off.

"What on earth is that?" Libby asks from under my arm where she sits on the sofa watching a movie with me, quite comfortably I might add.

"Don't make any noise and maybe they'll go away. This is my last night with you until we can work out our schedules. I'm not about to share."

"Did I forget to tell you?" She grins impishly. "I swapped out with other providers for the next three days until we both go back to work."

She yelps as I pin her to the sofa underneath me. "I get you to myself for three more days? You're not leaving?"

"Nope."

Nuzzling into her neck, nipping on the sweet spot that I've learned is her weakness, I mumble, "Then we're definitely not answering."

"Open the door, you prick!" Reece yells from the other side. "It's the least you can do. I came home to two cans of Raid, a premade tub of home remedy crab treatment, and a safe sex pamphlet from Mrs. Thompson outside my door; complete with condoms and a shaving kit that she offered to use on me!"

"What did you do?" Liberty whispers.

"He shouldn't have offered to be my proxy for sex with my woman. Paybacks are a bitch." I nip at the sweet spot once more and relish her moan. "Do I need a proxy, Libby?"

She whimpers and grinds against me. "God, no. You're perfect."

"Come on, Tanner!" he whines. "She's 73 years-old! I can't

go home. I know you're in there. I saw your Jeep in the lot. We brought pizza and beer."

I'm tempted to let them wait it out while I enjoy a round with Libby. She's wound up, I'm wound up. It won't take *that* long. Two simple pieces of fabric; easy on, easy off, easy in, easy out.

"I even brought wine for Liberty," he teases. "A little warmer upper. I'm not an animal, you know. I'm actually quite the gentlemen. If you'd read the book on my counter . . ."

And that's all it takes. I yank my shorts down just past my hips, slip her shorts to the side and slide home. "Lucas!" she screams my name; the only name she will ever scream, whisper, or call out in ecstasy again.

"You dumbass!" Roger growls. "You never know when to stop!"

"Oh God," Libby whimpers as I drive harder. "I think they heard me."

"I don't care what they hear, Libby," I breathe fast, continuing the momentum at the speed she loves. "I only care how you feel."

"*So – so good,*" she pants hard; the thought of anything other than pleasure gone as she crests toward the point of no return. "*Lucas, I'm – I'm going to . . . ahh.*"

She holds back her scream, but I let go of a long satisfied groan and a few unsavory swear words as I bury my face in her neck and let go. I hate that she held back at all, but we've got three more days together that I hadn't counted on. She'll be hoarse by day two, on voice rest by day three.

I tug my shorts back up in an effort not to spill any remnants onto the cushions and slide her shorts back in place before I help her to her feet.

She glances down at the sofa and grins. "All clear."

Grinning back at her, I take her cheeks in my palms. "It's leather. Easier to clean than Reece's crotch." The mortification that fills her eyes indicates I should probably put my friend back in the go-zone for Mallory. "It was a joke, baby. I might have given Reece's neighbors the impression he has a bit of a personal infestation."

She gasps, her nose wrinkling in disgust. "You didn't!"

I smirk and tip her chin up, planting a soft kiss on her mouth. "I don't get mad, Liberty. I get even."

She storms toward the bathroom, grumbling, "Men. You are such children." While Libby's in the bathroom, my phone on the coffee table pings with a text from Reece:

Wiley's making us wait in his apartment. He's lecturing us about respecting boundaries and won't let us start without you. What the hell happened when we were at work?! Come on, Tanner. The pizza is getting cold!!!

I send back one quick response:

We're done.

Fast footsteps in the hallway are heavy before knocks on the door sound. I open it slowly to see Reece holding three pizza boxes, Roger with a case of beer, and Wiley proudly displaying two bottles of wine. My grin is cocky as I drawl, "Yes, gentlemen. May I help you?"

Reece scowls as he holds up the boxes and shoves his way past me. "Now we gotta heat up the pizza."

"You should have called first," I tell him as Roger and Wiley follow him in.

"That's what I told him," Wiley says. "As well as to stop flirting with your girl."

Reece slams the pizza boxes down on the counter and rolls his eyes. "Yes, Wiley. You've been a vast table of knowledge and advice ever since you made us leave."

I shrug. "Dads are usually a good point of reference due to experience."

Wiley sets the wine on the counter and nods at me, a slight tip of his lips as he says, "Thank you, son. I appreciate that."

Reece and Roger both freeze – Roger with the beer still in his hands – and look to each other, then back at the two of us. Reece sputters a laugh and points back and forth between us. "Did you two adopt each other while we were gone?"

"Didn't have to," Wiley offers, his expression a mix of joy, sadness, loss, and determination as he looks at me. "We're the real thing."

"You sure are," Libby says softly from the hall entrance where she watches the exchange.

"No fuckin' way," Reece howls. "April Fool's is over. Knock it off."

"I can tell you where his birthmark is," Wiley says confidently. "And I ain't seen him naked since the day he was born."

Pinching the bridge of my nose, I groan, "TMI, Wiley."

"I got the same one," he tells me. "Wanna see it?"

"Hell no!"

Roger chuckles, setting the beer on the counter. He tears open the packaging and removes four beers. "Pour Liberty a glass of wine," he orders Reece and waits for him to hand her the glass before passing the rest of us our beers. We pop the tops together and wait for his lead. "Odd as it may sound," he glances to me as he holds up his can and shoots me a puzzled but knowing look, "I'd say discovering our resident idiot is your real father is a win-win. Cheers."

Wiley raises his beer to his mouth and begins to drink before the entirety of that statement sinks in. He spews beer from his mouth that he tries to catch with his hand but fails miserably. "You asshole! I take issue with that."

The only ones laughing are Liberty, Roger and me, as Reece seems deep in thought, studying what could very well be dead air.

"How long have you known about this?"

"Yesterday morning," I reply.

"Yesterday!" he shrieks, then sets his beer down hard on the counter, and pulls his phone from his pocket. "So you've been sitting on this for two days?"

"It's not exactly news you text, Reece," I explain. "We were waiting until your shifts were done."

He punches a button on his phone and walks down the hall to my bedroom, slamming the door behind him. A one-sided, heated conversation starts on the other side of the barrier that has us exchanging confused glances. Everyone but Roger, that is, who simply drops his chin to his chest and shakes his head. "He is so pussy whipped. Can't wait to see how he fucks this up."

"What am I missing?"

"Mallory brought him lunch today at the firehouse." He chuckles. "Seems his little kitten may have neglected to share some news. Did she know?"

In unison, Wiley and I blow low whistles as we study the ceiling – AKA pleading the Fifth – while Libby sets the pizza boxes in the oven on warm, pretending she didn't hear the question.

The door to my bedroom bursts open as Reece is finishing his phone call with an angry muttered growl, "Get your skinny little ass over here before I come get you and paddle it so hard you won't be able to sit while you eat your pizza." He disconnects the call, scowls at the screen for a moment – seemingly unaware the rest of us heard the tail end of that conversation – before looking up to see three gaping jaws and one glaring Liberty. He shrugs and grins impishly. "What? It's not a daddy kink. We call it . . . *word play.*"

Silence befalls the group as the grin vanishes from Reece's face when he sees the way Liberty is looking at him. *So reminiscent of Mrs. M it makes my balls shrivel.* "I have access to scalpels and the morgue, Reece." She narrows those mesmerizing eyes I fell in love with the first time I saw them. "Hurt my friend, and you'll be the victim of one and a resident of the other."

Balls of steel, a heart of gold, and the loyalty of a golden retriever.

Reece looks her straight in the eyes and voices without waver, "And if I ever do, I will give you permission."

Wiley leans in to whisper in my ear, "Marry. that. woman."

Chapter 38

Liberty

Six months later

We've made the deadline that Lucas deemed acceptable eighteen years ago. We're still thirty. More in love than the day we found each other again. I wonder what our first fight may look like – we haven't had reason for one yet – though building a house together is presenting challenges. We're strong believers in the art of compromise. But I know when I've pushed his buttons; the heated flare in his eyes, the smirk. The way he dips his chin in challenge, the slow, steady steps as he stalks his way toward me. Maybe if I had one ounce of resistance, one shred of willpower, I could stay irritated. However, one lip tip is all it takes. That damn dimple! It's my kryptonite. I'd decided long ago if I ever do get mad at him, I need to poke it with my index finger to hide it while we argue. But then I would have to stand close and he'd kiss me and it would be over before it started anyway. He's like that, you know. So patient, so slow to anger, so . . . Lucas. The boy I fell in love with – now the man I get to spend the rest of my life with.

We'd considered a destination wedding, but why bother? This is where we started, where we reconnected, and will probably be where we spend the rest of our lives. The only family not living here is my mom and Tom, and they're looking at villas in the area. Spend six months of the year here with us, and the other six in North Carolina near Tom's kids. Compromise.

"You ready, kiddo?" Captain Sullivan's smile warms my heart as he extends a bent elbow for me to take. He's giving me away today to the love of my life. My decision wasn't hard. Tom is perfect . . . for my mom. But he's walked his own daughters down the aisle.

Captain Sullivan was there for me the night my dad died. I've never forgotten it. He held me while I cried, may have even shed a few tears of his own, uttered words that I may not remember but were comforting at the time. He kept a package for two years – knowing the chances of ever being able to deliver it for me were slim to none – but he didn't give up. In the process, he gave Lucas something to hold onto, something to bind us together over the years we were apart. He's kind of my hero.

"I'm ready," I say as I slide my arm through his and we make our way toward the arch that exposes the pathway leading to my waiting groom.

The moment Lucas catches sight of me, his chest caves and his fisted hand flies to his mouth. His watery eyes watch my every move as Captain Sullivan brings us closer together with each step, as if he's afraid to look away. As if he blinks, this will all disappear. I want to tug on Sully's arm to hasten the march; I'm a little worried myself. It seems too good to be true.

Lucas is so handsome in his black tux – the custom-dyed blueberry color bowtie and cummerbund a declaration of our beginning – the tutti-frutti pink bouquet in my hands that he asked me to carry, the perfect match.

Lucas insisted one chair in the front row next to Wiley be left empty, a huge bow placed on it, a picture of my dad and two pieces of the same gum he used to buy for us attached to the center. Is it any wonder I love this man so much?

Before we've made the final few steps to our destination, Lucas swipes at his cheeks and takes a couple steps toward us before Sully holds up a hand. "Patience, Tanner."

Lucas scowls and mutters, "Eighteen years, Sully."

Sully smiles and arches a brow. "Ten more seconds ain't gonna kill ya."

Roger grips Lucas' shoulder, tugging him back. "If she hasn't run by now, she ain't going anywhere, Tanner."

Mallory takes my bouquet when I hold it out to her. Tears in her eyes, she smiles softly. "All that time spent searching the internet and all we would have had to do to find him was get arrested for indecent exposure." She shrugs. "Who knew?"

I giggle and pull her into a hug, clinging tightly. "I'm going to miss living with you."

She sniffles and squeezes hard before releasing me. "Well, it's been an amicable divorce. Good thing we never had kids." She takes my shoulders and narrows her eyes. "Lunch in the cafeteria at least once a week. We have a deal."

"Wouldn't miss it for the world," I promise her.

"Uh, ladies," Reece whispers from the other side of the officiant. "Tanner's leg is shaking. Either he's losing patience or he forgot to piss before the ceremony."

The officiant clears his throat as he shoots a look of disgust at Reece while Mallory glares. "Tell him to pinch it," she whispers.

"Pinch it?" Reece's face folds in confusion. "Does that really work?"

"Yes, you moron," Mal growls through gritted teeth.

He winks and bobs his eyebrows. "Can we test your theory later?"

Before they can get carried away with their *word play*, Lucas gently takes my elbow and leads me to the proper spot in front of the officiant, who at the present time is busying himself, whipping his head back and forth, silently scolding Reece and Mallory for their inappropriate conversation with a furrowed brow and a curled lip.

"Shall we proceed?" he says, once done with his silent chastising, though I think the elbow to Reece's ribs – thank you, Roger – was more effective.

Lucas turns to him, after a quick scathing glance at Reece, before he says, "Please."

"Friends and family," he starts, "we are gathered here today to . . ." He continues with the usual rhetoric, the words that lead to what we each need to express, what we've written, or memorized in my case. "And now, it's time for the bride and groom to exchange vows of their own choosing."

My hands are shaky as Lucas holds them in his, but only because there are no words to express fully the way I feel. There is so much. But we have a lifetime.

"The day the moving truck pulled up in front of my house, I was so excited to see if I had new playmates. Then I watched as this shy boy climbed out of the cab and look around as if he was lost. I wasn't even disappointed you weren't a girl." I feel a tear run down my cheek at the same time I see Lucas blink back one of his own. *"I ran inside to grab two popsicles and came back out to*

find you standing in my yard as if you weren't sure where to go. I gave you a choice of flavors, and like you have ever since, you told me to choose first. I knew that day I had met my best friend. I could always tell you my secrets and know that you would hold them tight to your chest, as if they were your own. We had seven years together as children, years that most people forget as they grow older, but I never forgot a day.

"The one time you didn't offer for me to choose first is the day you explained the color pink to me. It was the oddest thing I'd ever heard, but as I got older I realized it was the most romantic thing a girl could ever hear. And it came from a twelve year-old boy's mouth. That was the same day I lost you, and I thought I'd never find you again. I thought I'd never be able to deliver the promise I'd made to you. It was also the day I realized how much I loved you and how broken I was without you.

"It's true that two halves make a whole, because I have never felt so complete as I do with you. You were my first love and you will be my last because I would never ask anyone to try and live up to the joy that you have given me. I will give you all of my tomorrows and I will love you until the day I die. Lucas, you are my everything."

He swipes the tears from my cheeks with his thumb as his own moisten his skin, and as he leans in to kiss me, the officiant grasps his shoulder and pulls him back.

"Not so fast. You still have your own to recite. Never rush a good thing."

Lucas nods and clears his throat, his eyes never leaving mine.

"Liberty Collins, the day I met you is the day my life began. You have always been my light in the dark, my port in the storm. Through all those years we were apart, I still found refuge in the memories of you, because you gave me the happiest times of my life. You were the calm to my chaos. My two favorite colors of green and blue." He winks and smiles. *"The promise of pink.*

"You taught me compassion, how to trust, how to love. You were my best friend, my soulmate, my reason. And now we're all grown up. You're still all those things, Libby. After all these years, no matter our time apart, nothing has changed other than you've grown more beautiful, more compassionate, and I love you more than I ever thought possible.

"I'll walk in the rain with you but I promise to never be the reason you need to. I'll let you win," he tilts his head and scrunches his nose, *"the majority of our arguments, should we ever have any. I will make it my goal to see you smile every day, to hear you whisper my name in the dark, and to make you as happy as you've made me. Go crazy with me, Liberty. It's a trip I can't take without you."*

Sniffles abound all around us, even one from the officiant, as Lucas lifts my hands and kisses my knuckles one by one.

Roger presses his fingertips to his temple, surreptitiously wiping a tear from his eye and mumbles, "I ain't ever gonna be able to top that."

Reece drops his chin, swipes at his nose, and grumbles, "At least the woman of your dreams didn't hear it."

We exchange formal vows and the rings; a beautiful bezel-set oval pink diamond in platinum for me – no prongs to catch on medical equipment or, worse yet, patients' skin – and a diamond studded platinum band for Lucas when he's not working. He insisted he have my name tattooed on his finger a week before the wedding. It's classy and bold; done in black and red. He's a lefty. I prefer he have nothing on his finger to interfere when handling firearms.

"You may now kiss your bride." The officiant nods at Lucas, adding an eye roll as if to say *finally.*

It's the kiss of a lifetime. Our first as husband and wife. It's consuming, claiming, and overwhelming as he bends me backward. Cheers, whistles, and applause ring throughout the large backyard of Captain Sullivan's home.

"Ladies and gentlemen," the officiant proudly announces over the noise. "I present to you Mr. and Mrs. Lucas Tanner Bergman."

"Pink," he whispers once the seal of his lips against mine is broken.

"You're gonna have to let me up." I giggle in return.

He moans and nuzzles into my neck. "We could send them all home and get naked and skinny dip in Sully's pool."

"Or . . ." I lift his head and look him in the eyes. "We could get through the reception and leave for Bora Bora tonight and skinny dip all we want in the private pool you reserved for us for a week."

He furrows his brow in thought. "Damn. You make a good argument, wife." His face splits in a grin as his eyes twinkle. "Liberty Collins is my wife."

"Liberty Bergman now," I correct him. "You got yourself a whole new family."

Lucas took Wiley's surname three months ago after much consideration and a lengthy discussion with his aunt and uncle. Ruby had met Wiley many years ago, before she and Amy went their separate ways, and had no clue he was Lucas' father. Needless to say, the news was warmly welcomed and they took no insult with Lucas taking his father's name.

As we turn to make our way to the waiting guests, the empty chair with my dad's picture catches my eye and it makes me smile. His toothy grin and bright blue eyes are aimed at us. He would have approved, I just know it. Wiley sits next to that chair, his arm slung over the back as if sharing the moment – maybe even a silent thank you for helping Lucas in his youth – tears pouring from red rimmed eyes as he relishes watching his only son be happy. A moment, I'm sure, he never thought he would see. Proof there is more than one reunion to be celebrated today.

I never could figure out how such a wonderful boy – my hero – could come from the likes of the senior Monterrey. Now I know. He didn't. There was never a connection between those two. He feared him, relished the moments he wasn't home, sought shelter in mine with my mom and dad, found happiness in the smallest of things like bubblegum and bike rides, sno-cones, grilled hamburgers with my family. My dad pulling his baby teeth and my mom dishing up ice cream as a reward for his bravery showed him more love than any dollar under his pillow ever could. He didn't need a tooth fairy; he had the real thing in the form of family.

But most of all, just like me, he had his best friend. His first love. The one you never forget and, if you're lucky, the one that lasts a lifetime.

Epilogue

"Wiley's got him, baby," Lucas reassures me, adjusting our three-week-old in his arms, as we sit on the loveseat under the shelter of the patio cover and watch our three-year-old in the pool with his grandpa.

"And you haven't put her down since we brought her home," I remind him for the hundredth time, "other than to breastfeed." Come to think of it, he rarely put her down in the hospital. I cast him a wry look. "And even then you're spellbound."

"I'm mesmerized. . ." he grins impishly then winks, ". . .and a bit jealous."

"She's never going to sleep in her crib." I sigh and shake my head. "Unless we make a pillow cast of daddy's shoulder and the inside of his elbow."

Lucas has six weeks paternity leave, just like the first time, and plans to relish every moment he's given. His parenting skills are second to none. He takes spit-up like a champ, cleans up a blowout diaper while laughing, and is the first to try and soothe what ails them. He's become a pro with Band-Aids as well in preparation for spills from their bicycles.

"Levi adjusted." He shrugs his free shoulder. He's right.

After six weeks in his father's arms, our little boy did adjust. It might have taken a few sleepless nights, but eventually he did learn there were more options than being held 24/7. It was easier for him than it was for Lucas. He studies our daughter, Lucy, and brushes her cheek gently with a single finger. "She's beautiful, Libby. So damn perfect. How did you do this?"

I chuckle at a totally whipped Lucas, and prematurely pity any boys who want to take her to prom. I'll have to double check the gun safe to be sure it's locked. "I had a little help, you know."

"She's all you, Libby," he whispers.

"And Levi has your dimple."

He winks and clicks his cheek. "Lady magnet."

"Papa!" Levi shrieks with laughter from the pool. "Do it 'gain!"

Wiley lifts him in the air and brings him down into the water to waist level with a splash. Levi demands another splash, then another and another.

"I think your dad is going to wear out before our son does."

Lucas watches the two of them, a quick flash of pain in his eyes before he blinks it away and smiles. "Seeing that makes up for it, you know? I can give my little boy what I didn't have, and I can give the dad I didn't know I had what he always wanted."

I extend my hand to take his. "Family," I whisper as I entwine my fingers with his.

He draws my hand to his mouth and kisses my knuckles. "Family." He releases my hand and wraps his in my hair, pulling me in for my favorite kind of kiss: slow, deliberate, just like the first one. "Still pink," he whispers against my lips.

I giggle. "You mean tutti-frutti."

"I mean Liberty. I am so glad you didn't kiss me that day. You were worth all the tomorrows I had to wait for. I love you."

The End

Mallory Tompkins has sworn off casual relationships and playboys since witnessing her best friend's fiancé cheat. This includes the persistent, obnoxious, Texas-born, firefighter Reece Callahan. However, Reece has other plans for the girl who doesn't remember him. Now all he needs is a strategy.

<u>I Shouldn't Have Kissed Him</u>

Coming in March 2025

About The Author

Annie Mick

A diehard laughaholic who has learned to take everything with a grain of salt, Annie Mick loves to dish it out with a good dose of sarcasm.

If you can giggle while you wiggle, it's added exercise and spares you ten minutes on the treadmill.

It is true that if you can laugh while you cry, the tears are saltier and it makes the margaritas taste better.

If you can find your hero in one of her books, therein lies her success. If you can find a bit of yourself in one her characters, therein lies her joy.

Life is too short to not get lost in a fantasy; if only for a day, if only in a book, one page at a time.

Sweet dreams.